The basta
t

Bernard felt the stab of grief as if he'd been told she'd died. His temper flared beyond control. "You had no right to bargain away that which is mine!"

"You have no rights but those I grant you!" Lord Setton replied. "Either accept my decision or begone."

Bernard reined in hard on his anger. Butting heads with Setton was getting him nowhere. Claire was lost to him. He could make do without—he had no choice.

But he needed the land. Without the land, he'd given four years of his life for nothing.

Into the stillness of the hall, Bernard cleared his throat, preparing to come to some compromise with Setton.

"I will relinquish my claim to Claire—"

Bernard heard a soft gasp and turned to the sound.

Claire.

A vision in emerald silk, her amber eyes wide with surprise. Older. More lushly curved. The woman whose body he'd dreamed of sinking into since the day her father had promised—

Mine!

Dear Reader,

This month our exciting Medieval series KNIGHTS OF THE BLACK ROSE continues with *The Conqueror* by Shari Anton, when a prized knight returns from war to clam his promised reward—marriage to his liege lord's daughter—but finds she's betrothed to another.... *The Marrying Man* by bestselling author Millie Criswell is a darling marriage-of-convenience tale about a spunky mail-order bride who tames a rough coal mine owner and his tomboy daughter. Pat Tracy concludes THE GUARDSMEN series with *Hunter's Law,* in which a haunted rancher decides to take the law into his own hands and falls into the path of a beautiful Eastern miss on a "rescue" mission of her own. And don't miss *Lady of the Keep,* another terrific L'EAU CLAIRE book by Sharon Schulze. Here, a knight falls in love with the pregnant widow he is sent to protect.

For the next two months, we are going to be asking readers to let us know what you are looking for from Harlequin Historicals. We hope you'll participate by sending your ideas to us at:

Harlequin Historicals
300 E. 42nd St.
New York, NY 10017

Q. What types of stories do you like; i.e., marriage of convenience, single father, etc.? _____

_____

Q. Are our books too sensual or not sensual enough? _____

_____

Whatever your tastes in reading, you'll be sure to find a romantic journey back to the past between the covers of a Harlequin Historicals novel. We hope you'll join us next month, too!

Sincerely,

Tracy Farrell
Senior Editor

SHARI ANTON

THE CONQUEROR

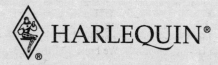

HARLEQUIN®

TORONTO • NEW YORK • LONDON
AMSTERDAM • PARIS • SYDNEY • HAMBURG
STOCKHOLM • ATHENS • TOKYO • MILAN • MADRID
PRAGUE • WARSAW • BUDAPEST • AUCKLAND

ISBN 0-373-29107-8

THE CONQUEROR

Please address questions and book requests to:
Harlequin Reader Service
U.S.: 3010 Walden Ave., P.O. Box 1325, Buffalo, NY 14269
Canadian: P.O. Box 609, Fort Erie, Ont. L2A 5X3

Without the vision of the following people,
the Knights of the Black Rose wouldn't exist.
Therefore, this book must be dedicated to…

Editors Tracy Farrell and Margaret Marbury,
for their courage and enthusiasm.
Authors Suzanne Barclay and Ana Seymour,
who were a joy to work with.
Authors Laurie Grant, Sharon S. Schulze and Lyn Stone,
for invaluable contributions.
Hussies (too numerous to name!),
for unfailing support.
Love you all.

Chapter One

Dasset Castle, 1222

"Bernard Fitzgibbons? Is it really you, lad? You truly live?"

From atop his courser, Bernard smiled down at Old Peter, both amused at and fully understanding the stable master's amazement. Few, himself included, had expected Bernard Fitzgibbons to return from Crusade.

"Aye, Peter, I survived. Hard to believe, is it not?" Bernard asked as he swung down from his horse.

"Aye!" Peter confirmed. "Nigh on a year ago we heard you had died in the Holy Land. Then a few weeks ago a messenger from some abbey near York comes with news you are laid up there with a leg broke. Hard to tell what to believe!"

The false report of his demise had come by way of the English commanders upon their return from the Holy Land last fall. The commanders had made a false assumption, one not entirely without merit. When Bernard and five other knights failed to report aboard the ships for the fall passage, what else could the commanders assume but that the knights had perished with the rest of their comrades-in-arms?

They hadn't died, but ridden off to rescue a fellow knight from a Saracen prison. They'd succeeded, but in doing so missed the fall passage and been forced to wait until spring for a ship.

"Obviously I did not die, and 'tis true I suffered a broken leg upon my return to England," he said, choosing not to tell Peter the whole of that embarrassing incident. It still seemed incredible to Bernard that he had come through Crusade with nary a scratch, then suffered his greatest hurt upon returning to England. "The good monks provided bed and board until I could walk again."

Peter inspected the courser. "'Tisn't the horse you left with."

Bernard patted the neck of the warhorse that had served him well these past four years. "The nag Lord Setton gave me did not last but two days. It collapsed on the road to London. To my good fortune, Bishop Thurstan's pockets proved deep and charitable—may he rest with God."

Peter bowed his head and crossed himself at the invocation for Bishop Thurstan of Durleigh, who'd gathered men from every corner of his bishopric to form the Knights of the Black Rose. Of that great, glorious company who'd journeyed from Durleigh to the Holy Land to fight the infidel, only six yet survived.

Simon, a champion without equal and without whose leadership they might have all perished several times over; Nicholas, a rogue who could charm a woman or wield a sword with equal ease; Hugh, a stout-hearted warrior to whom Bernard owed more than he could repay; Gervase, a baron whose healing skills caused him pain; Guy, the outlander, a man of dual heritage in search of a single identity.

They were knights of the most chivalrous bent, who'd taken an inept squire under their protection and kept Bernard safe until he'd learned the harsh lessons of war and become their equal. Fast friends who would come to his aid if the need arose. Men who could count on Bernard to answer a call for help.

Nicholas had already required Bernard's help, and oh, hadn't the two of them had a grand time rescuing the lovely Beatrice Thibault from an unscrupulous captor. The adventure had allowed Bernard to thoroughly test his leg, but also further delayed his return to Dasset.

Today, finally, he would collect his reward.

Riches in the form of land to call his own. Marriage to Claire Setton. At times, only the promise of receiving his reward had made the desert heat bearable, his life in the squalor of camp tolerable.

Eager now to get on with it, Bernard asked, "Have you a stall for my steed?"

"Aye. Lord Odo sold off a few of his lesser horses—"

Shocked at the news, Bernard interrupted. "Odo? He was on his death bed when I left."

"Humph. Well, he got up again. Odo always was a contrary cuss. Still is."

Bernard removed his gauntlets and tucked them into the large traveling pack on his courser's rump. He'd thought the old lord to have passed on years ago.

'Twas Lord Odo Setton's impending death that had brought Bishop Thurstan to Dasset to hear Setton's final confession. Desperate to fulfill the penance required by the bishop, Setton had all but begged Bernard to take the cross and fulfill Dasset's service to the bishop's company. So desperate he was that when Bernard hesitated to accept, Setton blurted out the promise of a reward— a holding and marriage to his youngest daughter—upon his return from Crusade.

Only the veriest fool would have turned down the offer, even believing he had little hope of living to collect.

He'd lived. Even thrived. All these years Bernard had fully expected to collect his reward from Julius, the eldest son and so the heir to Dasset. Dealing with the son had always been easier than dealing with the father.

Bernard led his horse into the stable and inspected the first empty stall. Approving the freshness of the straw and lack of muck on the floor, he handed the reins over to Peter.

"Leave my saddle and pack in the stall and I will see to them after I speak with Setton."

Peter pointed at the scabbard hanging from Bernard's belt. "And that...thing?"

Bernard drew out his scimitar. The curved blade hadn't been beyond his reach since he'd picked it up during a frantic struggle on a battlefield and made it his own. Weapons weren't allowed in Dasset Castle's great hall—except for those borne by the guards on duty.

"This *thing* is a scimitar," Bernard said with reverence.

"An infidel's weapon," Peter observed with disdain.

Heathen and beautiful and deadly. "A weapon knows no God, or right from wrong, or sinner from saint. It only responds to the hand of its master, for good or ill."

Peter took the scimitar, but he wasn't pleased about it, as if he feared some heathenish taint would rub off. Bernard inwardly scoffed at the man's foolishness, but didn't comment.

"Is his lordship in the hall?" Bernard asked.

Peter answered with a nod. "He holds court."

Bernard set to rights the distinctive Crusader's tabard that covered his chain mail. Fashioned of gray cloth trimmed in black and red, with a black rose embroidered high over the left breast and a red felt cross stitched over his heart, the tabard would not only impress his overlord but help all identify him.

With a parting wave to Peter, Bernard strode across the bailey toward the stairs of the keep. 'Twas hard not to run, as he once might have done. He'd learned well the value of patience and self-discipline, among other hard lessons. Lessons he might not have learned had he not gone crusading. Sweet Jesu, for all he'd been twenty upon leaving Dasset, he'd also been a green youth, lacking skill with a weapon and knowing next to nothing about the horror of true battle.

He'd passed the tests of fire and flood, famine and pestilence, battle and boredom. He'd earned his knighthood and become a man confident he could meet any trial and win, face any foe and prevail.

Except, he hadn't made a demand of Lord Odo Setton in his entire life. He hadn't even asked for the one favor he might have a right to. Maybe, if all went well today, he might press another claim later.

Bernard made short work of the stairs, passed through the castle's huge oak doors and entered the great hall. A familiar sight, yet not exactly as he'd left it.

Lady Leone Setton—short, plump and now white-haired—sat near the hearth with her women, quietly working distaff and spindle to make yarn of carded wool.

From the dais at the far end of the hall, Lord Odo Setton, still dark-haired and formidable, presided over his court from his ornate, canopied chair. He wore a court mantle of deep blue velvet trimmed in ermine.

Peasants, retainers and guards comprised the small crowd before him. Setton's voice echoed through the hall, his words muffled at this distance, though the anger in his voice rang clear. Bernard pitied the object of Setton's ire, a peasant, who stood apart from the crowd with his head bowed low.

Of the Setton's four children, Bernard saw not one. 'Twas odd that neither of the boys, especially Julius, did not hover nearby while Odo held court. 'Twas also odd that neither of the girls, especially Claire, did not sit at Leone's side.

Claire. The youngest. The minx most needful of watching.

Did Claire yet bedevil her father's soldiers with frivolous commands—just because she could? Did she still walk across the hall with the grace of a swan and most regal bearing, then ruin the effect with a playful smile?

He'd thought of Claire often while away, wondering how she fared and pondering the wisdom of taking the minx as his wife. Maybe she, too, had changed over the years. Maybe her mother's persistence in training the winsome yet willful girl to wifely duties had won out. Bernard could only hope.

Over the years, he'd wondered how Lady Claire Setton had reacted when told she'd been promised to Bernard Fitzgibbons. What would she say now that he'd come to claim her?

He'd been far from worthy of Claire four years ago, a mere squire of far less than perfect form and talents, with hardly a copper to his name. He was more worthy of her now, as a man duly knighted, though the state of his pockets remained sad. The relics in his pack, purchased in the Holy Land, were worth something, but surely less than the amount necessary to maintain a manor and wife for more than a season—a warm season.

'Twas August. In only a few short weeks the leaves would turn, with winter hard on autumn's heels. How well he and Claire would survive the coming winter depended much upon which lands Lord Setton bestowed and on how well they'd been cared for.

Mostly, Bernard hoped for a stone manor, a shelter to hold sturdy against winter storms. A manor worthy of a landed knight, the son-by-marriage to Lord Setton. A place in which to fashion a comfortable life for himself, Claire and the children she would bear him.

A dream fulfilled, and as necessary to him as his next breath.

'Twould help, of course, if the manor's stores were full, for he had no idea of how to go about filling them. Claire should, and he would gladly yield to her superior knowledge.

As Bernard began to cross the hall, one of the guards came forward. Bernard recognized Edgar, a household guard of long standing.

Edgar held out his hand in greeting. "Bernard! 'Tis good to see you again. How is the leg?"

"Healed," Bernard said, chagrined. Apparently everyone knew he'd broken the limb. Thankfully, only a few trusted friends knew how, and would keep the tale to themselves.

Bernard nodded toward the forlorn-looking peasant. "Is his lordship nearly done with that poor fellow?"

"Aye, nearly. Come. I will inform Miles that you are here," Edgar said, and rushed off toward the man who stood at Setton's right hand, Dasset's steward.

Nearing the dais, Bernard comprehended Odo's ire with the peasant. The man's ox had run amuck in several of the villagers' gardens, threatening the peasants' winter food supply.

Setton turned to Miles. "You have a list of the villagers' claims?"

"I do, my lord," the steward said.

"All those who suffered damage are here?"

Miles nodded.

Setton peered down at the peasant. "You will make amends. To each of your harmed neighbors, you will give a cabbage for a cabbage, or perform a service which equals its value."

"My lord," the peasant said in a shaky voice, "my own garden suffered, and there are not enough hours in the day—"

"If you are unable to make amends, then I shall take your ox in payment for that which must come from my stores." Setton waved a hand at the group about the dais. "Miles will aid you in arranging payment to each claimant."

The peasant paled at the possibility of losing his ox, but he nodded his agreement. There was really nothing else the man could do. Where he would find the means to replace the vegetables, or time to spare between working his own fields as well as those of Lord Setton's, Bernard had no idea.

Before Setton could rise from his chair, the steward leaned toward the lord's ear and waved a hand in Bernard's direction.

Bernard stepped forward, his heart beating faster now that the time to claim his reward had arrived. He'd waited four long, harsh years for this moment.

Lord Odo Setton turned to face Bernard.

Bernard bowed at the waist. "My lord," he said.

When Setton remained silent, Bernard straightened to

find Setton studying him intently, as if assuring himself of Bernard's identity. Bernard withstood Setton's scrutiny without fidgeting, no longer a squire who might cower. Indeed, no man had been able to intimidate him for some time now.

"Fitzgibbons," Setton said on a sigh. "I had begun to despair you had lost your way between the abbey and Dasset."

Bernard ignored the twitter of the crowd and the tinge of derision in Setton's tone.

"Not lost, my lord, merely delayed."

"You broke another body part, perhaps?"

The twitter broke into light laughter. Setton, however, didn't appear to be making an attempt at humor.

"Shortly before my leg healed, I received a message from a fellow knight, requesting my presence at his hall. I answered his call and helped him overcome a difficulty."

Setton leaned forward. "You considered this knight's difficulty of greater import than reporting to your overlord?"

The crowd's laughter died. The hair on Bernard's neck itched in warning.

"Lives were at stake, my lord, those of a woman and an infant. As a knight, I am sworn to protect both if the occasion arises."

Setton's eyes narrowed. He snickered. "What fool knighted you?"

An English nobleman of high rank who owed his life to Bernard's skill with the scimitar, a man Setton would know of and could send to for confirmation.

"I was knighted by Ranulf, earl of Chester, after a hard-fought battle with the Saracens for possession of the Nile."

"Did he mistake you for another, then?"

Bernard tamped down the ire that threatened to rise. Losing his temper would do no good. Damn, but he wished Julius occupied the ornate chair, not Odo.

"Nay, Lord Setton. No mistake was made. I fully earned my knighthood that day."

Setton waved the declaration away, as if the accomplishment meant nothing at all. "Did you pledge to the earl?"

"I pledged fealty to no man, only to uphold my knightly vows. The earl understood my loyalty belonged to…the lord of Dasset."

Setton stood and extended his hands. "Then I will have your pledge now."

All along, Bernard had envisioned himself kneeling before Julius Setton to do homage. Still, Odo remained the lord and in order to collect his reward the oath must be given. Bernard stepped onto the dais, knelt before Setton and raised his folded hands, which Setton clasped in a cold grip.

"Have you returned my courser?" Setton asked.

Taken completely off guard, Bernard blurted out, "Your courser?"

Setton gave a confirming nod. "Bishop Thurstan demanded payment for the warhorse he was forced to purchase because you lost the horse I gave you."

Bernard hadn't lost the nag. The poor beast had succumbed to the rigors of the road. But if Setton wanted the courser he'd paid for, then he had the right to demand it. Bernard felt sharply the impending loss of the faithful beast, but had no choice but to give it over.

"Cabal is in your stable."

"I suppose I shall have to give him to you now that you are a knight."

Bernard bowed his head, more to hide his irritation than out of reverence.

"If that is your wish, my lord."

"My wish, for now, is to hear your pledge of homage."

'Twas oh, so tempting to get up and walk away. Only for the reward due him, for the lands and marriage to Claire, Bernard remained on bended knee. In a firm, clear voice, he gave his pledge.

"To Lord Odo Setton, I give my homage. I swear to keep faith and loyalty to you against all others, and to guard your rights and those of your heirs with all my strength."

"From Bernard Fitzgibbons, I accept homage. In return, I promise protection and maintenance as is due a knight in my service. Rise, Sir Bernard, and take your place in my household."

Released from Setton's grasp, Bernard rose.

Setton reached for the brooch securing his mantle, signaling the end of court. The crowd began to disperse. Bernard knew he was being dismissed, but he'd come too far and through so much to be shunted aside so quickly.

"Might I ask but another moment, my lord, to settle the particulars of my maintenance?"

Setton tossed the mantle to his steward. "A pallet in my hall and board at my table, at which you may now take a higher place and partake of wine instead of ale, if you prefer. We can talk about your duties on the morrow."

He'd earned much more than a higher place at table and wine in his goblet.

"I had hoped to take immediate possession of my lands, my lord."

"Your *what?*"

A cold chill gripped Bernard's spine. "I claim the reward you promised me upon my return from Crusade. A holding of my own, and marriage to Lady Claire."

Setton stared at him for a moment, then burst into laughter so hard he sank into his chair. Others joined in Setton's outburst of mirth. Bernard stood stoic, his stomach churning with the surety that Setton was about to refuse the reward.

Setton's laughter faded to a chuckle. "Land and Claire? Oh, Bernard! Did you suffer some injury to your head in the Holy Land? Did you have a fevered dream and count it as reality? Lad, I promised you no such reward. I fear you must be content with such comforts as those of my other household knights."

Bernard remembered the promise as clearly as if given only a moment before. Setton weak and pale in his bed, Bishop Thurstan hovering nearby. An oath taken, a reward granted.

"You granted the reward, my lord, on the day you sent me off with Bishop Thurstan to join the Knights of the Black Rose."

Setton shook his head. "Impossible. Even delirious with fever, I would never have granted such a prize as my daughter to a squire who could barely hold a sword correctly. You must have misheard, Bernard."

"I did not mishear."

Setton's amusement fled, his mouth flattening to a straight line. "Do you say I lie?"

Bernard took a deep breath. On the edge of his awareness, he noted that a large crowd was now gathered before the dais, enthralled by his claim, waiting for Bernard's answer.

Calmly, firmly, Bernard stated, "You were deathly ill, so perhaps your memory is not as clear as mine."

Setton rose from his chair and countered with equal measure. "Bernard, I made no such bargain."

'Twas impossible that this travesty was happening, and all he could do was persevere.

"The bargain was witnessed, my lord, by Bishop Thurstan."

"Thurstan is dead, and if he were here, he would surely remember as I do." Setton huffed. "And truly, Bernard, even had I made such a ridiculous bargain, the reward you claim is no longer mine to give. Some months ago, Lord Eustace Marshall and I agreed to a bargain for Claire and her dowry."

Setton had married her off! The bastard had given Claire to another! Bernard felt the stab of grief as if he'd been told she'd died. His temper flared beyond control.

"You had *no* right to bargain away that which is mine!"

"You have no rights but those I grant you! Either accept my decision or be gone."

Bernard reined in hard on his anger. Butting heads with Setton was getting him nowhere.

Claire was lost to him. If she'd married, he couldn't very well claim her from a husband who'd wed her in good faith. The Church wouldn't annul her marriage on his appeal. As much as it pained him, that part of his dream was gone, irretrievable. He could make do without—he had no choice.

But he needed the land. Without the land, he'd given four years of his life for nothing. Without the land, and its income, he'd be forced to hire out as a mercenary, for he knew no other skill than fighting. Without a holding to call his own, he would have no peace, no pride, no life.

Into the stillness of the hall, Bernard cleared his throat, preparing to come to some compromise with Setton.

"I will relinquish my claim to Claire—"

Bernard heard a soft gasp and turned to the sound.

Claire.

A vision in emerald silk, her amber eyes wide with surprise, her fingers lightly resting on the bottom lip of her bow mouth. Older. More lushly curved. The woman whose body he'd dreamed of sinking into since the day her father had promised—

Mine!

Nay, no longer. Claire belonged to another man. Married to Lord Eustace Marshall, a member of one of England's most powerful families.

He turned away.

"Lord Setton, I am due a holding worthy of a landed knight. On that I will insist."

Setton's face went scarlet. "Guards! Seize him! Toss him into the dungeon until he comes to his senses."

Two guards grabbed hold of Bernard's arms. With a sharp, mighty heave, he sent them both flying and took a step toward Setton—his hand automatically going for the hilt of his scimitar. Not there. Damn.

Bernard saw panic in Setton's eyes, a panic quickly replaced by fury.

Then pain ripped through his head. Just before the world went black, Bernard heard his name ring out in a shrill scream.

Chapter Two

"Nay, Henry! Hold!" Claire shouted at the guard who'd raised his lance to hit Bernard again.

After the guard checked his swing, she rushed over to the prone figure lying facedown and too still on the dais. Trembling with dread, she bent down on one knee and gently brushed at the blood that seeped through the strands of Bernard Fitzgibbons's sable-hued hair.

"Claire! Get up! Leave the villain be!" her father commanded.

Claire ignored the order only long enough to find the faint assurance of a heartbeat in Bernard's temple.

Relieved, she slowly rose to face her furious father. If she weren't careful, she could end up on the floor beside Bernard. Or maybe not. He'd been less harsh with her since her betrothal to Eustace Marshall; her value to him had risen.

Still, she shouldn't have meddled in her father's affairs. Mercy, whatever had made her scream Bernard's name and rush to his aid? She knew, of course. No one else would dare plead Bernard's cause, and if he suffered greatly from her father's harshness, her own plans to escape Dasset could be in jeopardy.

For three weeks yet she must strive to keep the peace, until after her wedding. Then her father could indulge in whatever nastiness he pleased and she wouldn't know about it much less have to deal with it.

"Bernard needs tending, Father," she said gently but firmly.

Her father's hands clenched into fists. "He needs to be put in chains! Did you hear what he demanded of me?"

She hadn't heard the whole of the argument. She'd been drawn from her pallet in the solar by shouting in the great hall. Coming down the stairs, she'd trembled at her father's tone of voice, glad his ire wasn't directed at her for a change. Not until she'd reached the dais did she realize who traded verbal barbs with her father— Bernard Fitzgibbons.

The particulars of Bernard's demand had shocked her, made her wonder if the man's mind had been warped somehow.

But, oh, he'd been a glorious sight in his battle-scarred Crusader's tabard, standing steadfast in his misguided beliefs. She'd barely recognized this changed Bernard Fitzgibbons, both in body and spirit. The Bernard she'd known hadn't been so tall, and hadn't fitted into his chain mail so fully. Nor would the Bernard who'd left Dasset all those years ago dare to press her father to blinding anger.

"I heard," Claire answered her father, keeping her voice low and soothing. "His demands made no sense. Still, for all his foolishness, he must be tended and made well. Bernard wears the red cross of a Crusader over his heart, and as such, is considered a hero of the faith by the Church, so his rights must be respected."

Setton waved a hand toward Bernard. "This lout has

no rights! No lands to be preserved. No wealth or family to be protected. He left with nothing and comes back with nothing except a claim to knighthood and the audacity to demand a reward from me! For what reason should I even allow the man to live?''

Fear wrapped around Claire's heart, but she managed to keep from trembling. Her father couldn't be serious. Bernard may have committed an error in making a false demand, but that wasn't a crime so heinous as to warrant his death!

Under other circumstances she might walk away now, but with more than the nature of Bernard's punishment at stake, she pressed on.

''As a Knight of the Black Rose, will not Bernard's welfare be of particular interest to Bishop Walter of Durleigh? Dare we risk incurring the bishop's wrath, and possible interdict, so close to my wedding?''

Setton flinched at the threat of an interdict—which meant no Mass could be said at Dasset, and thus no wedding ceremony could take place. No wedding meant no escape for Claire, something her father wouldn't consider important. No wedding also meant no alliance with Lord Eustace Marshall, which her father craved. She pressed her case further.

''If I remember aright, the new sheriff of Durleigh is also a Knight of the Black Rose, one of Bernard's fellow knights. Would Simon Blackstone have some concern for his comrade-in-arms?''

Her father didn't answer. He glared down at Fitzgibbons.

''Get him out of my sight! Edgar, toss him in the dungeon. I shall decide what to do with him later.''

As four guards arranged themselves around Fitzgibbons, the man they intended to haul away began to rouse. Edgar bent down and whispered harshly into Bernard's ear. Whatever Edgar said seemed to have the desired effect.

Helped to his feet, Bernard looked around, dazed, then allowed Edgar to lead him away.

Claire watched him make an unsteady trek across the hall, out of her father's immediate reach. She started at the hand on her shoulder, her heart skipping a beat.

Her mother. ''I have a posset readied for you,'' she said softly. Leone Setton always spoke softly.

Claire blew a breath held too long, listening to her father shout orders to ready the dogs to hunt down a boar that had been seen near the old mill. 'Twas mid-afternoon, a late time to begin a hunt, but Claire could only be grateful he was leaving the hall.

At her mother's urging, Claire crossed to the hearth.

''You should not be up and about,'' Leone said, handing Claire a cup which contained a bitter potion.

Claire drank the warm, herb-infused liquid to ease the discomfort of her sniffles. For the most part her illness had begun to abate, though she still sneezed and coughed on occasion.

''I could not rest with all of the shouting going on down here,'' Claire said.

Nor could she afford to spend too much time abed. Most of the preparations had been made for the marriage ceremony and accompanying tournament, but not all. If she wanted the ceremony perfect, the feast plentiful, the tournament gay and conducted without mishap, then she must put the remaining days to good use.

Now there was this problem with Bernard to deal with. She'd known he was returning to Dasset, but hadn't expected him to cause trouble.

For several months they'd believed him dead. Last fall

she'd attended a special Mass said for the repose of the souls of the crusading knights. Mercy, she'd even shed a tear at Bishop Thurstan's impassioned plea.

"Heroes of the Crusade," Thurstan had call Fitzgibbons and his comrades. "These men gave their lives in the service of Jesus Christ. Let all honor their memory."

She'd included Fitzgibbons in her prayers until a bit over two months ago when a message arrived from an abbey near York. He'd broken his leg, but was far from dead.

Now he was down in the dungeon.

"What will Father do with him, do you think?" Claire asked.

Leone shrugged a shoulder. "He will do as he will. You must not interfere again, Claire."

No, she'd not put herself between the two men again. 'Twas far too dangerous a place to be. But she could talk to Bernard, maybe convince him to withdraw his demands. He'd already relinquished part of his demand—his claim on her.

Claire quickly squelched an unwarranted pang of hurt that Bernard had given her up so easily. It mattered not.

Within three weeks she'd be the wife of Eustace Marshall, a lord who kept a refined court in his magnificent castle. She'd want for nothing. She'd spend her days acting as Marshall's chatelaine, her evenings entertained by poets and troubadours.

Marshall was a great lord, a handsome man, and a knight who practiced the rules of chivalry. A woman couldn't ask for more.

All she had to do was convince Bernard Fitzgibbons to cooperate, then quell her father's desire for the retribution that could bring the censure of both the Church and the law down on Dasset. A daunting task.

She handed the cup back to her mother. "I will take food down to Fitzgibbons. Mayhap I can talk some sense into him."

Concern clouded her mother's face. "Oh, Claire. I wish you would not."

"Father will be gone for some time, and I promise to hurry." She kissed her timid mother's cheek. "Worry not. All will be well. You will see."

"Well, now you have gone and done it," Edgar said, locking the iron cuff around Bernard's wrist. "Setton will be in a bad way for days. None of us will have any peace. How is your head?"

"Hurts," Bernard said, lightly fingering the back of his skull. A lump had formed and the blood was already drying. "Did Henry have to hit me so hard?"

"Henry probably saved your life. If you had managed to get your hands around Setton's throat—"

"I was not going to hurt him."

"Appeared to all of us that you intended to throttle his lordship. Truly, you are fortunate Henry did not whack you a second time. He would have if Lady Claire hadn't stopped him." Edgar smiled. "Not that any of us would miss the old buzzard, you understand, but 'tis our job to guard him."

Claire. He thought he'd heard his name called. Had the scream come from Claire?

He'd been surprised to see her after being told of her marriage. Why was she at Dasset and not at Huntingdon with Eustace Marshall? Not that it mattered, though if he had the chance he might thank her for saving him a second blow.

Each of the guards had taken the same oath that he'd given Setton only a short time before. Bernard supposed he couldn't fault Henry for doing his job. Just as he couldn't fault Edgar for putting this damnable cuff on his wrist.

If he had his way, the cuff wouldn't be there for long.

"Where is Julius?"

"In Italy. Been gone several months now."

Italy? Bernard didn't think his spirit could sink much lower, or his headache pound much harder, but both did.

"When will he return?"

Edgar shrugged a shoulder. "No idea. Why?"

"Because Julius can be reasonable."

"Aye, that he can. But he is not here."

With a sigh, Bernard eased down onto the dirt floor and rested his head against the stone wall.

"The old man, he is worse—more bad-tempered—than when I left."

"Aye. The last couple o' years…well. Look, I have to get back to duty. After the gates are closed, I will bring you something to eat and we can talk then. Try not to get into any further trouble while I am gone?"

Bernard almost laughed. Simon Blackstone, a friend and the sheriff of Durleigh, had admonished him with much the same words not a fortnight ago, though for different reasons. He'd been so sure upon taking leave of Nicholas and Simon at Hendry Hall that he would return to Dasset and collect his reward without incident.

Wouldn't they both be surprised to hear that instead of returning to the gratitude of his lord, he would spend his first night home in chains?

From the kitchen, Claire pilfered a chunk of yellow cheese, and slices of roasted pork dipped in pepper sauce tucked into a quarter loaf of white bread. Armed further with a goblet of heady red wine, Claire headed down into the abyss of the castle.

She'd been in the dungeon before, though not in a long time. As a child, she and her siblings had played games of seek and find. Inevitably, one of the two boys would choose to hide in the dungeon, then jump out from behind the huge, hideous rack to frighten whichever seeking sibling dared come after him.

She wished Julius were home. Her eldest brother had always enjoyed the most success in tempering her father's actions. But he wasn't home, so she must try.

Claire descended the last section of the dark, curving stairway, careful to avoid contact with the torches that lit her way. She ignored the stench that grew stronger as she neared the underground chamber where her father kept men captive for crimes ranging from petty theft to murder. So far as she knew, Bernard was the only current resident.

Bernard had truly committed no crime other than to argue with her father. Once Bernard apologized and withdrew his demands, Father might let him go, might even allow Bernard to take his place among Dasset's other knights. Claire hoped her father bagged the boar he'd gone off to hunt. A successful hunt would improve his mood greatly.

At the bottom of the stairway she opened the thick oak door, not surprised to find it unlocked. The precaution was usually unnecessary, for any prisoner would be manacled to the far wall, his wrist encased in a heavy iron cuff attached to a short chain.

She stood still while her sight adjusted to the dim light of the dungeon. The torches on either side of the door flickered, casting a wavering shadow of the rack across the dirt floor of the large room. Chains, whips, knives and pincers hung behind the rack, ready to torture whichever poor soul found himself their victim.

Claire shivered and turned away even as her stomach roiled from the odor of blood and excrement that hung heavy in the chamber where no freshening breeze ever wafted through.

Against the far wall, beyond the rack's shadow, a man sat on the floor, his legs stretched out before him and crossed at the ankles. One arm reached above his head, his hand dangling from an iron cuff. Only from the silver shimmer of his tabard was she sure of his identity.

Bernard Fitzgibbons. Hero of the Crusade. Former squire of her father's, now a knight—if Bernard was to be believed. The man who'd demanded a reward of land and marriage to her.

His request for land, she could understand. In land was wealth and power, and every man craved a hide or several for his own. But the marriage? Claire found that part of his claim truly baffling, and had to admit it rather intriguing.

Bernard tilted his head, a questioning gesture.

"I brought you something to eat," she said.

"Food for the condemned?" he said, a hint of amusement in the well-deep voice he now possessed. A little erotic. A bit dangerous.

"You are not condemned, merely held until Father decides what to do with you."

His head tilted farther. "Claire?"

A strange tingle ran down her spine at the sound of her softly spoken name. How foolish, she thought as she crossed the chamber, to be so affected by the simple utterance of her name.

This was Bernard, whom she'd known for most of her

life. She'd always liked the boy she'd ordered about as a page and the young man she'd teased as a squire.

Then Bernard rose to his feet with a catlike grace she wouldn't have thought him capable of. When he took a step into the circle of torchlight, her steps nearly faltered.

He now stretched taller than most men and had developed a broad set of shoulders and a wide chest. He held himself stiffly erect, his manacled hand opening and closing, betraying an intensity held firmly in check. Before her stood a warrior of the ancient tales, possessed of a face certain to set any young maiden's heart to racing.

She'd always thought Bernard's features pleasant to look upon. Pleasant, not handsome, certainly not entrancing.

Every trace of boyishness had vanished.

His thick mane of rich sable hair brushed his shoulders, framing a noble brow and prominent cheekbones. None of his former shyness softened the hard set of his clean shaven, squared jaw. No uncertainty lingered in the depths of his hazel eyes. His gaze swept over her in much the same appraisal she'd given him. An appraisal in which she was sure to come up lacking.

While the years had been as kind as heaven to him, they'd been less than gracious to her.

Claire firmly reminded herself that she was no longer a young maiden, and had no business admiring Bernard's physical attributes. She was about to marry Marshall, a fair handsome and powerful lord willing to overlook her plain features and advanced age for a generous dowry.

"You should have sent a maid or guard down. The dungeon is no place for a lady," Bernard declared.

"A dungeon is no place for a hero of the Crusade, either. Besides, I wished to speak with you." Claire handed him the goblet of wine. "Hold a moment while I fetch something to use as a table."

Bernard took a sip of wine and watched Claire walk off, her spine straight, her chin tilted upward. She'd retained the regal bearing he remembered so well, but no smile played at the corners of her mouth. A pity, that.

Claire hadn't become the woman of his dreams, the exquisite beauty he'd fashioned her into during lonely nights in the desert. As always, she'd gone her own way and perversely become her own woman.

Though her hair was pulled back into a crispinette covered by an emerald silk cap that matched her gown, Bernard noticed the russet color hadn't dimmed. Nor had the sparkle left her eyes of purest amber, set wide from a pert nose. Her skin hadn't paled to porcelain, but brought to mind a finely-wrought ivory carving.

Not exquisite, just adorable, and far more suited to Claire.

Nor had she gone fragile. Sturdily built and softly rounded, she curved with enticing fullness in all of the places a woman should curve. A fine figure that a man might grab hold of tightly without the worry of breaking her.

Claire should have been his to hold, but he'd already determined the futility of claiming a married woman.

Though, the stir of his loins told him, he wouldn't mind having her as his wife and in his bed. All those soft curves pressed close, her ivory skin sliding against the darker tone of his. His name uttered at passion's height from her bow-shaped, rose-tinted mouth.

He shook his head at his senseless musings. Marriage to Claire wasn't to be, and he must accept that. Dwelling on what might have been would only distract him from the more important task of laying claim to his land.

The aroma of the wine tickled his appetite, just as the thought of Claire's observance of courtly manners tickled his humor. For as long as he could remember, Claire had tried to observe the civilities of a court far grander than Lord Setton's. For a time, she'd even wanted to be called Eleanor, in honor of her idol, Eleanor of Aquitaine.

Bernard doubted the long deceased duchess of Aquitaine and queen of England would have taken food to a prisoner in a dungeon, even if she considered the man a hero.

"Hero of the Crusade, is it?" he asked, amused, knowing he'd done nothing more than was necessary to survive and guard the lives of his fellow knights.

"So says the Church of any man who fought the infidels. I happen to agree." Claire picked up a stool and carried it back. "I simply wish you had used greater tact when speaking to Father, then neither of us would be in this foul place."

"I have seen worse," he said. Far worse had been the fortress from which he and his fellow knights had rescued Hugh of Halewell. Setton's dungeon compared to a garden when measured against a Saracen prison. "As for your father, I tried to be forthright without giving offense. Obviously, I did not succeed."

Claire settled the food on the stool. No place in her experience was worse than this dungeon. Likely, Bernard had seen other horrible places in his travels and could tell many a tale. She quelled her curiosity, for now wasn't the time for stories.

He plucked a slice of pork from the bread. "Pepper sauce. My favorite. Did you remember?"

She hadn't, but couldn't help being pleased she'd chosen his meal well. It might make him more agreeable.

''Most men enjoy pepper sauce,'' she commented as the spicily seasoned meat slipped into his mouth between full lips.

Claire backed up a step to keep from wiping away a drop of sauce from the corner of his mouth. She thought about turning away when he captured the drop with a flick of his tongue, but she held her ground.

Sweet mercy, she was noticing far too much of Bernard's person. Best to get her piece said and be gone.

''Your only way out of here is to make amends with my father, you know.''

One sable eyebrow rose. ''Amends? If you mean prostrate myself before him and humbly withdraw my demands for my just reward…nay, Claire, I will not. I fought, well and hard to earn it. Edgar tells me Julius is in Italy. When will he return?''

She'd sent word to Julius about her wedding and the tournament, as she'd also done with her brother, Geoffrey, and sister Jeanne. She hadn't yet received replies. ''A fortnight, I hope.''

Bernard tore a chunk of bread from the loaf, then glanced about the dungeon. ''Two weeks,'' he said on a sigh.

Was Bernard thinking of waiting it out, hoping Julius would support his claim? Father would never allow Bernard to simply rot down here…or would he?

She crossed her arms. ''Bernard, if Father offered you a reward, why did neither he nor Bishop Thurstan say a word of it to anyone?''

He thought about it while chewing on a chunk of cheese. How he could eat in this foul smelling place, she had no idea.

"I know not," he finally said. "All I know for certain is that your father granted me a reward, and I intend to hold him to it...or at least part of it. Without the land, I have nothing."

She heard his longing and determination.

"I highly doubt Father will give any land to you. He has stated before too many people that he owes you nothing."

"Julius will help me. I can wait."

And would be disappointed, she was sure of it. "What if Julius is delayed? What if he does not return for a month or more?"

Bernard frowned, his gaze sweeping round the dungeon, across the rack, over the tools of torture behind it.

Claire pressed her case. "Bernard, do you truly believe my father will simply allow you to wait, unmolested? You know my father. He will have his way." She tossed her hands in the air. "He always does, no matter what he must do to get it."

Bernard took a long sip of wine. "That is why you came down here, is it not, to help your father get his way? Did he tell you to threaten me, see if I would weaken?"

Her father would fly into a rage if he knew she'd come into the dungeon. "Father does not know I am down here. I came of my own accord."

"To what purpose? You obviously believe I have no right to insist he honor his word. But then, you do not believe he made the promise at all, do you?"

No one did. Speculation among the servants had it that Bernard had gone daft in the Holy Land, either from some horrible experience with the Saracens or being out too long in the cursed heat of the desert sun.

"I think, perhaps, Father promised you a reward, but you misunderstood."

He scoffed. "So said Setton. I tell you true, Claire. I did not mishear."

Leaving only one explanation she could think of. "Bernard, is it possible you dreamed of a reward, and the dream was so vivid it seemed real? We all have such dreams."

Bernard's chin tilted upward, his eyes closing. "Aye, I dreamed. Of hides of land beyond what mine eyes could see, plentiful with waist-high wheat. Of a woodland teeming with game for my dogs to flush out and birds for my hawks to snatch from the air. A stone manor with an ample hall and welcoming hearth."

With a small sigh he lowered his head and fixed those incredible hazel eyes on her. "You were there, too, Claire. At times weaving at your loom, a babe or two at your feet. Or plucking the strings of your harp, singing one of those fanciful songs you had learned from a passing troubadour." His gaze sharpened. "I dreamed, but those dreams came not from wishful thoughts, but the promise I had been given. Look to your father for a faulty memory, not me."

Bernard's dream sounded so lovely, and so much more modest than her own dreams had been—and all of those from wishful thoughts, until recently. She would have her grand court in a lovely castle, her every whim attended to by maids or courtiers as soon as she married Eustace Marshall.

How could she ask Bernard to give up his dream of a better life? Claire knew what Bernard's answer would be, but asked anyway because she must. "Is there no other reward you are willing to accept? Mayhap I could convince Father—"

"You need not come down again, my lady" he said, handing her the empty goblet. "Edgar will ensure I do not starve. Stay out of it, Claire. I will deal with your father."

Dealing with her father had earned him a berth in the dungeon and a knock on the head.

"How is your head?"

"It hurts."

"Good. Remember the pain when you deal with him next."

Chapter Three

Bernard's dream refused to leave Claire's head.

Through what remained of the day, she helped her mother ready the hall for evening meal, and heard Bernard describe his manor and its surroundings. Sweet mercy, she could even envision him flying a hawk against a starling or dove.

The warrior in the dungeon craved hearth and home, such as he hadn't known since boyhood.

Claire remembered Bernard's arrival at Dasset, a forlorn child riding at the tail of a supply cart. She'd been all of seven summers, and told only that Bernard's parents had been killed in a raid and so the orphaned boy would reside at Dasset. She knew little of Bernard's family. The elder Fitzgibbons had been her father's man, but in what role Claire had never heard, nor been curious enough to ask.

Curiosity now nagged hard.

She'd also begun to wonder if there wasn't some basis for Bernard's claim. Had her father promised Bernard a reward and then forgotten he'd done so? He had been very ill at the time of Bernard's departure. She still doubted the whole of Bernard's claim, but what reason would Bernard have for demanding a reward if something hadn't been granted?

Throughout evening meal her father celebrated a successful hunt. His retainers matched him goblet for goblet of wine. Many would sleep where they fell tonight, unable to seek out their pallets.

Claire barely knew what she ate, watching intently for that moment when her father was most easily approached—when he'd downed enough wine to muddle his head but before he turned surly.

Bernard had told her not to interfere, but no one else seemed willing to moderate their disagreement. Certainly not her mother, who usually went about her day as if her husband didn't exist.

When her father leaned back in his chair and belched loudly to praise the cook for a fine meal, Claire steeled her resolve and approached him. She drew his attention with a hand to his shoulder.

"Father, might we speak a moment?"

"Hmm? What of?"

Knowing how much her father hated being towered over, Claire grabbed the arm of his chair for balance and scrunched down.

"Bernard Fitzgibbons."

"Sir Bernard," Setton huffed. "Can you credit it? The ungrateful bastard. What of him?"

Claire ignored the base entitlement, not quite sure why her father expected Bernard's gratitude. For allowing Bernard to live at Dasset as a boy, or for sending him off on Crusade?

She recalled the last with some sympathy for Bernard. He'd ridden out the castle gate clad in overlarge chain mail and helm, with a chipped sword and dented shield, on a horse better suited for the plow. Bernard had survived through no fault of his lord's.

"He deserves a reprimand, assuredly. I wonder, though, if keeping him locked in the dungeon is wise." To her father's sharp, censorious look, she quickly added, "For your sake."

He scoffed. "Mine?"

"Aye, Father. As I said earlier, the Church has often declared that any returning Crusader be considered a hero of the faith. By tossing Bernard in the dungeon you may invite the censure of the Church."

Setton waved his goblet toward where Father Robert sat with several knights, tossing dice.

"Tell me, daughter, does our priest seem upset?"

Father Robert held his position as Dasset's priest by virtue of a speedily said Mass. He wouldn't hazard his position by putting Church matters over the wishes of Lord Setton.

"'Tis not the good priest I worry over, but Bishop Walter. If the bishop hears of Bernard's plight, he may take umbrage."

Her father looked about the hall, his gaze resting briefly on a visiting peddler, then on a knight who'd sought hospitality for the night. They would carry the tale out of Dasset. Claire didn't worry for them, however. Her father knew as well as she did that many people traveled often between Dasset and Durleigh, only a half day's ride away. The tale could spread by any number of other means.

"You worry overmuch, Claire."

"Mayhap," she said, wishing her father worried more. "But Father, I want nothing to interfere with my wedding to Marshall, and I fear this situation with Bernard may either prevent or delay it." Claire pressed a hand to her father's forearm and rushed into her solution, praying hard that he proved agreeable. "Something must be done about Bernard in short order. I thought, perhaps, you might see fit to grant him a hide of land, a noble and charitable act on your part, and send him on his way."

Setton leaned toward her, his eyes narrowing to mere slits. He whispered harshly, "Give the miscreant *land?*"

Claire resisted the urge to back away. "A hide, no more. On the farthest reaches of your estate, mayhap. Bernard would be satisfied, the bishop placated, and the wedding and tournament could go on with no one the wiser."

On a loud belch, Setton began to laugh. He tossed his head back and bellowed his mirth, drawing everyone's attention.

Mortification warmed her face, but she waited him out.

"Ah, Claire. Only you would come up with so witless an answer to a difficulty. I shall have to warn Marshall of your peculiar attempt to interfere in dealings best left to men."

Claire managed to control her flash of temper. "I seek only justice and peace for all concerned. Truly, Father, if you think on it, if you gave Bernard some small reward, 'twould go far to glorify your name. All would see you as the most magnanimous of lords."

"All would see me as a weakling," he declared. "You are right, however, in that Bernard must be dealt with. Worry not for any ill-effects on your wedding, daughter. By morn, Bernard will no longer be a difficulty. Go now."

She'd been dismissed, but Claire couldn't move, fro-

zen in place by the finality in her father's tone. She dared
a last question.

"What will you do?"

"Did you see him this morn when he lunged at me?
If not for Henry's lance to the back of his head, he may
have done me harm." Setton quaffed the dregs of his
wine. "Bernard gave me his oath of homage and then
went for my throat. No man threatens his lord's life and
escapes the harshest of punishments."

Sweet mercy, by trying to help Bernard realize his
dream, she may have done him great harm. If she didn't
act quickly, Bernard could be dead by morn.

Bernard ran a finger around the edge of the iron cuff.
Though restrained for mere hours, he felt the degradation
keenly, giving him greater respect for Hugh of Halewell's ordeal. Bernard also better understood Hugh's relief upon seeing his fellow knights arrive at the prison
in the Holy Land, come to end his suffering.

Bernard glanced at the dungeon's door. A useless gesture. None of his friends knew of his plight. He couldn't
look to a rescue even if he wanted one.

'Twas a strange feeling to be wholly on his own, with
no comrade to guard his back.

The dungeon's door opened. Someone stepped inside,
shrouded from head to toe within a dark, hooded cloak.
He caught a flash of emerald—Claire, he realized—as
she turned to close the door.

She pushed back her hood and reached for the large
ring of keys that hung under a torch.

"What are you about?" he asked.

Claire crossed the chamber swiftly, sorting through
the keys. "Setting you free. Do you know which key
unlocks the cuff?"

He'd used every key on the ring while a squire in Setton's service. 'Twas tempting, but he'd not make use of the key today. "Put the ring back on its hook. I do not wish to be freed."

She stopped before him. Her hands trembled, jangling the keys. "You have no choice. Unlock the cuff and be gone before the bell is sounded to close the gates."

"I do have a choice, and I choose to remain until I come up with a plan to force your father to give over my reward."

"If you stay, you may not live to see another sunrise! What good will your reward do you then? Please, Bernard. Argue no more. Just go."

Another plea from another Setton to depart Dasset, and Claire seemed as much in earnest as her father had been those many years ago. Something had happened to send Claire down here with the notion that his life was endangered. Or Lord Setton had sent her down to test his resolve.

"What happened?" he asked.

She glanced at the door, as if waiting for a guard to burst through. "I sought to reason with Father on your behalf, but only made things worse for you. Much worse."

The rack was one of Setton's favorite toys. Bernard had seen men stretched out on it. Some screamed from the moment they'd been strapped on while others suffered in silence. All broke. Bernard wondered how much he could withstand.

"Bernard, hurry!"

Only a coward ran. "I cannot—"

Both of her fists slammed into his chest. "Fool! Do you not understand? He will *kill* you if he must to be rid of you!"

Dare he believe her? Dare he not?

Bernard took the keys and unlocked the cuff, his anger rising. "What the hell did you say to him?"

"I will tell you on the way out. Come," she said, and turned toward the door.

"Hold a moment. Did anyone see you come down?"

"I kept to the shadows. I think not."

Not good enough. If he was going to escape, he would do so cleanly.

"Hang up the keys and grab a torch. We will take another way."

"What other way?"

"Through the tunnels."

Bernard strode to the wall of seemingly solid stone behind the rack. He reached behind the whips and probed for a lever he knew to be about waist high. From behind him, he heard the jangle of keys and the slide of a torch from its sconce. The light around him grew brighter.

"Stay where you are, Claire. Let me open this first."

If the dungeon was no place for a lady, then the tunnels were less so. Dug by an ancestor of Setton's, the tunnels provided an escape route to the river if Dasset were about to fall to an attacking enemy. In times of peace, the lords of Dasset put them to other uses, smuggling in particular.

He found the lever and pushed hard. With the grinding of stone and screech of laboring pulleys, a section of the wall slid open. He could see but a few feet into the tunnel before the darkness extinguished the light of Claire's torch. No pile of bones littered the floor, only a thin layer of mud. He heard no rats. Bernard stepped into the tunnel.

"Come, Claire. The way is clear."

When she reached his side, he shut the wall behind him. The noise was nearly deafening within the tunnel hewn of rock and dirt.

Claire grabbed a fistful of the back of his tabard.

"Mercy," she said with awe. "There is not a mother's child who has not been threatened with being sent to the tunnels for misbehavior. Can one truly become forever lost?"

Bernard grabbed the torch and began walking. "Have you never been in them?"

She shook her head and fell into step beside him, not hard because he walked more slowly than he would have liked. The torch lit up only a few feet around them before fading into the complete blackness beyond.

'Twas awkward having her pull on his tabard. He reached around and took her hand, then wished he hadn't. She clasped his hand in a firm grip, her chilled fingers warming readily to the warmth of his. A warmth that spread farther than his hands.

He took refuge in answering her question.

"The main tunnel slants down to the river," he explained. "Another tunnel branches off to a stairway leading up to the lord's bedchamber. Yet another comes out under the stable. So. What did you say to your father that makes my escape urgent?"

Claire sighed. "I pointed out to him that imprisoning a hero of the Crusade—"

"I am no hero."

She squeezed his hand. "I believe you are. Be that as it may, your imprisonment would not sit well with either Durleigh's bishop or sheriff. Both could cause trouble at a time when Father needs peace. I suggested he give you a hide of land somewhere and send you on your way."

Bernard could imagine Setton's reaction. "Your father took umbrage."

"Oh, aye, he surely did."

Not surprising. Yet, had he been too hasty in accepting Claire's judgement of the situation? He stopped walking.

"Just because your father is angry does not mean he intends to dispose of me."

Haltingly, she told him of her talk with Setton, of how she'd suggested the bishop might punish Dasset with an interdict.

"The alliance to Marshall is important to my father," she said. "My wedding could not take place if Dasset is under an interdict, and thus no alliance with Marshall."

She was not married.

He'd made a hasty assumption when told of the bargain, thinking it done and over. Claire was only betrothed, not yet beyond his reach.

Except he'd already told Setton that he would relinquish Claire in exchange for the land. He was a man of his word, even if Setton was not.

Bernard's anger, so recently banked, flared again. "So I am to give up my reward so your father may have his alliance and you have your marriage."

"That is not the worst of it. Father believes you tried to harm him this morning and deserve the harshest of punishments. By leaving now, at least you will have your life."

Bernard resumed the journey through the tunnel at a faster pace. "What life? I have no funds to buy land, so must resort to the skill of my sword to earn my living. By the devil's toenails, I have no wish to become a mercenary, assuming I could raise the funds to buy passage to the continent to do so.''

''What of pledging your sword to an English lord? Many would welcome a knight such as you,'' she said.

''As a new man, I would become a household guard, which I could have done here if I had been of a mind. 'Twould take several years to prove my worthiness and rise so high in another's service that land might be considered.''

Claire coughed in hard, sharp bursts that came clear from her toes. Bernard slowed, noting the flush on her cheeks from lack of air.

''Are you all right?'' he asked.

She took a deep breath and waved a dismissing hand. '''Tis no more than the remains of my sniffles. Only the cough lingers.''

Bernard turned into the tunnel which passed under the castle's storage rooms and armory. Claire's head swivelled to inspect the stairway as they passed it.

''Do these stairs lead up to the lord's chambers?''

''So I am told.''

She smiled up at him. ''Now I know how to get back into the castle without being discovered.''

'Twas the first smile she'd given him since his return. Her bow lips curved upward, parted slightly. A mouth made for smiling, lips that invited kissing, belonging to a woman who should have been his to kiss. Contrary to all sense, he was again thinking about kissing the woman whose meddling had made it more difficult for him to collect his reward.

The tunnel turned sharply and sloped upward toward the stable at its end. This wasn't how he'd planned to leave Dasset, making a dash for the gate before it closed for the night. Empty-handed, with nothing to show for his sacrifice. Under threat of death from the lord he'd served.

"Hold this," he said, handing her the torch.

Bernard grabbed hold of the ladder rungs. He hadn't yet stepped up when Claire said, "I am sorry, Bernard. If I had not spoken to Father none of this might have happened."

She sought forgiveness. 'Twould be the kind thing to do, simply give her the words. But the words stuck in his throat, so he climbed the ladder.

Slowly, as quietly as possible, Bernard pushed up on a plank at the roof of the tunnel. A shower of dirt and straw fell into his face, but he continued to move the plank up and to the side. Hearing no voices from above, he climbed higher and poked his head through the opening.

Long shadows spread across the stable's floor, heralding the end of the day. Horses drowsed in the stalls, having been fed and watered before the stable master and his lads went off for their evening meal. A couple of the lads would return shortly to spend the night in the loft.

Bernard climbed back down the ladder. "Up you go, my lady."

She glanced up the ladder, then over her shoulder at the tunnel. "I had thought to leave you here and go back to the stairway."

"I need you to stand watch while I ready my horse. After all the trouble you have caused, 'tis the least you can do."

She took a deep breath, her lips pursed. Bernard braced for an argument, but then she handed over the torch and wiped her hands on her cloak before grabbing hold of the ladder.

A loud creak accompanied her first step up.

"I dislike the sound of it. 'Tis not sturdy," she said.

"All ladders creak. It held my weight, did it not?"

"You will catch me if it breaks?"

"'Tis the least I can do."

One rung at a time, her knuckles white, she started up the ladder. By the time her feet hit the third rung, Bernard felt some remorse for making light of her request. She was shaking. On the fourth rung, Claire swayed.

Without conscious thought he steadied her with a hand to her rump. She stiffened instantly and clung to the ladder. Even through the layers of her gowns and cloak, he felt the muscles beneath his hand quiver and contract.

"Oh, very nice," he heard himself say.

She cleared her throat.

"You may remove your hand, Bernard. I am steady now."

"Are you sure?"

She scowled down at him. "No true knight would take such unfair advantage of a lady. Had I the courage to move my foot so far, you would have my heel in your chest."

"A woman about to fall cannot be choosy about the manner in which she is saved."

"Bernard!"

He removed his hand. "Very well, my lady. Can you manage the rest of the way without falling—or a push?"

Claire looked up the ladder and sighed.

Bernard stood ready to toss the torch and climb up after Claire or catch her if need be. 'Twas hard, slow work for her, but she reached the top and wiggled through the opening.

Truly, Claire *did* have a very nice rump.

He couldn't take a lighted torch up with him. So great was the fear of fire that torches weren't allowed in the stable. A flicker of light would be noted and acted upon by passersby. He leaned the torch against the wall.

His own climb took less time than Claire's.

She stood at the far end of the stable, peeking round the edge of the doorway into the bailey beyond.

The stable master had done as told. Bernard's saddle and pack were in the stall, his scimitar laid across the pack. With the weapon slid home in its scabbard, Bernard made quick work of readying Cabal.

Time to flee. It yet irked him, but what else could he do? Dead he couldn't collect his reward; alive there might be a chance.

He strode toward Claire. She heard him and turned around.

"Ready?" she asked.

"Aye. How do we do?"

"Father must have ordered another ale keg opened to celebrate his hunt. Hardly a soul strolls about. Godspeed, Bernard. Go far and fast."

Fast, aye, but not far. He should head for Durleigh, he supposed, and make further plans from there.

Plans for what? Challenge Setton for the reward again? Who beyond Julius might listen and believe he'd been grievously wronged? 'Twas Bernard's word against Setton's that a reward had been granted.

If Bishop Thurstan had lived to bear witness…but he hadn't. No help there.

Bernard scanned the bailey. Claire had the right of it. Hardly a soul wandered about. 'Twould be easy to gallop out the gate to freedom. For a hastily wrought plan, Claire had chosen the perfect time with prime conditions.

Too easy? Too prime?

Truly, he needn't have bothered coming through the tunnels. Without a problem, he could have followed Claire straight up the dungeon's stairway and across the bailey to the stable, unseen. He'd been in the dungeon for several hours, yet his saddle, pack and scimitar were all here and handy, undisturbed.

Bernard didn't doubt Claire had talked to her father, but he now wondered if she told the truth of what had been said. He could well imagine the two of them conspiring to be rid of him—Odo to save his alliance, Claire to save her upcoming marriage.

Fury rose, bright and hot, as he imagined their scheming on how to dispose of the nuisance in the dungeon without raising his suspicions of being played for a fool. What a profound fool he'd been, listening to Claire's false pleas.

With him out of the way, either dead or gone, the Settons could go forward without a care. The only question that remained is whether they intended to let him ride out of Dasset or if guards armed with crossbows waited to take down an escaping prisoner.

They weren't going to get away with it.

He would take Claire with him. No guard would dare let loose a bolt for fear of hitting the lord's daughter. Then, by damn, she could help him obtain his land.

A fair trade for her betrayal.

Chapter Four

"Back the horses out of their stalls," Bernard told her, then headed for the back of the stable.

Exasperated, Claire tossed her hands in the air. Why couldn't the man simply get on his courser and leave? Bernard seemed in no hurry at all! He wasted precious minutes when he should be rushing toward the gate.

"Why?" she asked.

"For a diversion. We let the horses loose to draw attention away from us," he said, then disappeared down the ladder into the tunnel.

There were few in the bailey to divert! Yet, as she went from stall to stall, she decided his reasoning made sense. While people chased horses, Bernard wouldn't have anyone to contend with until he reached the gate. Too, during the confusion, she could slip away unnoticed, get back into the castle without having to go back down a wobbly ladder. Going down, if the ladder broke, Bernard wouldn't be there to catch her.

Claire could still feel his large, warm hand on her backside. He'd steadied her for far longer than necessary, adding to her discomfort. Still, he'd given her something other than her fears to focus on—a diversion of sorts—as she climbed out of the tunnel.

Whatever was he doing down there so long anyway?

She sneezed. Her head was beginning to ache again, her nose to fill up. When this was over, she promised herself, she'd crawl onto her pallet and not move till morn. Maybe not until nooning.

Claire backed another horse out of a stall to see Bernard come up out of the hole. He pushed the plank back to where it belonged and kicked some dirt over it.

"Finished?" he asked.

"Two more, besides yours."

Soon, eight confused horses shuffled about in the aisle. Bernard inspected his packs and his courser's tack. Guessing what he was about to do, Claire moved to the side of the door. Here she'd be out of the horses' way yet see the excitement about to take place in the bailey— and be in position to sneak away from the stable when the moment seemed right.

Bernard neither got on his horse nor sent the others out the door. Instead, he strode toward her. Now what? Fare-thee-wells? The signal to close the gate would sound any moment now. If Bernard didn't leave with haste, he'd be trapped!

Before she could tell him so, he bent over and lunged for her stomach, nearly knocking her over as he picked her up. Draped over his shoulder, Claire couldn't breathe much less protest. With a move as slick as silk, he mounted his courser and settled her sideways on his lap.

Claire found a puff of breath. "Put me down."

"I think not, my lady," he said in an unyielding, chilling tone.

With both hands she pushed against the arm clamped

around her waist, holding her firmly against him. "I demand you release me!"

"Not until your father comes to his senses. Once he does, I will bring you back to Dasset."

Bernard intended to hold her hostage against his reward! She'd freed Bernard from the dungeon only to become his captive.

Claire kicked at the horse and swung at the man. For her efforts, Bernard pinned her arms to her sides and turned her around to ride astride.

Fear quickened her heartbeat. She drew a deep, calming breath—and caught a whiff of smoke. The horses smelled it, too, becoming agitated.

"Fire." The word came out as little more than a whisper.

"The ladder."

That's what he'd been doing in the tunnel, starting the ladder afire. Soon the stable would go up in flames. His true diversion, she realized. He'd set her to freeing the horses as a way to keep her busy.

"Treacherous knave! This is how you repay my kindness?"

"I will measure your kindness by our reception at the gate."

The gate bell tolled, warning all to be on whichever side of the gate they wanted to be before it closed for the night.

Bernard had waited too long to make his escape. He'd be captured. Father would hang him on the morn for this kidnaping attempt and setting the stable afire. She'd tried to save Bernard, and now Bernard gave Father just cause to hang him. Nor would Father's fury be appeased by Bernard's death. She wouldn't escape a reprimand for her part in this affair.

"Hold tight!" Bernard shouted and kicked at the rump of a nearby horse. The horse bolted for the doorway. The others followed, as did Bernard.

They broke free of the small herd and flew across the bailey. Claire held tight to the only solid support available—Bernard's arm.

No one, thank providence, was foolish enough to step before the charging courser to try to stop them. Truly, they needn't. The gate was coming down. Already the points of the huge, iron gate were visible, lowering slowly, steadily. Bernard would have to turn aside soon.

He didn't. Incredibly, he spurred his courser to a swifter speed. The guards at the gate spotted them. Some pointed and shouted, lances at the ready. She heard Bernard's name, and then her own, among the guards' cries.

With her heart in her throat, Claire realized Bernard didn't intend to stop. Not in her wildest imaginings had she dreamed she would die atop a courser, crushed between a knight gone mad and an iron gate.

She closed her eyes. *"Ave Maria, gratcia plena—"*

Bernard chuckled. "Save your prayers for when we need them. Duck down."

He didn't give her a choice. He leaned forward, folding her in half, smothering her with his body. Unable to breathe or see ahead, she ignored his admonishment and continued to pray, keeping track of their progress by sounds.

The pounding of hooves on dirt. The shouts of the guards, ordering Bernard to halt. The unholy screech of the gate as they passed under. And finally, the sharp clip of the courser's iron shoes on the wooden drawbridge.

The horse's pace slackened only a little, carrying them swiftly down the road. Bernard rose up, bringing her with him. She drew in a long breath and blew out a relieved sigh.

"Now you can pray," he said.

Incensed, she told him, "I never stopped. Truly, Bernard, 'tis only by the grace of the Blessed Mother we still live."

"Then ask for her blessing a while longer. I expect we shall have a company of guards coming after us shortly."

Claire hoped so.

Bernard pushed Cabal down the road until it was too dangerous to go on. Alone, he might brave the night a while longer. Risking his own neck was one thing; risking Claire's was quite another. Best to pull off the road, get some sleep and ponder over his next move.

He'd made two hasty decisions today—one to escape, the other to kidnap Claire. Both had been made in response to events over which he'd had little control. From now on, he intended to control his fate.

Since one spot along the road was as good as another, he supposed, he reined his courser to a halt.

Claire's anger would glow red if given form. She sat stiffly before him, her spine as straight and firm as an iron rod. She hadn't said a word after chastising him for slipping under the descending gate.

With his arm around her middle to hold her steady, he'd felt Claire's every movement, her every breath. She hadn't given in to tears, though early on he'd felt a hitch in her breathing that warned him she might. She'd coughed instead, though whether to strengthen her resolve not to cry or because of her sniffles, he didn't know. He'd loosened his hold but refused to feel guilt.

She held on to her anger, refused to give way to fear.

He admired her for it, though he preferred not to. Claire's meddling in his business with her father had made flight from Dasset necessary. Whether she'd innocently interfered or plotted his demise, he still wasn't sure.

Bernard dismounted, then put a hand to Claire's elbow to help her down. He had no trouble understanding the scathing look she shot him. Claire held him in contempt, resigned him to perdition with a frown and narrowed eyes.

He couldn't blame her, especially if she was an innocent victim of his troubles with Setton.

"Take your hands from me," she said, spitting the words.

Bernard obliged and backed up two paces. If she could get down on her own, he would let her.

She made a lightning-swift grab for Cabal's reins and kicked the courser. The warhorse stood perfectly still, too well trained to obey anyone's commands but his master's.

"Move, damn you!" she shouted and kicked again.

Bernard grabbed her ankle to save the horse's ribs. "You should know better, Claire. A courser obeys only his knight. Now come down."

A slight dip of her head. A small huff of resignation. Then she leaned forward, clutched Cabal's mane and swung her free foot over his back as if to comply. Sensing her true intent, Bernard caught hold of her swinging boot before the heel could connect with his chin. For her vain effort, she landed stomach down on the saddle.

If he were Claire, he knew what his next course of action would be—take off afoot.

Hoping to discourage her flight, he gave her a warning. "There are more ferocious beasts of the night than me. You would make easy prey and a fine dinner for a wolf.''

Though draped awkwardly over Cabal, she managed to mutter, ''Mayhap I prefer the wolves to a demon.''

Demon, now, was he? He kept his amusement out of his voice. ''I cannot let you court the wolves, Claire. I shall let you down on your oath to behave.''

She shifted, rising slightly to look over her shoulder at him. ''This from a man who, just this morn, swore an oath of fealty to my father. What good is an oath given to an oath breaker?''

His amusement fled. ''I would have kept my oath had your father not broken faith first.''

''Truly? What of your knightly oath to protect noble women? 'Twould seem you have broken that one, too!''

Had he detected a dram of worry in her voice? Mayhap Claire wasn't so brave after all.

''You are safe with me, my lady. I will let no harm come to you while under my care. As part of that oath, neither will I allow you to harm yourself—as in becoming a wolf's meal.''

She didn't answer.

He shook her ankle. ''Might prove hard to sleep on your current perch. And while I must say the view from where I stand is most enjoyable, 'tis most undignified. You do have a beautifully curved rump, Claire.''

She gasped. ''Let me down!''

''Your oath first.''

''Fiend.''

''Is a fiend of lower caste than a demon or treacherous knave?''

''Several steps lower!'' she declared, then sighed. ''Oh, very well. I shall desist from feeding the wolves.

Besides, Father's men will come across us soon. I suppose I can tolerate your company until then.''

Bernard let go of her ankle and put his hand to her waist. When she neither wiggled nor kicked, he grasped her with both hands and guided her slide to the ground. Once down, Claire adjusted her cloak about her shoulders and strove to regain her dignity. When she turned around, no trace of her embarrassment or anger showed—only the coolness of a noblewoman.

She looked back on the road they'd traveled, her brow furrowing. ''He sent no company out after us, did he?'' she asked, her confusion mingled with disappointment.

Bernard had wondered, too. He'd checked over his shoulder several times, fully expecting the garrison to ride hard on his tail. So far as he knew, Dasset's gate had lowered and remained down. He'd heard no pounding of hooves behind him on the road, no shouts of angry soldiers to halt and release his captive.

Now, with night falling hard and fog beginning to swirl, he highly doubted Setton would be foolish enough to send his men out of the gates. Besides, his men might yet be very busy.

''Mayhap all hands are needed to fight the fire.''

''Your diversion,'' she said with a sneer. ''Father will be more than angry with you now that you tried to burn down his castle. What were you thinking, Bernard? You keep giving him reasons to have you hanged!''

She had a point. Bernard ran a hand down Cabal's neck.

''I do not suppose he will be grateful that we let loose his horses.''

Claire stood silent for a moment, then crossed her arms. ''Nay. He will not remember the horses as he puts a noose around your neck, only that you started the fire.

Truly, Bernard, I do not see what you hope to gain by this madness.''

His goal, as always, was possession of the portion of the reward he needed to survive. What he'd fought for in the Holy Land. What he fought for yet.

"Land."

"After all you have done, do you believe Father will give it to you?"

Bernard shook his head. "Even I am not so foolish. Nor can I say I want your father's land. In truth, I do not think I could bear Odo Setton as my overlord. What I will demand, however, is enough gold and silver to buy an estate elsewhere."

"How much?"

He shrugged a shoulder. "I had not thought that far. I wonder how much you are worth to him."

She answered with a wry smile. "At the moment, I imagine he would rather let you keep me. Father would consider it my just punishment for helping you escape his dungeon." She glanced back down the road. "Mayhap that is the true reason why he sent no soldiers to fetch me."

Bernard hadn't considered the possibility that Setton might let his daughter go. He was greatly relieved when she continued.

"He will take me back, however. He may even, against his will, give you something for my return. Without me there can be no wedding, and thus no alliance to Marshall."

For a practical reason, having nothing whatever to do with the love a father should bear for a child. The lack of caring between father and daughter wasn't his problem. So long as Setton paid a goodly sum to get her back, the reason for paying the ransom made no difference.

"Your father has what I want. I have that which he needs. We shall make a trade, he and I, and then forget we ever heard one another's names."

"So simple?"

Bernard knew better, but he could hope for the best.

He held out his hand. "Come, we will build a fire to keep away the wolves."

Claire found little ease in the night music of whichever bugs and animals sang their summer songs. The night was mild and dry, yet she huddled in her cloak within the circle of a small but crackling fire. Bernard had assured her wolves disliked flames and would keep a distance.

She dearly hoped so. As yet, she hadn't heard one howl, but that didn't mean none lurked nearby. Too, Cabal hated the beasts, or so Bernard claimed, and would give warning if a bolder wolf came too near.

Cabal—a fanciful name for a courser, straight out of the ancient legend of King Arthur, the name of the king's pet dog. Bernard's courser was no pet, but a knight's vital companion. Bernard had been right, she should have known the horse would obey no one but its owner. The owner now scrubbed the horse's hide with a fistful of coarse grass, rubbing the sweat and grime from his most valued possession.

Bernard glanced over his shoulder, checking on her. He needn't. She wasn't going anywhere tonight. Not only because of the wolves, but 'twas so dark that beyond the light of the fire she couldn't see her hand in front of her face, much less find the road. So she would spend the night in the forest, in the company of the uncouth, unchivalrous lout of a knight who'd deprived her of the comfort of her bed and a hot posset to ease her stuffy nose and aching head.

'Twas hard to think of Bernard Fitzgibbons as a knight, though the look of him left little doubt. His size, his mail, his horse—all confirmed he'd come into his own while on Crusade.

She couldn't deny he'd become a handsome man, or that she didn't notice his fine features. Or his broad shoulders. Or the strength of the arm clamped about her midriff during the dash from Dasset.

Bernard had become a stubborn man, too. He yet maintained her father owed him a reward, and he would collect it in one form or another. While Claire wasn't sure what to believe on that score, she knew full well her father's impending reaction to a ransom demand.

He would toss a grand fit.

Though he'd likely pay the ransom, she would also pay a price, especially if the fire had caused a goodly amount of damage requiring costly repairs.

Then again, maybe the fire had been easily doused. With the horses out of the stable, people could concentrate on putting out the fire. Bernard had started the fire, but he'd also ensured the horses safely out of harm's way, an act of kindness of which she approved.

Still, if Bernard had done as told, as any truly chivalrous knight would, she wouldn't now be sitting near a small fire, her temples throbbing, her musing rambling away in no certain direction. Her sniffles were going to be back in full force on the morn, she just knew it.

Claire closed her eyes and rubbed at her headache. Sweet mercy, she was tired, but saw no hope for rest.

The jangle of chain mail warned her of Bernard's

presence behind her, but didn't prepare her for the warmth of his fingers on the sides of her head.

"Allow me, my lady," he said.

Claire lowered her hands and nearly melted under the ministration of his gifted fingers. With light pressure and slow circles he kneaded away the pain, leaving behind a pleasant numbness.

Her head wasn't the only part of her body to respond to the magic of his hands. The tips of her breasts tingled, as if hoping those gently circling fingers might ease their itch, too. Down low within her nether places another ache formed in a swirl of liquid heat.

"Better?" he asked.

Hardly. The pain had left her head, but now she ached in places she had no right to ache. Heaven help her, she liked the sensations, this awareness of her body. 'Twas sinful to feel yearnings for a man not her husband, a man she should consider her enemy.

According to Bernard, she'd been promised to him as part of his reward. She'd have become his wife, lain abed with him, known those hands on her naked body.

She wouldn't be Bernard's wife, but Eustace Marshall's. Would Marshall's touch affect her so profoundly?

Bernard cleared his throat. "Claire? Have you fallen asleep?"

She shook her head; his hands slipped away. "Nay, but the pain is gone, so mayhap now I can sleep."

Maybe she could, if the rest of her body allowed it.

"Good. You will need whatever rest you can manage. We will have a hard day on the morrow avoiding the soldiers your father will surely send out at first light."

Mention of her father snuffed her desire. How foolish

she was, wallowing in sensual fancies about the man who'd kidnaped her and led her into danger.

How odd that she'd not truly considered the dangers, not once been frightened. Except for those few moments when she'd been sure Bernard would run headlong into the gate. Those moments would twist her dreams into nightmares for some time to come, she was sure.

"Where do you intend to go?" she asked. "You may avoid the soldiers tomorrow, but surely they will catch you eventually."

Bernard moved to sit beside her. "Only if I allow them to, or become careless. 'Tis not in my plan to be careless."

"Have you a plan?"

"Of sorts. We will need food and shelter first. Then find some way to relay my ransom demand to Setton. Arrange a place to make the exchange. Then you return to Dasset and I—I take the ransom and buy some land, far away from Dasset."

She shook her head at his casual attitude. He seemed to think he had the upper hand, as if there were no way her father could thwart Bernard's plans.

"'Twill not be so easy, Bernard."

"I know. But the simplest plan leaves room for amendment."

"And for failure. Look at what has happened this eve."

At his raised eyebrow, she went on. "I did not plan your escape as thoroughly as I ought have. I should have known things would go awry but thought only of setting you free and not far beyond."

"You did not fail. You set me free."

"Only to be made your captive. 'Tis one of your amendments I had not foreseen."

"You could not have, since I did not think of it myself until we were in the stable."

"An ill-fated notion if ever I heard one."

"We will see."

Claire withheld comment. She'd already tried to sway Bernard from his course and gotten nowhere. 'Twas like pushing against a stone wall.

Besides, what Bernard did on the morrow did not concern her. She had a plan of her own, which didn't include spending several days wandering about the forest with Bernard.

As Bernard had said, Father's soldiers would be out at first light looking for her, and would surely come down this road. She would be on that road, waiting for the first one to come her way. If she intended to be up before dawn, she needed sleep.

Claire lay down where she was, curling up within the cover of her cloak, pulling the hood forward to pad her face against the forest floor. She closed her eyes and told herself to sleep.

She heard Bernard's chain mail, but could tell he hadn't gotten to his feet. She opened her eyes to see he'd merely shifted and was removing his tabard. Once off, he folded the silken, gray tabard into a neat square.

He held it out to her. "For your head," he said.

Claire tucked it under her cheek, and immediately wished she'd refused his kindness. She didn't want to think kindly of Bernard. Nor had she any notion of how she would sleep with the scent of him playing havoc with her senses.

He shouldn't have touched her. Shouldn't have gotten anywhere near her. But the sight of Claire rubbing at her temples had overcome his good sense.

Claire was ill, and he'd spirited her out of Dasset without considering the possible consequences of her illness becoming worse. He knew how to treat battle wounds, even how to ease an aching head, but not how to cure coughs and sneezes. If Claire became gravely ill, if she died...he shook his head. He'd not let things go so far.

While in the tunnel, she'd said her sniffles were nearly gone, that only the cough remained. She might suffer a slight setback from spending the night out of doors, but she shouldn't worsen too much. If she did, he'd simply take her to someplace where treatment could be had. A physician or herbalist in Durleigh town. Or to any abbey. Maybe to the old, crotchety monk who'd treated his broken leg but seemed to know what he was about.

His fingertips had felt the faint pulse beneath her temples, speeding the beat of his own heart. Her soft moan of relief had sounded akin to a soft moan of yearning.

He should have pulled away then, but his thumbs had brushed against the netting covering her hair, allowing him a brief but tantalizing touch of the silken strands. From there his imagination had taken to wing and had yet to roost.

Wanting Claire, as a man wants a woman, was a mistake. He couldn't have her. She'd been betrothed to another man—a wealthy, powerful lord—and he'd relinquished his claim.

Better he should contemplate Claire's worth to her father.

In gold.

Then figure out how to go about getting his hands on it.

Chapter Five

Claire's cough came from deep in her chest and threatened to choke her. Or so it seemed to Bernard.

After what had been an exhausting day, he'd removed his chain mail in favor of a long-sleeved, peasant-weave brown tunic. He'd fallen asleep nearly as soon as his eyes closed, then awakened to the dry rasp of Claire's cough. He didn't like the sound of it, especially that nasty underlying wheeze as she struggled for air.

When her cough didn't seem about to ease, he got up and rummaged through his pack until he found his cloak. He knelt at Claire's side.

"Sit up," he told her and gave her his hand to help.

She obeyed, covering her mouth with his tabard. He tossed his cloak over the one she already wore.

Claire's face had turned a mean shade of red. Tears slid down her cheeks. He wished he had something soothing to give her, but he didn't. Not knowing what else to do he rubbed her back. She slowly gained control.

"Better?" he asked.

She nodded.

He swiped at a tear, pushing it across her cheekbone into the fall of her silken hair.

"I thought for a moment that your insides would spill out."

"Almost," she said weakly, a small smile on her lips.

"Did you not tell me your sniffles were done?"

She cleared her throat and looked about their small campsite. "All but for this cough. Breathing this damp air has not done it any good."

She didn't have to accuse him of worsening her illness. He already knew he was responsible for her health and must ensure she got well. Only, how to do so without giving away their whereabouts?

Going into Durleigh seemed too risky so soon after their escape. Setton would send patrols into the town, or at least in the town's direction. He could take Claire to the abbey near York, but he would rather not travel so far away from Dasset. Besides, Claire needed more immediate relief.

For now, he could but keep her warm and dry, and maybe if she slept more upright the cough wouldn't take her so thoroughly again. Resigning himself to a sleepless night, Bernard swept Claire from the ground.

"What are you doing?" she asked, tossing her arms around his neck, her face so close to his that he could feel her breath.

"I am moving you. Save your voice, and mayhap your throat and insides."

With little trouble Bernard settled on the ground with his back against a tree. Claire fitted nicely between his upraised knees. Too nicely. Her body warmed the inner thigh against which she leaned. The heat spread, rushing through his blood like fire. He fought hard against the lust any man would feel for any woman who lay between his legs.

Surely, 'twas merely lust.

She put her hand on his chest when she realized where he intended for her to sleep. "Ah, Bernard, I um…"

"Can you breathe better?"

"Aye, but I do not think—"

"I do not either, but can think of no other way to ease your breathing and mayhap prevent your cough. 'Tis the only way I know of to help you."

She studied his face intently, her amber eyes looking for answers to a question she seemed unable to ask. He gave her the answers she needed—so she would sleep.

"I will not hurt you, Claire. Nor will I take liberties. I need you to sleep so you will be prepared for whatever happens on the morrow."

"What *will* happen?" she whispered.

He shrugged a shoulder and smiled. "Depends on how many men your father sends after us and how early. Who knows, they may catch us both here sleeping."

Claire's eyes went wide at the picture he painted. He chuckled and pulled her against his chest. Her head landed softly on his shoulder, and stayed there. If he moved his head a mere inch, his cheek would brush against her hair.

Through no conscious effort, his arms circled Claire.

"You must remember that I need you alive and well enough to hand over to your father, eventually," he told her. "'Twould seem I must take care of you in order to get my reward."

"How chivalrous of you," she said in a cutting tone, then snuggled deeper into the cloaks, pulling both hoods about her face.

Bernard let the mocking remark pass and directed his thoughts toward solving his immediate problem.

He would get little sleep with Claire pressed against him. He'd given Claire his word that he wouldn't take advantage of the situation, but no man could resist wondering what this lovely woman might do if he kissed her. Ponder on how she might respond if he touched her in one of a woman's many sensitive places—which he knew about thanks to an Arab woman who'd demanded equal pleasure.

He'd learned the skills of satisfying a woman with the idea that he would ply them well on the woman who would be his wife. Claire. The woman who trustingly slept against his shoulder with no notion that he wanted her. 'Twould be easier, now, if she were married to another, giving him another reason to keep his hands to himself and his urges under control.

Claire *was* betrothed, but betrothed wasn't married.

Except he couldn't touch her, bound by his own oath.

He put his head back and closed his eyes, willing his body to remain calm and for one certain part to stand down. He couldn't succumb no matter how great the temptation.

For his own sanity, he had to cease thinking of Claire as his. All she could be to him was Setton's daughter, the means by which he gained the important part of his reward. Returning her to her father in good health must be his foremost consideration.

If he were alone, he could wander about the countryside for days, sleeping on the ground and scavenging for food where he might. Claire needed shelter. She was used to sleeping on a soft pallet with a roof over her head, accustomed to meals of hearty fare and to clean, dry garments.

He must also find an herbalist for the posset Claire needed for her sniffles.

Bernard knew where to find both, close by, if the

manor yet stood and the herbalist yet lived. If he could find the courage to revisit his childhood home.

He'd never returned to Faxton after the raid that had taken his parents' lives. In outraged grief he'd done as Odo Setton had commanded—gone to Dasset—when assured his parents' deaths would be avenged, the bandits captured and hung.

Was he ready to go back and face his past? Maybe not, but for Claire's sake, he must.

Lord Odo Setton paced the archer's walk of the outer curtain wall, cursing the fog that hampered the search for Claire and Fitzgibbons. All morning his men-at-arms and knights had ridden the road and wandered the woodland. They'd seen nary a sign of the pair.

"My lord," Miles called up from the ground far below. "The men who searched the area of the old mill have returned. Shall I send them to Durleigh?"

Another failure. He hated failure.

"Have them gather in the hall. I will speak with them first," Setton said, then took another look out over the fog-shrouded fields surrounding Dasset Castle.

The men he sent to Durleigh must be cautious, have care not to alert either the bishop or the sheriff of their purpose. Claire had been right to be concerned about those two men.

Now, if his daughter had only shown the wisdom to let him deal with the problem in his own way—well, she hadn't. She'd meddled in outrageous fashion. Now both Claire and the troublesome Fitzgibbons were on the loose and creating more problems.

The miscreant had threatened his overlord's life, set fire to the stable, and kidnaped Claire. For any one of those crimes Fitzgibbons deserved hanging.

For aiding Bernard's escape, so did Claire. He'd be tempted to put a noose around her neck, too, if he didn't need her to marry Marshall.

'Twas all Bishop Thurstan's fault, of course. Four years ago, Thurstan had refused him absolution at the height of his illness and panic, until the terms of the penance had been met.

Send a knight on Crusade. Make amends to Bernard Fitzgibbons.

Odo thought he'd done so in a brilliant stroke by sending Bernard Fitzgibbons on Crusade. The lad hadn't been a knight. The squire couldn't point a lance at a quintain without being knocked from his horse, or wield a sword with enough authority to be aught else but a menace. Still, Thurstan hadn't objected to the choice of Crusader, especially when Setton promised to reward the lad when he returned.

The latter still rankled. No man in his right mind would have guessed Fitzgibbons would survive and come back to claim the reward Setton had never expected to grant.

The lad was perverse, just like his father.

Once again Setton relegated the death of Bernard's parents to an unfortunate twist of fate. It had happened years ago, and he had no intentions of paying further for the mistake.

After all, he'd taken the orphaned boy in, fed and clothed him, given him shelter. What more could the boy have asked for? Truly, Fitzgibbons should be grateful he'd been given a pallet in his lord's hall when he could easily have been left to fend for himself.

Fitzgibbons had never shown any gratitude, not once over all the years. Had the boy known all along what had happened the day he'd been orphaned? Setton didn't think so, and he truly hadn't been concerned about the lad finding out—until yesterday.

Fitzgibbons had changed. Become a man. A knight. A threat.

Setton abandoned the curtain wall from which he could see no farther than half a field away and made his way to the hall.

He'd been far too lenient with Claire of late, influenced by the foolish courtly notions of Eustace Marshall, he supposed. The girl had taken advantage, however, and now put his alliance with the powerful Marshall family at risk.

When he got the girl back, he would remind her where her first duty lay.

"Where are we?" Claire asked.

"Garden of Eden," Bernard answered flippantly.

Claire quelled the urge to laugh.

She'd spent most of last night curled in Bernard's arms, and now sat in front of him on Cabal. To her chagrin, she no longer felt threatened or any powerful need to escape.

Indeed, she felt safe with Bernard. Unwise, certainly. She shouldn't be this at ease, shouldn't feel secure enough to trade quips with the man who'd kidnaped her. The serenity wouldn't last long, she knew, for her father's men would track them down and take them back to Dasset.

Still, for the space of a few hours, she could enjoy the peace of the forest and the company of a man she hadn't expected to like so much.

Though she wished she knew where they were going. They'd risen early, dined on oatcakes from Bernard's pack, then ridden slowly through the forest for hours. She was lost, and suspected Bernard was, too.

"Try again, Bernard," she said.

"You do not believe me?" he asked, incredulous.

"If the Garden of Eden were so close to Dasset Castle, one would think I would have heard of it. So, where are we?"

"South of Dasset, north of York and west of Durleigh."

"You are lost."

"I am not lost," he insisted. "This fog simply makes it hard to be certain of our exact location."

Or tell east from west or north from south, she thought. The fog would also hamper her father's search.

"Is there some destination we seek?"

After a long silence, he answered, "Home."

'Twas the last answer she'd expected. "You are taking me back to Dasset?"

"Nay. I meant my home, the place where my parents lived…and died. There should be something left of Faxton's manor, I think."

She'd never heard of the place. Odd. She thought she'd known the names of all of her father's holdings. The place must exist, however, if it had been Bernard's home.

"Have you not been back since?"

"Never had a good reason to go back."

"Then why go now? Would not your former home be a place my father would search for you?"

"Worried for me, Claire?"

Aye, she was, and it didn't sit well. After all, she'd tried to do him a good turn and he'd repaid her by putting both of them in jeopardy. If Bernard insisted on giving her father reasons to hang him, she couldn't save him. If he intended to go to a place where her father would search for him, she shouldn't object.

She should be trying to escape from him, not enjoying a ride through the fog.

"Of course not," she said, hearing the falseness in her statement and choosing to ignore it. "Where is Faxton? I do not believe I have heard of the place."

With amusement in his voice, he repeated, "South of Dasset, north of York and west of Durleigh."

This time she laughed. "Oh."

"As to why," he went on, "there is—was—an herbalist who resided nearby. Mistress Morgan may know of a potion to ease your cough."

"She does," Claire said, recognizing the herbalist's name. "My mother keeps many of her potions and possets at hand."

"Truly? I do not remember ever seeing the woman at Dasset."

"So far as I know, she never comes. Mother always sends a messenger to collect what she needs. But the widow resides at a place called Fallenwood, not Faxton."

"So where is Fallenwood?"

She had to smile. "South of Dasset and west of Durleigh. Bernard, could Faxton now be Fallenwood? Could Father have renamed the place for some reason?"

She felt him shrug a shoulder, and sensed something else. A tension that hadn't been there before.

"'Tis possible," he said.

"How old were you when…when you left?"

"Nearly ten and two."

He'd been so young when his parents died, killed in a raid of some kind if she remembered aright. Had he been happy at Faxton? Loved his parents and they him?

She couldn't bring herself to ask, not wanting to stir up painful memories simply out of curiosity. He was likely dealing with them anyway, now so close to his childhood home. She wouldn't intrude.

So they rode in silence.

Claire noticed the fog was beginning to lift when she spotted a pond some distance away. Bernard rode up to it and stopped at its edge.

"Fish pond," Bernard said. "I remember catching trout and perch in those waters."

"'Tis stocked with eels now," she said, sure of where they were. A place known to her as Fallenwood. "Father dislikes perch, so had this pond changed over some years ago."

"Hmm," was his only comment.

Not long after, Bernard reined in before a cottage of wattle and daub with a thatch roof. A large garden, mostly of herbs, grew beside the cottage. From around the corner two huge, gray geese flapped toward them, honking their displeasure.

"We are announced," Bernard said, amused.

"Mistress Morgan's?" she asked.

"So I hope."

An ancient woman appeared within the doorway. She stared at Bernard, her eyes going huge and round. With a gnarled hand, she crossed herself.

"Saints preserve us. Bernard?"

"Aye, 'tis me. Why is it everyone doubts me?"

A smile lit the woman's face as she waddled forward. "Oh, lad, there can be no mistaking you. Come down where an old woman can get a better look."

Bernard no more than put his feet on the ground when the herbalist threw her arms around him in a fierce hug. To his credit, Bernard didn't shy away. He not only allowed the hug but returned it. When she drew back, tears shone in her eyes.

"Your return has been a long time coming, Bernard Fitzgibbons. 'Tis good to have you back." The widow turned toward where Claire yet sat on Cabal. "My lady, how are your sniffles?"

While Claire could only gape, Bernard answered. "'Tis why we came to you, Lillian. Her cough frightens the birds from their nests."

"Then get her down here, Bernard. Hide that beast of yours behind the cottage and come inside."

"She is amazing," Claire said, placing her hands on Bernard's shoulders.

"That she is," he agreed, placing his hands on her waist. "'Tis nice to know that some things remain the same."

With an ease she yet found disconcerting, Bernard swung her down to the ground. The man's strength amazed her. She was heavier than most women of her age and size, always had been. Yet Bernard flung her around as if she were feather light.

"Come, come," Lillian said, waving a beckoning hand. "Let us get inside."

"Go ahead," Bernard said. "I will take Cabal around back and then join you."

Claire followed Mistress Morgan—Lillian, Bernard had called her—into the cottage and sat in the chair near the cook fire the woman waved her to. 'Twas strange to put a first name to the woman who she'd known about for years but never seen.

"Down to the cough, is it?" Lillian said kindly.

"How did you know about my sniffles?"

Lillian chuckled and turned to rummage about in a large wooden chest. "Girl, I have been preparing your possets since you were no bigger than one of my geese. Think you I do not know you suffered the sniffles these past days? Tsk.''

Still confused, Claire asked, ''Then you know who I am?''

''Oh, aye, Lady Claire. When your mother sends for supplies, she always lets me know which member of her household is in need. The potions I prepare for you are different from the others. We learned, early on, there are some herbs you may not have, so I take special care with yours.'' She put various leaves and flower petals on the table. ''Let me tell you, I was most relieved when your mother stopped asking for unguents for you.''

Claire's spine stiffened, remembering where those unguents had been applied, and how they'd eased her pain and faded her bruises. Her discomfort must have shown. The widow came round the table and bent to take Claire's hands.

''There now, my lady. Be at ease. I fear I have caused your heart pain, but I mean what I said.''

Claire took the comfort in the spirit given. Yet, she still didn't understand how Lillian had recognized someone she'd never set eyes on.

''Out in the yard. How did you know it was me atop the horse with Bernard?''

''Oh, that. Well, it has been an interesting morning.''

Bernard's voice came from the doorway. ''I imagine it has.''

Startled, Claire looked his way. How long had he been standing there? How much had he heard? Or understood?

''Your father's men have been here already, Claire,'' he said. ''I saw the marks of fresh hoof prints out front of the cottage. That is how Lillian knew you were with me. What I don't understand is how she recognized me so readily. I have been gone a long time.''

With a gentle squeeze, Lillian released Claire's hands and crossed the rush-covered floor to stand before Bernard.

''You, Bernard Fitzgibbons, are the very image of your father. No one who knew Granville could mistake you for anyone but his son.'' She crossed her arms. ''Now all that remains to be seen is if you have his character and fortitude.''

''How so?''

''How much do you remember of the day your parents died?''

Bernard ran a hand through his hair. ''Every scream,'' he said, the words so soft Claire strained to hear.

''Good. Then mayhap, with a bit of help, Fallenwood will once again become Faxton.''

Chapter Six

Bernard forced aside memories of the raid, guessing at what Lillian Morgan wanted him to do.

Claim Faxton. He wished he had the right.

His father, Granville Fitzgibbons, had held Faxton of Lord Odo Setton—for a knight's fee and twenty barrels of salted fish per year. Setton, in turn, held it of the bishop of Durleigh, but for what fee Bernard didn't know.

At Granville's death, the land had reverted to Setton to do with as he pleased. At Setton's death, the land would revert to the bishop of Durleigh. Most times, if the holder left behind a son, the son would be granted the privileges and responsibilities of his father's lands.

In Bernard's case, Setton had chosen to keep Faxton and give the son of his fallen knight a place in his household. 'Twas well within Setton's rights as lord.

Lillian must know that, but looked at him as if by strength of will and flash of sword he could turn Fallenwood into Faxton once more.

"I cannot claim that which is not mine, and with how things stand between me and Setton, can never hope to," Bernard said.

"Bernard—"

He raised a halting hand, not wanting to hear more of her vain hopes. "I brought Claire here for a potion for her cough, no more. Once she has it we will leave. I will not put you or any of my father's people in danger."

"Did you hear what you just said—your father's people? As his son, you should abide in the manor."

"The manor yet stands?"

"'Tis in need of repair, but your father built it sturdy, to last his lifetime, and yours, and your son's beyond that. With little effort you could move in straightaway."

Bernard shook his head. "Just give Claire the potion."

When Lillian tossed her hands in the air and seemed ready to argue further, Bernard left the cottage. Arguing did no good. She asked the impossible.

"Stubborn," he heard Lillian tell Claire. "Just like Sir Granville."

The comparison made him smile. Aye, his father had been a stubborn man, wanting things his way and no other. Fortunately, his father had also been a fair and loving man, so his way benefitted his people and brought pride to his son and wife, Alice.

Bernard looked up the road toward where the home of his youth promised shelter. The memories would be both joyful and vicious within the walls of the stone manor house his parents had so loved and given their lives defending.

He'd never quite forgiven himself for living through the raid when they hadn't, even though he knew in his head that the guilt was unwarranted. His aching heart, however, had never stopped asking "Why?"

He couldn't move back in, but he could probably stay the night. Maybe two. Setton's men would return, Bernard was sure, but probably not until they'd searched other areas where two people on the run might hide. He and Claire should be safe for the night at least.

Tonight Claire would have a roof over her head. He could snare a rabbit or catch an eel for their supper.

He and Claire. In a stone manor house. Sharing a meal. He shook his head at the fanciful thought that a part of his dreams would be real for one night.

Since the day Setton had promised the reward, he'd pictured himself as the holder of several hides of land on which sat a stone manor house. 'Twould be foolish to deny he'd based his hopes on memories of his childhood home.

Yesterday, he'd even thought to ask Setton to include the one place he might have a right to ask for within the reward. Then Setton had laughed in his face and tossed him into the dungeon.

And Claire had released him.

He still didn't know why. Out of compassion? To irritate her father? Because her father had told her to?

Bernard strolled over to the garden, bent down and plucked a weed from among the clusters of parsley.

He'd come here often as a boy. The last time had been on a clear summer's night with the sting of smoke in his chest and sound of death in his ears. His father had told him to run, and he'd obeyed.

And you are still running.

Or maybe not. Maybe he'd stopped while in the Holy Land. His musings on a home all centered around the manor he'd left so long ago. He'd even imagined Claire by the hearth where his mother used to sit. Had imagined babes at Claire's feet.

Always she'd been at the back of his mind. Now he

was about to take her to the place where he'd envisioned her as his wife, his lover, the mother of his children.

Foolish.

Maybe so, but they'd be safe there. Better than sleeping out in the open another night. And after tonight?

He couldn't stay home long. They would be discovered. Too, he had to send someone to Dasset with a ransom demand. He gave a brief thought to asking Lillian to find someone to act as messenger, then dismissed the idea. Someone from Fallenwood—its name now— might be accused of aiding Bernard Fitzgibbons. Better he should hire a stranger.

He'd have to go into Durleigh, he supposed. Sweet mercy, he would have to watch himself in the town. Likely, Setton had sent soldiers there to search for him, and might have summoned the sheriff. Simon was going to be surprised, and probably angry, at what Bernard had done.

Still, he needed to hire a messenger and maybe sell a relic or two for the coin to buy food. Dare he visit the Cathedral? Had a new bishop been installed in Thurstan's place?

This ransom business wasn't going to be as easy as he'd first imagined it to be.

"So, what do you think of our Bernard?"

Watching Lillian crush leaves and flower petals in a wooden bowl, Claire noted the pride in the question and thought back on the woman's greeting for Bernard.

"*Our* Bernard? Are you related to him?"

"Well, I helped the boy get born, so I feel a bit motherly toward him. He was forever underfoot as a lad. Used to come down here and pull weeds from my herbs when he was troubled about something. Would not surprise me a bit if he had a hand full of 'em now.''

Claire resisted the urge to get up and look.

Bernard's troubles weren't her concern any longer. She'd done what she could for him, and now must get back to Dasset. She had a wedding and tournament to plan—a father to make amends to. Could Lillian help her?

"Did Father's soldiers tell you why they searched for us?"

Lillian put the bowl on the table and crossed to the hearth. She swung the kettle hanging on an iron arm out from over the fire. "The soldiers said little more than Bernard had escaped from your father's dungeon and grabbed hold of you on his way out." Lillian smiled, dipping a tin cup into the kettle. "Good bit of fortune for you, I would say."

"Fortune? He kidnaped me!"

Lillian chuckled as she returned to the table. "He did at that. Why did Setton toss him in the dungeon?"

Miffed by the lack of sympathy for her plight, Claire huffed. "Bernard demanded a reward from my father, for going on Crusade. Father denied promising him one. Bernard argued the point, Father got angry."

Lillian scooped some of the crushed mixture into a cup of steaming liquid. "Ah, he must have been a glorious sight. Bernard, I mean."

He had been. She'd thought so. Father hadn't.

Claire accepted the cup Lillian offered and took a sip. The brew slid down her throat with comforting ease. The woman was a marvel with medicinals—no question there. Her easy acceptance of what Bernard had done, however, didn't sit well.

"Bernard shook off two guards, took a threatening

step toward Father and went for his sword. The action earned him a knock on the head and a seat in the dungeon. Not so glorious.''

"Always was a bold one, our Bernard. I should have liked to have seen it.''

Claire put the cup on the table. "Bold? Bernard? The Bernard Fitzgibbons I knew would *never* have threatened my father. Do we speak of the same man?''

"I speak of the boy before he went to Dasset to live. The death of his parents affected him greatly. I always hoped, prayed, he would regain his spirit. Sounds like he has.''

Lack of spirit. Aye, that was the Bernard she knew. He'd always done as told, took orders without complaint or protest, as if nothing mattered but doing each task as it came to him. He'd always struck her as...lonely.

If this woman knew of Bernard's low spirits, why had she never come to Dasset to see the child she claimed to have motherly feelings toward? Come to think on it, Claire couldn't remember anyone coming to Dasset to see Bernard. She knew many people from her father's other holdings, but none from Fallenwood.

"Did no one from here ever come to visit Bernard?''

Lillian shook her head. "Your father would not allow it. Said seeing us would only upset the boy further. We did not believe the claim, but had no choice. How is your throat?''

Claire swallowed. Her throat clear of phlegm, she felt no urge to cough.

"Much better,'' she said. "My thanks.''

Lillian again rummaged about in her chest. She came up with a small leather pouch and poured the herb mixture into it. "When the cough comes on you, add a bit of this to warm broth.''

Claire tucked the pouch into an inner pocket in her cloak, thinking she could only add the mix to broth if she were home. She wasn't making progress to that end by discussing Bernard's childhood with Lillian Morgan.

"Mistress Morgan, I…"

"Oh, fash, Lady Claire. Call me Lillian. Everyone does."

"Lillian, then," Claire said and began again. "I realize you are fond of Bernard and do not wish to see him captured and returned to Dasset. I understand that, and indeed, wish him well with his life. On the other hand, I must return as quickly as possible—"

"Whatever for? I should think you would be happy to be away from your father." Lillian's smile returned. "And truly, for one who so enjoys the romantic tales and courtly ways of the days of Eleanor of Aquitaine, one would think you might enjoy the adventure."

Claire felt her cheeks grow hot. Did everyone know of her girlhood fascination with the great Eleanor?

"How did you know—?"

"Come, Claire. You are the youngest and most headstrong child of Lord and Lady Setton. Surely you must know that stories about you abound."

"Gossip, you mean."

"If you will."

"Bernard took me from Dasset against my will and intends to hold me for ransom. This is no romantic tale!"

"Was not your Eleanor captured by some great lord and held for ransom?"

Not quite. Eleanor had been held in great castles by powerful lords, usually at her husband's request, to keep her from meddling in his affairs. There had never been a ransom paid for her release. Only her husband's death had ended Eleanor's imprisonments.

Claire rose from her chair. "Nay, she was never ransomed. Lillian, I need to return to Dasset, today if I can. Will you help me?"

"Ah, child. What can an old woman do against a man set on a course that will bring him a reward?"

"I see. I will remember your lack of aid, Mistress Morgan."

The old woman smiled sadly. "No doubt you will, Claire. Remember to add the herbs to warm broth. They are most effective that way."

Her head held high, discouraged and offended, Claire walked out of the cottage.

Bernard, indeed, knelt near the garden.

Claire lifted her skirts and ran in the opposite direction.

"Claire! Claire, halt!"

Bernard wasn't surprised Claire ignored the order. Well, at least she ran in the right direction. Cabal would be spared the weight of two people for most of the distance to the manor.

"I fear I upset her, Bernard," Lillian said. "She is most angry with me for not driving you away or returning her to her father. Have a care with her."

Bernard leaned down to place a kiss on the old woman's cheek. "I will. Has she something for her cough, then?"

"Aye. Mix the herbs with warm broth. Where will you go?"

"For tonight, to the manor. From there?" He shrugged a shoulder. "Mayhap to Durleigh. Mayhap

York. Have a care for Setton's soldiers. Have one of the men hereabouts rake out all of these hoof prints.''

''Not to worry. Come back when you can.''

He handed her the weeds. ''I did the parsley. Your basil needs attention, too.''

She laughed lightly. ''Go on with you, before her ladyship runs too far.''

Bernard took to the road at a moderate pace, glancing occasionally at Claire's footprints in the dirt, holding back the memories that threatened to overtake him the closer he rode to the manor.

He'd expected Claire to run, had been surprised when she didn't bolt this morning. Something had stopped her, maybe the fog. Judging from the depth of her footprints, he knew she now ran as if a demon chased her.

She wanted to go home; he couldn't let her. Not yet. Not until he got the ransom.

Somehow, he had to make Claire believe he wouldn't hurt her, that as soon as her father gave over she could go home. The faster done, the better for both of them.

Up ahead he saw a faint cloud of dust. Claire. He spurred Cabal into a gallop.

Bernard spotted her as he went around a curve. Running hard. Her cloak flapped around her like great, useless wings. She must have heard him, for she turned her head to look, never losing her stride.

Then she took a sharp right turn into the woods. Where her footprints left the road, he wrapped Cabal's reins around a low tree branch.

Bernard easily followed the trail Claire left, to both his eyes and ears.

''Claire! 'Tis no use running!''

He heard no answer except the breaking of more twigs. She was fleet of foot, he'd give her that, but soon now she would run out of air. Then she would cough. Bernard picked up his pace, and when he saw her, broke into a full run.

He wasn't quiet, either.

"Claire, stop. You will either hurt yourself or worsen your cough."

"Leave me be!" she screamed, and if anything, ran faster.

He caught a fistful of her cloak as she ducked under a low branch. She twisted to get away. The movement caught Bernard with awkward footing and he fell, taking her with him.

She landed on her back. Bernard tossed a leg over hers and grabbed hold of her wrist.

Claire panted. Her chest rose high and fell hard with each large draw of air. She wouldn't look at him. He couldn't tear his gaze from her.

Magnificent, he thought, enchanted by the rhythm of her breathing, noting the strain placed on her emerald gown by the upward swell of her breasts. One of those mounds would fill his hand, and his palm itched to prove his conjecture.

If he loosened the cloak's ties at her neck, she could breathe more easily. So he did, his fingers brushing the soft, pulsing skin at the base of her throat.

Desire swirled, deep and hot, for the woman on the ground beside him. She gulped air, yet he yearned to cover her parted lips with his own and steal away whatever breath remained.

"Claire," he said hoarsely, her name sweet on his tongue and manna to his starved soul.

She turned to look at him. Indignant. Ire flashed in eyes of purest amber. "Hate…you."

"Nay, you do not," he rejoined with more bravado than confidence.

"Do...too."

Bernard refused to believe the woman who'd curled up and slept in his arms last night could hate him. Indeed, he couldn't fathom Claire hating anyone.

"I grant you are very put out with me right now, but I do not believe you hate me."

"Believe," she said, but her ire had dimmed. She yet breathed hard, but 'twas no longer a struggle.

He should get up, but didn't move from Claire's side.

"I believe you want to go home, and would say and do most anything right now to convince me to take you there."

Her gaze slid from his. "Mayhap."

Bernard shifted a bit closer to her and plucked a leaf from her hair, thinking that one of these days he'd like to tear away the netting of her crispinette and see her hair down and flowing around her shoulders.

"Lillian could not have helped you had she wanted to," he told her. "I would not have allowed it."

"She would not even try. I am the daughter of her overlord and she gave you her loyalty over me."

Claire's annoyance was understandable. As Setton's daughter she would expect obedience from any of her father's vassals.

"Lillian holds a special place in my heart, as I do in hers. She would not betray my trust."

"Your affection is misplaced, then. She said she had motherly feelings toward you, but not once did she come to Dasset to see you or ask about your welfare. None from Faxton did. They abandoned you."

He recognized her strategy, but he wouldn't be swayed against the people his parents had held dear.

''When your father took me away to Dasset, Lillian told me that if I should ever need her, or any of Faxton's people, I need only come back and weed her garden. I never did. One could argue that I abandoned them.''

''You were but a boy.''

''For one who claims to hate me, you make pretty excuses for me.''

Her hand rose to his face, her fingers skimming his jaw. ''You *were* but a boy.''

A boy no longer, but a man whose body burned. Did she know what she did to him with her touch? Had she any notion of how terrible a temptation she was, arrayed in disheveled splendor on a forest floor? How far was she willing to go to get her way?

How far could he allow her to convince him without losing his sanity? A kiss? An embrace? More? How much more?

He slid his hand along her middle, just beneath the breasts he yearned to stroke, lightly, but hard enough to raise the nubs. She neither flinched nor drew away. Her hand remained on his jaw.

A question appeared in her shimmering amber eyes. He answered with a touch of lips, a sip of nectar. Claire shivered in response. The question left her eyes. Her hand moved to the back of his head.

A light pressure at his nape was all the encouragement his passion-fogged senses needed. He kissed her, long and deep. Her initial awkwardness said she was an innocent, untried. While he struggled to hold back, she didn't allow it, but returned the kiss with full, stunning measure. When her body arched to his, he dared the caress his hand had begged for. So firm. So full. All Claire.

Bernard gave himself up to the sheer ecstasy of

Claire's kiss, no matter what her reason for the offering. He didn't give a damn why she pressed against the hand that stroked her breast. Or why she fired his blood with a passion-laden kiss. Or why she seduced him.

With the flick of his tongue he begged entrance to her mouth, and when she opened to him, he forgot to think at all.

Claire knew she lay on a forest floor, Bernard's mouth on hers, his hands where they should not be. Sweet mercy, there was nowhere else on earth she would rather be right now than pressed close to the man she'd run from.

Where had her senses fled? Where had her anger gone? Burned away by the fire of carnal lust she'd been warned against and wondered so much about. Without doubt, it could bend a person's mind with need, turn saint to sinner.

Make a woman forget to say the man nay, turn him aside with protests of innocence and pleas for her honor. Only a wanton welcomed a man's intimate advances.

Then a wanton she was, and never suspected. Or maybe Bernard's kisses could tempt any lady to lay her honor aside, give an angel a reason to shed wings. Claire simply didn't care why he chose now to show her the power he possessed. She could only be glad he had, or she might never know.

From somewhere a niggling voice pleaded for reason with an urgency she couldn't ignore. She was betrothed and would marry soon. Eustace Marshall would be horrified to see her now, gasping for breath and savoring the full possession of Bernard's mouth.

She'd kissed Eustace, once, but hadn't experienced the raw hunger to devour him like she wanted to with Bernard.

This wasn't right. It made no sense. This had to stop.

He deserted her breast and entangled her hair, dragging away the crispinette that held her tresses bound. She felt the net come free, the tug of his fingers close into a fist around the loosed strands of her hair.

She pushed at his chest until he ended the kiss. Her mouth shouldn't feel so deserted.

"Bernard, I cannot—" she managed to say before her throat convulsed and she coughed.

He backed away. The haze of desire in his eyes cleared. With renewed concern, he pulled her up to sit and rubbed at her back until her cough eased.

"Ah, well," he said. "Mayhap next time."

She shook her head. "There will be no next time. I will not allow you to seduce me."

"Seduce *you?* I beg to differ, my lady. You not only invited my kiss but gave no sign of revulsion. You wanted the kiss as much as I did."

"I made no invitation," she said, not arguing the last because it rang of truth. "And you went far beyond the bounds of a kiss."

"Tell me you did not enjoy it."

She couldn't, not honestly. She reached behind her, found her crispinette and shoved her hair back into the netting.

"I am nearly a married woman. A truly chivalrous knight would respect my betrothal."

"That is why you want so badly to return, is it not, your marriage to Eustace Marshall." He got up and brushed leaves and twigs from his tunic and breeches. "He can have you, but not until after I get my reward. 'Twould be best if you apply your energy to thinking on how best to bring the ransom to pass than attempting to seduce me into taking you back."

Claire got up. She didn't bother brushing at her clothing.

"I did *not* seduce you. You seduced me!"

"Truly?" he said, then took her cheeks in his hands and kissed her again.

Hard. Demanding. Her mind went blank and her knees went weak. She grabbed hold of his tunic to keep from falling once again to the forest floor. She heard herself gasp when he ended the kiss sharply and pushed her away.

"Should I ever attempt to seduce you, my lady," he said, "I will do it so completely not even your cough will stop me. You will beg me for the pleasure of a full and thorough coupling, I promise you."

He waved a hand toward the road, an order to retrace her steps. She did so on shaky legs—his promise reverberating within her head.

As she'd feared, Bernard's kiss could blank her mind, make her forget who and where she was. She couldn't allow him to do it again.

But sweet mercy, if he put his mind and muscle to it, how would she stop him?

Chapter Seven

Once more on the road, Claire wondered how the devil she'd managed to get into this mess and, more to the point, how she would get out. She needed to return to Dasset quickly, but Lillian's mild suggestion to remain out of her father's reach made her wonder if she was being too hasty.

Father was likely furious with her right now for having let Bernard out of the dungeon last eve. Had it only been last eve?

Except the need to escape had become more urgent after kissing Bernard. Remaining within his reach was nearly as dangerous, though in a different way, than returning home.

"We need a pact, Claire," Bernard said from behind her on Cabal. "I cannot watch you every moment, and you need to feel less a captive. Mayhap, with a firm agreement to terms, you will not feel the need to escape."

Wary, doubting his intended pact would bend to her advantage, she asked, "What terms?"

"Those normally agreed to between a captive held for ransom and the person who holds the captive. I promise you my protection and treatment afforded one of your rank. In return, you promise to remain with me until the ransom has been paid.''

She voiced her immediate reaction. ''You jest.''

''I do not. Think back to your Eleanor. When her son, the Lionhearted, was captured when returning from Crusade, did she not raise the funds to pay his ransom?''

''Nearly beggared England to do so,'' she said, now having an inkling of where Bernard was headed.

''King Richard made a pact with his captor. He would not attempt escape if treated well and with due deference. His captor agreed, and the king spent many months enjoying the hospitality of the German lord's castle while his mother cajoled, demanded and bled the ransom money from noble and peasant alike. When the ransom was paid, the two parted as friends, and the king made his way home to England. True?''

''True.''

''Then see you the advantage to us both to come to terms? I get my money, you get to go home. All we need is the cooperation of your father to give over the ransom.''

There was the sticking point. Her father.

''The difference here is Eleanor, and the rest of England, wanted King Richard's return and were willing to pay the ransom to bring it about. I am not so sure about my father's desire for my return.''

''How badly does he want the alliance with Eustace Marshall?''

There was that, and perhaps the only reason Odo Setton would agree to Bernard's demands for ransom. By advancing her brothers' interests, Father stood to gain both prestige and wealth, to move in those lofty circles of royalty and high nobility as he thought his due.

"This alliance with Marshall will raise Father's standing at court. He intends to garner a high court appointment for Julius and a similar position for Geoffrey within the Church."

"Then 'twould be in your father's best interest to pay the ransom to get you back and me out of his life."

If the ransom were within his power to raise without beggaring Dasset. If she were returned soon enough to marry Marshall as planned.

"How much of a ransom will you ask?"

"I had thought your weight in gold might be a tidy sum."

Her weight?

Claire had this horrible, vivid vision of sitting on one plate of a huge scale, the other plate stacked with gold, and her father complaining bitterly about each coin required to balance the scale to her weight.

"Is that not a bit excessive?" she asked.

"I thought it rather appropriate."

She thought it rather degrading. "Father will not have an easy time of it. 'Twill take him a while to gather so much gold coin."

"A fortnight should do it, I would think. If he comes up short, well, I could make allowances. So long as he comes close, I will be satisfied."

Two weeks was not a lot of time, but Bernard was right. It could be done.

Her weight in gold, indeed.

Still, no matter how much of a ransom Bernard asked for, her father would begrudge the payment of each sou. And he might very well seek restitution—from her. He would collect it in blood and bruises—her blood and bruises.

Despite what she did, her father would have his revenge.

Why not put it off and let Bernard collect the ransom? Certes, he was due some reward for the years he'd spent on Crusade, whether her father had promised him one or not. She would have her reward, too, once she married Marshall.

Could she trust Bernard to uphold his part of the pact if she kept hers? Probably not. Men rarely kept bargains with women. Still, 'twas to Bernard's advantage to keep his word. Without her to turn over to her father, he couldn't collect the ransom.

Claire nearly laughed at the realization that both her father and Bernard needed her to bring their grand plans to completion.

Agreeing to the pact Bernard proposed had definite advantages. The only drawback, so far as she could tell, was having to spend a fortnight in Bernard's company.

She was attracted to him as she'd been drawn to no other man. While she hadn't invited his kiss, she couldn't deny the swift and strong reaction of her body. Or the loss of her senses. Or the hunger for his touch.

Two weeks. Could she be around him for that long and keep her hands off him? Or more dangerous to her state of mind, would he refrain from kissing her? If Bernard caught her off guard with one of those disturbing, mystical kisses, would she find it impossible to deny him? Or would she, as he promised, beg for a thorough coupling?

Claire grew warm all over just thinking about it.

"Bernard, this pact you propose. In return for my agreement not to escape, may I assume the protection you offer includes protection from you?"

"From me?"

"I will have your assurance that you will not attempt to seduce me again."

She felt Bernard squirm. "No more kisses?"

"Not one."

"No more rolling about on the forest floor?"

He was teasing her. The lout.

"Most certainly not. I am no whore to be taken lightly."

The statement gave him pause, but not for long.

"Then I will do my best, if you promise not to tempt me beyond my ability to control my baser self."

On that he had no worry. She hadn't the vaguest notion of how to tempt a man to a kiss, much less beyond his control.

"I give you my word, Bernard Fitzgibbons."

"Then it seems we have a pact, Lady Claire, and just in time, too. We are arrived."

Claire paid better attention to her surroundings. Ahead she could see a stone manor house. From its size, she suspected it held only one large room. Vines had crawled up the stones, particularly in the front, where entwining growth partially obscured the doorway. No one had used the door in a very long time, possibly years.

The less said of the roof the better.

On the far side stood a well in what may once have been a lovely courtyard. Here and there a flower poked its colorful head above the weeds.

Bernard reined in Cabal not far from the doorway.

"Welcome to Faxton's manor, my lady," he said without any emotion, much less welcome, in his voice.

He'd dreaded memories of fire. Of a night of chaos. Instead, he could see his mother standing in the open doorway of the house, greeting him with a smile. His father hailed him from the nearby well.

No specters. No visions. Just memories of the two people he'd loved most in the world on a day most ordinary.

Grief tightened around his heart hard enough to squeeze the life's blood from it.

"'Tis a lovely manor, Bernard.''

She was being kind. 'Twas a shame she hadn't seen it when the roof was whole and the courtyard bloomed.

He swung off of Cabal and reached up to help Claire down.

Her amber eyes narrowed with uncertainty. "Bernard, are you all right?"

What could he tell her if the words could get past his constricted throat? That he was hearing the laughter of children at play, those belonging to the tenants who'd come to help at the manor. The women would be inside—weaving cloth, churning butter, changing rushes—doing whatever needed to be done on that particular day. Most of the men worked the fields—planting, hoeing, harvesting—their tasks determined by the season.

Alice Fitzgibbons directed the women's work. Granville oversaw the men. Day after day, season after season. Life had been good for a boy growing up under their love and guidance.

He set Claire on her feet. "I will be fine," he said, and realized that he would.

The grief had hit him hard, but where before he'd only dwelled on the bad, he could now remember the good.

Bernard walked around the manor, noting the growth of vines on the front that he would have to tear away to get through the doorway. The near side looked much the same. He poked at solid stone and, in places, at mortar come loose. On the whole the house was still sound, built for the generations as Lillian had said.

He rounded to the back of the house and suffered a fresh pang in his heart. He put fingertips to fire-blackened stone. Here the outlaws had set a pile of hay and branches afire, hoping the blaze would draw Sir Granville from his pallet. The fire had done its work well.

Who had been the outlaw leader? What of value had Sir Granville possessed to warrant the taking of two lives?

Setton had told him the outlaws had been caught and hung, but never given forth particulars. As a boy, Bernard hadn't asked, too deep within his grief to care. Now that he would like to ask, he probably wouldn't get the chance.

To the pressure of a gentle squeeze, Bernard looked down at his hand. How long had he been holding on to Claire? He couldn't remember taking her hand, or her sliding her hand into his.

When he looked up, it was into Claire's smile. "Look at the roses, Bernard," she said, nodding toward the well.

Roses, small and yellow, had done some climbing, too. They'd taken over one side of the well.

After a short burst of laughter, he tugged Claire toward what was once his mother's "fancy garden," or so his father had called it.

"Father teased my mother unmercifully about those roses," he told Claire. "She fussed over them, watered them, and they did not get more than two or three blooms a year. Now look at them."

"Mayhap all that early care is why they yet survive,"

Claire commented, pointing farther into the garden. "Was there a trellis in that spot?"

She pulled him forward until they reached what remained of the lattice-crossed slats of his mother's trellis. Claire let go of his hand and bent to clear away weeds from the bottom.

"What was planted here?" she asked.

"Zounds, Claire, 'twas so long ago," he said, closing his eyes, trying to remember which creeping plant had claimed the trellis. "A blue-colored flower, as I recall. Tiny, fragile blooms." He opened his eyes. "I can see it, clear as day, but the name escapes me."

"Aha!" she exclaimed. She jumped up and presented him with a tiny, delicate blue flower.

Bernard took the bloom from her hand and tucked it into the netting that held her hair. "Shall we go in now?"

She tilted her head, her eyes questioning.

Bernard took hold of her hand and brought her fingertips to his lips, a courtly gesture she couldn't possibly object to.

"My thanks for your diversion," he said. "I think I might tear those vines away from the door now."

Claire blushed. "You looked so sad. I did not know what else to do to help you."

"I fail to see why you should want to."

She shrugged. "'Tis becoming a habit, I suppose. I stopped Henry from bashing you over the head a second time, then aided your escape from the dungeon." With a wry smile, she added, "I do believe I have saved your life twice now."

"Hmm. Which means I am in your debt?"

Mischief sparked in her eyes. "Perhaps I am due my own reward."

He raised his hands, palms up. "My lady, I am but a poor knight with nothing of worth to give."

Except he did have a gift for Claire. Her marriage gift.

Among the relics and travelers' necessities in his pack were two gifts. One he'd meant to give Julius Setton, whom he'd wrongly assumed would be his overlord. The other was Claire's, to be given to her on their wedding day.

Should he give it to her? Why not? They wouldn't marry, so she wouldn't be his wife. But he couldn't think of any reason why she shouldn't have the gift purchased with her in mind.

Bernard lowered his hands. "Truth to tell, my lady, I do have a reward for you. I brought you a gift, from Egypt."

The mischief in Claire's eyes changed to awe. "Did you? All the way from Egypt?"

"Aye."

"But why?"

Because I wanted you to wear it for me.

Damn bad idea, he thought as he turned away and headed for the door of the manor. He'd bought the gift with himself in mind as well as Claire.

Bernard grabbed a fistful of vines, then stopped himself from tearing them away from the door. Best he leave the vines as undisturbed as possible, so any passerby wouldn't notice that someone resided in the manor, if only for one night. Best to err on the side of caution.

"Bernard?"

He'd just been unforgivably rude by walking away with no comment. He owed her an apology and explanation.

"I beg your pardon," she said. "I also know the answer to my question, now that I think on it. 'Twas to be my wedding gift, was it not?''

Bernard put his hands on his hips and took a deep breath. "I had planned it as such. But not one thing has gone as planned since I came home. Not with the reward. Not with you. Not even here. Forgive my rudeness, Claire, but I am hard pressed to mind my manners these days.''

In a smooth motion Claire's back straightened and her chin tilted up into a regal set. "All considered, you have done well," she said. Then the mischief returned. "Mostly. I consider taking me captive most inconsiderate. I am inclined to make allowances, however, and will understand completely if only I might have my present. Bernard, might I have my present? Please?''

She pleaded so prettily Bernard couldn't resist.

"All right. Let us get settled in the manor and you may have the package.''

"Wonderful. What might I do to help?''

Together, they removed vines in an orderly fashion, not a haphazard tearing. It seemed to take forever, but Bernard thought the work well worth the effort.

"We should be able to open the door now," Claire said, removing another vine.

"Not yet," he told her. "You and I might pass through, but we must remove enough vines to open the door wide, to get Cabal inside.''

"Cabal?" she exclaimed, her nose scrunched.

"We cannot leave him out here.''

"But to take him inside…oh, Bernard, must we?''

"'Tis but one horse for one night. Think of all of your father's tenant farmers who keep oxen and sheep and hens inside their huts with them. You will be better for the experience, Claire.''

She huffed her disbelief but kept working.

When the door was clear, he pushed on the latch and opened it.

Stepping through was almost like stepping into his past. Part of the roof was gone. Someone had stripped the bed in the corner of draperies and covers.

One iron pot hung near the hearth. Wooden bowls and pottery jars were scattered around the floor. A table and two benches stood where they always had. His mother's broom leaned into the corner. His father's tankard stood sentry on the mantel.

Bernard crossed the room and picked up a battered tin cup from where his pallet had lain at the foot of his parents' bed. After four and ten years of abandonment, the manor should be empty, devoid of possessions. And, indeed, most things had been carried off over the years. Still, he hadn't planned to see even these few remnants.

"Shall I see if the well is dry?" Claire asked from near the hearth, holding a water bucket.

In the space of a heartbeat his old life and his dreams of the future collided in the present. How many times had he pictured Claire in just this way? Near the hearth of a stone manor. He tried to shake it off, to make light of watching Claire move about in the home they might have shared if Lord Setton hadn't broken faith.

"While you do that," he said. "I will get Cabal settled then try to snare a rabbit or two."

"Rabbit, hmm? I do not suppose your mother's spice chest might still be about," she said.

"I doubt it," he managed to say before he fled the manor.

Claire knew it must be hard for Bernard to come home to a house he hadn't seen in years, to have watched someone other than his mother make stew in the iron cooking pot.

Even after they'd eaten, she could sense the tension in him, tightly held. She'd given up prodding Bernard to talk, to forget his upset. He answered her with one or two words and then drew in on himself again.

He hadn't yet given her the gift he'd promised, and she hadn't asked again, feeling a bit foolish for having pleaded for it in the first place.

She sipped at the herbs mixed with stew broth, watching Bernard brush the snarls from Cabal's mane. Sharing living space with an animal seemed so strange. Bernard had the right of it. Peasants did so in huts smaller than the manor. She could endure the smell for one night.

Bernard brought his pack over to the bench on which she sat and put it down beside her. Claire held her curiosity in check as he pulled out a large leather sack and set it on the table.

He unwrapped the strings that held it closed.

"We need to go into Durleigh," he said. "I have little ready coin, so must sell a relic or two to some cleric." From the sack he drew an ornate wooden chest that fit in the palm of his hand. "This might do."

"What is it?"

He flipped up the brass latch and set the open chest on the table. On a bed of red silk lay several strands of white hair.

"'Tis said to be St. Peter's hair." Bernard dug a small pouch from the large pack. From it he emptied a small sliver of dark wood.

"The Church gave each knight a piece of the True Cross, as part of our pay as Crusaders. Many had it fitted into the hilt of a sword. Somehow, it seemed blasphemous to me to put it into my scimitar."

Claire dared to touch the sliver of sacred wood.

Holy relics were precious and much desired by both clerics and nobility alike. Every church had at least one or two for its altar. Most nobles owned some, both for the blessings they brought to the family, and for the swearing upon of a most solemn oath when the occasion arose.

Her father kept the relics belonging to Dasset Castle in a brass chest at the bottom of one of his clothes trunks.

"Must you part with it? 'Tis a rare and valuable treasure."

"I have others more rare, but know not their value."

From the sack, Bernard pulled out other chests and small squares of folded oilcloth. One contained the finger bone of some saint Claire had never heard of. Yet another a snip of fabric from the gown the Blessed Mother had worn on the day of the crucifixion. He claimed another was a piece of pottery from a wine jar used at the wedding at Canna.

"How did you come by these?" she asked, amazed at the array of precious items.

"'Tis not hard. One only needed to make known that one sought to buy them and those Saracens who dealt in relics found you."

"Saracens? You dealt with the enemy?"

"Aye. Those who lived in the cities we occupied strove to please their conquerors. You would be amazed at the concourse between Christians and Saracens when no battle seemed imminent. Too, in each city there were merchants of every Christian country who were not part of the Crusade, but only come to trade. Some made a very good living at dealing in relics."

"That seems sacrilegious."

''Where there is a demand, someone will supply,'' he said, and unwrapped a large bundle. ''This, I think, is the most valuable.''

The reliquary, a work of art, looked like a man's hand and forearm made of silver, covered with a gold, highly decorative bishop's robe. Jewels circled the hem of the sleeve as well as studded the length on two sides.

''Oh, Bernard, this is wondrous!''

'''Tis said to contain the arm bone of St. Babylas. I meant to give it to Julius.''

Surprised, she looked up at Bernard. He wore a deep frown.

''Why my brother?''

''I thought your father died shortly after I left. I thought I would collect my reward from Julius, and give him this in return. Now…'' Bernard shrugged a shoulder. ''Mayhap the new bishop of Durleigh will be interested. Do you know anything of him?''

''His name is Walter de Folke. I hear he is a man of high principles,'' she said, and touched the golden sleeve. ''You purchased this from a Saracen? On Crusader's pay?''

He laughed lightly. ''Nay. I won it in a game of dice.''

She gaped at him. ''Dice?''

''I told you there was much concourse between enemies.'' He picked up the reliquary and wrapped it.

''You will take this to the bishop, then?''

''Mayhap I will test his honesty on something smaller first, perhaps on St. Peter's hair,'' he stated, then pulled out of the sack yet another square of oilcloth. ''This is for you.''

Claire stared at the packet, then glanced up at Bernard. He busied himself putting the various relics back in his pack.

Slowly, savoring every moment, she unfolded the oil-cloth.

"Oh, my," she breathed, entranced by the scarlet fabric of so light a weave she could see the hand she slid beneath it. A band of glimmering gold, embroidered with red thread, trimmed the hem all around. "I have never seen the like!"

"'Tis a veil like that worn by the women of a sultan's harem," he told her.

She'd heard of the harems kept by the Arab sultans who took many wives. How exquisitely exotic, and temptingly improper. Wondering how Bernard might have come by a veil worn by a sultan's wife gave her pause.

"Did you win this at dice, too?" she asked, almost hoping he had.

"Nay. Purchased from a merchant in Damietta on Crusader's pay."

Relieved, she gently lifted the veil. When she thought she had the way of it figured out, she made to put it on.

"Like this," Bernard said, taking it from her hands. He arranged it around her head and drew a wisp of it across her face. "Arab women cover their faces when out and about," he explained, fastening the veil. "Only husbands and close male relatives are allowed to see their faces."

Words meant to thank him stuck in her throat. The desire in his eyes shook her to her core. Claire knew then when he'd planned to first see her in it—on their wedding night. Only he wouldn't have put the veil on her, but taken it off.

Heaven help her, she could envision him gently removing the gauzy veil, kissing her deeply, untying the strings of her chemise. Even as her body responded to the vision, she removed the veil. She couldn't keep it.

"You must put this away, Bernard, for the woman who will be your wife."

He shook his head and picked up his pack. "'Twas meant for you. Do with it what you will," he said, then walked away.

Claire carefully folded the beautiful veil and wrapped it in the oilcloth. With great care she put it into the inner pocket of her cloak.

If he wouldn't take it back, then she'd treasure the gift as a remembrance of the man who'd given it to her. She could only hope it wouldn't be a dead man she would remember, hung by her father for kidnaping her.

Chapter Eight

The following morning, Bernard closed the latch on the door, rearranged some of the vines, got on his horse behind Claire and didn't look back. His past was his past, he'd decided. There was nothing he could do to change it, or set it to rights. All he could do now was see to his future.

The success of his future depended upon the ransom from Lord Setton for Claire. Caring for Claire for the next fortnight meant selling a relic or two. The best person to approach was the bishop of Durleigh, Walter de Folke, and hope the man didn't yet know of Claire's kidnaping.

'Twas a lot to hope for.

At least Claire seemed content. Of course, he'd told himself the same thing yesterday morn and she'd proved him wrong, running off into the woods until he caught her.

When they'd kissed, and more.

If he didn't forget what she felt like beneath his hands he would drive himself insane. She'd promised not to seduce him and he'd vowed to keep his hands to himself.

For last night, at least, they'd kept to their pact, sleeping on opposite ends of the manor.

Maybe that was all Claire needed, the assurance of the bargain they'd made. Now that she knew she needn't fear he would abuse her in any way, she hadn't tried to escape or called him a vile name since.

Unfortunately, he couldn't keep his hands completely off of Claire. She needed his help when getting on and off Cabal, and the best way to hold her steady while riding was to wrap his arm around her middle—where he held her now.

To add to his misery, the day was warm, so she'd left off her cloak. She no longer held herself stiffly, but leaned back into his chest, her netted hair brushing against his chin. She'd plucked one of the yellow roses and tucked it behind her ear.

The scents and textures of the woman were driving his senses wild. Keeping the state of his arousal down to a mere simmer took most of his concentration. What he could spare he used to guide Cabal down the road to Durleigh. Thank the Lord the road was straight and thinly traveled. So far, he'd avoided being seen by other travelers by ducking into the woods.

He wasn't worried about being recognized. Few people beyond those who lived at Dasset knew him, and he'd changed a great deal while away. Claire, however, was the daughter of a lord, and even those who didn't know her might recognize her and question her presence on his lap…horse.

Best she put on her cloak and pull up the hood before they entered Durleigh.

His main concern was the possibility of happening upon a company of Setton's men-at-arms. Cabal was a big strong warhorse and for short sprints could run with the wind. But any courser would lose a long race, especially carrying extra weight.

"Will we go directly to the cathedral?" she asked, breaking the silence they'd maintained for most of the night before and since leaving the manor.

"Nay," he said, having decided last night that he couldn't take Claire into the bishop's presence. "Would you be averse to my leaving you in a room at an inn while I bargain with the bishop? This assumes I can trust you to stay put."

"I agreed to our pact. You need not worry over me," she said. "What inn?"

Except he did worry, and he wasn't sure about the inn. "Care to recommend one?"

"I know of two in Durleigh with rooms for let. I prefer the Royal Oak Tavern."

"Do the owners know you?"

"Aye, they do. The Selwyns are good people and…ah, that means you cannot leave me at the Royal Oak, right?"

Smart lady. He also noted Claire had begun to think more like a partner in his scheme rather than his captive. That boded well. Perhaps she truly trusted their pact.

He suspected there was more to it, however. Something had changed since yesterday when she'd been so eager to return to Dasset. Now, it seemed, she wasn't in such a hurry. Why?

Or maybe he was making too much of her willingness to now go along with his plans. Women were changeable creatures, and Bernard didn't pretend to understand females and their whims. Maybe he should count her change of heart as a good omen and leave it be.

"I wish I knew if your father alerted anyone in the town. If not, we could come up with a passable story for the Selwyns and you could wait for me in a place you feel comfortable.''

She was quiet for a while, then said, ''I doubt Father has purposely let anyone know, as yet. He will try to find us first. Mayhap in later days he will feel compelled to at least alert the sheriff. That does not mean, however, that the news has not spread to town. Too many people travel between Dasset and Durleigh for my kidnaping to remain secret for long.''

''Unless he closes Dasset's gates, opening only for his patrols to come and go. An extreme measure, surely, but he could get away with it for a day or two.''

''Oh, Bernard, that is brilliant!'' she said with a laugh. ''He just may do so. Consider. Father knows that if the sheriff becomes involved—Bernard, you know the sheriff. Would he choose to become involved if he hears rumors of the kidnaping?''

Knowing Simon as he did, the answer came easy. ''Aye,'' he said, knowing, too, that Simon would also take the time to be fair and hear his side of the tale.

She nodded. ''All right then. Once the search for you passes into the sheriff's hands, then it becomes the king's business and father loses the right to judge and punish you himself. He will not give up that right easily.''

''So possibly, for a day or two, we are safe in Durleigh.''

''Possibly. If Father did not send a patrol into Durleigh, which is probable.''

Bernard couldn't help but chuckle. ''Claire, you give me hope with one hand then snatch it away with the other!''

''Sorry, but you did ask my opinion.''

He heard the irritation in her tone and, as an apology,

squeezed his arm about her middle. "That I did, and you gave good counsel. Now all I need do is decide what to do about it."

Claire pointed up the road. "Someone comes."

Bernard immediately kneed Cabal off the road and into the woods, then reined in where he could see who passed by but not be easily spotted.

Claire sat very still, as she had each time they'd left the road. Bernard listened intently, and soon heard the clop of horses and the voices of their riders. A man and a woman.

He smiled when they came into view. Simon Blackstone rode beside a woman of stunning beauty who must be his wife, Linnet. Or at least she'd best be his wife. If Simon was looking at another woman in such enthralled fashion, he'd be in a passel of trouble.

Under other circumstances Bernard would rush out onto the road to greet the pair, for he hadn't yet met Linnet and he would dearly love to have a word with Simon. Except Simon was now the sheriff of Durleigh, and Bernard didn't want to involve his friend in his troubles unless necessary.

The last time he'd seen Simon, the sheriff had told both him and Nicholas Hendry to stay out of trouble. Simon wasn't going to be pleased that Bernard hadn't obeyed.

He whispered in Claire's ear. "We need not worry about the sheriff. That is Simon—"

Bernard shut his mouth when Simon slowed his horse and looked around, as if he'd heard his name. Damn Simon's instincts. His ability to sense when something was amiss, a trait that had saved their lives so many times in the Holy Land, now posed a threat.

Go on with you, my friend.

Bernard heard Linnet ask, "Something wrong, love?"

"For just a moment I thought—" Simon shook his head. "Nay, must be a trick of the breeze. You were saying?"

Bernard bowed his head in relief when Simon urged his horse forward, then waited longer than was probably necessary before he spoke again.

"That was Simon. He looks to be on an outing, not out hunting me."

"Who was the woman?"

"His new wife, I think. Why?"

"Curious. They looked so…pleased to be in each other's company, is all."

That they had, which delighted Bernard. Simon deserved whatever happiness came his way.

Bernard urged his horse back to the road and checked for travelers. With the road clear, he resumed the journey.

"I think we might try the Royal Oak," he told Claire. "In fact, we might spend the night. If we do not see any of your father's soldiers in town, I believe 'twill be safe."

"You have the funds?"

"I have a coin or two to spare."

"Oh, good," Claire declared. "Mistress Selwyn prepares the most delicious meals."

"You tire of rabbit stew already?"

"I have a feeling that during the coming fortnight I shall eat more rabbit stew than I care to."

Claire was probably right. After tonight, he needed to find a place to hide for the next two weeks. A haven with shelter and access to food, safe from Setton's patrols.

He wished he had a clue where to find such a sanctuary.

Claire pulled the hood of her cloak forward as they passed by the Royal Oak, grateful that Lillian's potion had eased her cough so greatly that she wouldn't unintentionally draw notice. One of her father's house guards stood near the doorway. Thankfully, he was so occupied with flirting with a tavern wench that he paid no attention to aught else.

Behind her, Bernard had gone tense, but not spurred his horse to greater speed. An eternity passed before he turned off the main road onto a side street.

"Sorry about your meal," he said.

Claire let out a relieved breath. "I can survive on rabbit stew. Now what do we do?"

"Visit the bishop."

To her way of thinking, Bernard seemed much too calm. "Is it safe?"

"One can pray."

One could, so she did silently as they wound through the narrow streets of Durleigh until they reached the high stone wall surrounding the cathedral and bishop's palace. A monk acting as porter greeted them at the gate.

Bernard swung down from Cabal. "I have business with the bishop," he told the porter. "Is he in residence?"

The porter looked over Bernard's fine courser, then gave Claire the merest glance. The warhorse declared Bernard a knight, of a rank high enough to deserve deference. Claire bristled at the monk's complete dismissal of her, but kept her peace.

"Bishop Walter is in residence, but a very busy man," the porter stated. "You may ask at the palace about an audience, but do not count on seeing him today. Leave your horse and...weapon with the stable master.''

Bernard smiled. ''The weapon is a scimitar, brought back from the Holy Land.''

The monk's eyes widened. ''You are a Crusader, then?''

''Aye, recently returned.''

A look of pure awe washed over the monk's face. ''A hero of the faith,'' he said reverently. ''Surely Bishop Walter will wish to see you. Would you be a Knight of the Black Rose?''

Bernard fairly puffed up with pride. ''I would.''

''Oh, then most assuredly His Eminence will be eager to meet you, as I am most delighted for this chance to welcome you home, sir. Be sure to mention your esteemed status to the bishop's secretary, Brother Oliver.''

''My thanks,'' Bernard said, then led Cabal to the stable.

A lad rushed forward to take charge of the horse while Bernard helped Claire down.

''I cannot go in with you to see the bishop,'' she said for his hearing alone. ''I met him only once, but he may recognize me.''

Bernard glanced around, his perusal ending at the cathedral doors. ''Perhaps you might light a candle or two. I could collect you from the cathedral when I am finished.''

A sound plan.

''Have a care,'' she said, and with the barest glance toward the four-storied stone palace, sought the refuge of a familiar and peaceful alcove within the vast expanse of the cathedral.

Though she walked softly, the sound of her footsteps rang off the stone floor and echoed into the heavens of

the ceiling high above. When she reached the side altar
dedicated to the Holy Mother, Claire lit two votive candles, one for herself and one for Bernard.

If ever there were a time for her to escape Bernard,
the time was now, when she could easily ask for aid
from one of the priests milling, or run to her father's
guards at the Royal Oak.

Bernard must realize she could escape, and to her way
of thinking, placed an unseemly amount of trust in their
pact by letting her out of his sight and beyond his grasp.

He trusted her word that she wouldn't try to escape,
an oath given a captor by a captive, even if given by a
lady to a knight.

Did he now trust her sense of honorable behavior?
Would the more honorable behavior be to return to her
father and thus betray her word to Bernard? Or keep her
word to Bernard, the man who'd kidnaped her and yet
believed she could be trusted?

It all came down to, she supposed, whether or not she
believed her father had broken faith with Bernard.
Whether or not she cared any longer if she gained her
father's love and approval.

She'd tried so hard for so long to please him, but
nothing she'd ever done had made a difference—until
her betrothal to Eustace Marshall. Only then had Father
considered her to be of any value.

The marriage would still take place, of course. The
promissory oaths had been given and witnessed. In the
eyes of the Church and the law she was as good as
married from that moment on to Eustace Marshall, a man
whom she hadn't found objectionable in any manner
during her brief visit to Huntingdon.

Two weeks should be plenty of time for Father to raise
and pay the ransom. She would be home with time to

spare before the wedding ceremony that would set her free of Dasset and give Odo Setton the alliance he craved.

For that alliance, her father might have done most anything, including breaking faith with Bernard Fitzgibbons. Father wouldn't give her over to a landless knight, the promise given or no, if he must forego the alliance to one of England's most powerful families.

Still, she couldn't envision Bernard making an outrageous claim and standing firm in his conviction if his claim had no basis.

So she had to decide, now, who to believe. To her sorrow, both her heart and head leaned toward believing Bernard over her father.

Which meant that if Bernard had returned from Crusade months sooner, before Father had bargained for the betrothal with Marshall, she might now be Bernard's wife instead of Eustace Marshall's betrothed. Odd, but the more she came to know and like Bernard, the less unreasonable she considered that fate.

She and Bernard would have dealt well together, she thought. Not only did her body respond favorably to his kiss and touch, but she thrilled at his willingness to ask for and listen to her opinions, and then consider them as good counsel. A rare and amazing trait in a man, one nearly as endearing as Bernard's sense of humor.

Bernard did have the tendency to make hasty judgements and act without thinking things all the way through—like with her kidnaping. She doubted he'd foreseen the problems of keeping her safe and fed, much less the burden to his horse, or the disturbing affliction of their growing physical attraction.

Even Bernard's decision to take the cross had been a

hasty one, possibly made under duress. Likely, he hadn't considered that his overlord would forswear the reward.

Claire crossed herself and knelt on the floor, more to ensure privacy than in reverence. She looked up at the statue, but found no answer to her dilemma in the beautiful, porcelain face of the Holy Mother. She hadn't really expected to, knowing her answer must come from within.

With a sprouting sense of peace, Claire turned her thoughts further inward. Yesterday, she'd been so sure the wisest course was to return to Dasset as quickly as possible. Surely, 'twas still the wisest course, but was it the right one?

Bernard had given four years of his life in Lord Setton's service. For that alone, he deserved some reward. If not marriage to her and the land he'd hoped to gain, then the gold he needed to begin a new life elsewhere.

Against his four years and the risk of his very life, two weeks out of her own seemed short, with barely any risk at all. They'd made a pact, the two of them, just as Bernard had made a pact with her father so long ago.

Already one Setton had broken faith with Bernard; she wouldn't be the second to betray him. He would find her in this very spot when he came to fetch her.

Claire looked heavenward and prayed she'd given herself good counsel.

On the second floor of the palace, Bernard paced the small chamber outside of the bishop's private apartments, clutching two relics, waiting to be announced.

He knew he was taking an awful risk by leaving Claire on her own, but saw no option, not if the bishop might recognize her and question why she had accompanied Bernard to Durleigh. He could have come up with some

tale, he supposed, but hated the thought of lying to a
bishop.

The huge brass doors opened. Bernard focused on the
man in splendid robes who followed the secretary into
the chamber. Bald, of middling years and leanly built,
Bishop Walter strode forth with the bearing of a man
secure in his position. Sharp brown eyes assessed his
visitor. The wide smile on the man's narrow face boded
well.

Bernard took the bishop's offered hand, bowed over
it and kissed the almost obscenely huge ruby ring.
"Your Eminence," he said. "I thank you for allowing
this audience."

"Nay, my son. 'Tis I who give thanks you came to
see me. Brother Oliver here tells me you are Bernard
Fitzgibbons, but I would have known in any case. Simon
Blackstone's description of you has proved most flaw-
less."

Bernard wasn't sure if he should be thankful or not.
To whom else had Simon described him flawlessly?
Were he and Claire in more danger of discovery in Dur-
leigh than he'd thought?

"Simon spoke of me?"

"As he has all of the returning Knights of the Black
Rose. I hope to meet all of you. Now come inside and
tell me what brings you here."

Bernard followed the bishop into his grandly ap-
pointed withdrawing room, noting the thick carpets on
the floor and the intricate tapestries covering the white-
washed walls. Bishop Walter lowered himself into a
throne-like chair behind a massive, ornate writing table
of highly polished dark wood. The bishop waved at a
slightly less impressive chair.

"Be comfortable, Sir Bernard," he said. "I have only

a few moments to give you, but we shall make the best of them.''

Bernard nodded and ignored the chair. "So Brother Oliver said. At the risk of rudeness, Your Eminence, might I get right to the point of my visit?''

The bishop's smile faded slightly. "Of course, my son. Proceed.''

Bernard placed the chest and the pouch on the bishop's desk, noting the man's immediate interest. He flipped open the latch on the chest and eased back the cover.

"While in Damietta, I was able to collect various relics. This is reported to be a lock of St. Peter's hair. The pouch contains a piece of the True Cross, which I know is genuine because each of us knights received one from Bishop Thurstan, may he rest with God.''

Bishop Walter made a quick sign of the cross over the sentiment for his predecessor, then gently touched the hair, not disturbing a strand.

"A grand relic indeed,'' he said with awe. "Do you believe your source honest?''

"I do. I know of a king and a prince who dealt with the merchant for much bigger and richer relics.''

The bishop closed the chest and leaned back in his chair. "Do you mean to donate these to the Cathedral, in thanks for your safe return?''

A natural assumption on the bishop's part. 'Twas a thing often done by returning Crusaders. Bernard shook his head.

"Would that I were in a position to do so, Your Eminence. I fear, however, that my present lack of funds prevents such generosity.''

"You wish to sell these?''

"I have little choice.''

The bishop's brow furrowed in thought. "Were you not the knight who was to return to collect some prize from your lord?"

Simon's doing again, Bernard suspected. How else would the bishop know?

"My lord and I are having a disagreement over the way of payment of the reward. Until we settle to terms, I need funds on which to live."

"I see."

The bishop rose from his chair, picked up the relics and walked into an adjoining room.

Impatient, Bernard wandered over to the window. The vantage point allowed a commanding view of the cathedral grounds and the town of Durleigh. In the distance wound the blue ribbon of the River Dur, and beyond it the town's surrounding wall.

Immediately below, walkways wound through a circular-patterned rose garden, a far more ambitious project than his mother's "fancy garden."

Between the garden and wall, the people of the town and monks of the cathedral went about their business, the crowds flowing in and out of Durleigh's centrally located Market Square where one could buy most anything from a sack of grain to a knight's armor.

Depending upon the generosity of the bishop, the market would be his next stop—after he collected Claire. Or mayhap not. Claire might enjoy a walk through the rose garden.

Bernard wondered at the fanciful thought. He needed to get out of Durleigh quickly, and here he was considering meandering through a flower garden with Claire.

Bernard turned to the jangle of coins coming from the adjoining room.

The bishop walked toward him, his wide smile again

in place. He handed over the pouch containing the shard of wood.

"Keep this, Sir Bernard. 'Tis your protection against the evils of the world," he said, then poured several coins of both gold and silver into Bernard's other hand. "No Knight of the Black Rose should have to beg for his supper. I give you the worth of the other relic, and thank you for giving me the chance at its purchase. Have you more?"

Bernard stared at the coins. Bishop Walter had paid him nearly five times the amount the relics' merchant had asked for the lock of hair. No wonder merchants made the long trek from the Holy Land to the continent and England to deal with churchmen and nobles. What profit they must make!

"A few more," Bernard answered, thinking of the richest relic in his pack. If a lock of hair proved so valuable, what might he get for the forearm of St. Babylas, encased in a reliquary of silver, gold and jewels?

"Should you find you must sell others, might I hope you will once more come to me?"

Bernard smiled back at the bishop. "You may depend upon it, Your Eminence."

"Splendid. Now, I have a Mass to say, and I imagine you have business to attend. Promise me, however, that you will return when we can visit more thoroughly. Simon has told me many tales of his adventures. I should like to hear them again from your view."

"I should like that, too," Bernard said, hoping he would get the chance. "Might I also make a request? I would rather Simon not know just yet of my difficulty with my overlord. He might wish to...meddle, in the name of friendship."

Bishop Walter chuckled. "I understand, and will

honor your request for silence. You will, however, let me know if you need my assistance, in the name of friendship.''

The bishop walked him to the door. Bernard put his hand to the latch, then remembered a question he wanted to ask of the bishop of Durleigh.

''Your Eminence, if a man wished to purchase church-held land, who would one talk to?''

''To the bishop or archbishop of the diocese that holds it.''

''As I thought. My thanks, Your Eminence, for your time and your coin.''

Bernard left the apartment in high spirits, nearly sprinting down the palace stairs and passageways. He couldn't wait to tell Claire of the bishop's generous payment. They could now visit the market and purchase whatever they needed for the coming fortnight.

His steps slowed only as he approached the cathedral.

Was she in there, waiting for him, or had she fled?

Bernard stepped inside. He ignored the splendor fashioned by man to honor God, searching for a lone woman in a hooded cloak. There, by a side altar, knelt Claire.

She'd stayed, kept her word.

She turned her head toward him, as if answering the call of her name. His heart flipped as she rose and made her way to the cathedral's doorway. Her smile gave it yet another jolt.

''You look pleased,'' she said. ''I gather you met with success.''

''Aye. Nice man, Bishop Walter.''

''So I have heard. Ready to leave?''

Now he had to show the woman who trusted him that he truly could keep his part of their pact. He would keep her safe and dry, warm and fed—and keep his lust under control—until the day they parted company. He didn't doubt which part of the pact would prove the most difficult to keep.

Chapter Nine

Claire marveled at how quickly Bernard convinced one of the pilgrims visiting the cathedral to sell his mule. After loading the beast down with blankets and Bernard's chain mail, they made their way out the gates of the cathedral courtyard and headed for Market Square.

She longed to visit the merchants, but didn't dare. Too many of them knew her. Though the day was becoming quite warm, she huddled in her cloak, the hood pulled forward to hide her face, while Bernard visited the vendors.

He bought meat pies and roasted doves. On Blake Street he purchased several loaves of bread, all the while keeping an eye out for her father's soldiers.

He pressed her into eating a pastry filled with apple slices and seasoned with cinnamon. She took the last bite of the sweet treat as they turned south onto Durgate to cross the bridge over the River Dur.

They'd reached Michelgate when Claire heard a man's cry for Bernard to halt. She felt him shift to look behind them.

"Damn," he swore softly, and urged Cabal to greater speed.

Claire didn't have to turn around to know who gave chase.

"Can we outrace Henry?"

"There are four of your father's guards chasing us. None of them are mounted, but the mule will slow us. Hold tight."

Bernard spurred Cabal down Michelgate and out the town's southwestern gate. Once into the countryside, at a wide spot in the road, he reined to a halt.

Claire didn't see the sense in it. They'd be caught! "Should we not keep going?"

"Nay," he said and swung off Cabal. "I now have my messengers. Who better to take a ransom message to your father than his own men-at-arms?"

She could hear them coming at a run, shouting. Her gut knotted. "Bernard, my father's soldiers do not chase us with bargaining in mind."

Bernard pulled his scimitar from the scabbard at his waist. "Then we will talk after."

"There are *four* of them."

"Good odds. Gives them a chance to live. You stay on Cabal."

Then he turned to face his attackers.

It was over, she knew it. No man could stand against four. While she knew Bernard had fought many a battle in the Holy Land and survived, she'd seen him wield a weapon only in Dasset's practice yard as an inept squire—easily disarmed during sword practice, being knocked from his horse when tilting at the quintain.

The soldiers wore thick leather hauberks to protect their chests. Bernard's chain mail lay draped over the mule's back.

Bernard didn't stand a chance. She could only hope

her father had ordered his soldiers to bring Bernard back to Dasset alive, and that the soldiers would obey.

The soldiers skidded to a halt a few yards from where Bernard stood with feet planted slightly apart, his scimitar held loosely at his side.

She knew them all, of course. Henry, the guard who'd knocked Bernard on the head in Dasset's hall, spoke for the group.

"We have no wish to harm you, Bernard. Give over."

"Oh, I think not, Henry," Bernard answered. He waved his scimitar at the men-at-arms in a broad sweep, drawing all of their gazes to the unusual weapon. "Put down your swords and we can come to terms."

Henry took a step forward. "Terms? Our orders are to rescue Lady Claire and bring you back to Dasset. If we must take you back slung over your horse, so be it."

Bernard scoffed. "If you are determined, then have at it. The choice is yours."

They had no choice, Claire knew. The soldiers couldn't return to Dasset and report they'd seen Bernard and then let him go without a fight. The punishment for neglect of duty would be severe.

Henry looked up at her. "Come down, my lady. Move to behind us where you will be safe."

"Stay where you are, Claire," Bernard ordered. "To get to you they must get through me, and I vow they will not."

His face twisted in anger, Henry charged Bernard.

Claire clung to Cabal's mane, her heart pounding, as sword clashed against scimitar. Within the space of two heartbeats, Bernard pushed Henry back and hooked the soldier's sword within the curve of the heathen blade. The sword flew to the far side of the road. Henry fell to the dirt, clutching his bleeding arm.

Had she blinked, she'd have missed it.

This wasn't the Bernard of old.

As if to prove her right, Bernard skittered away from Henry and beckoned to the other three. They accepted the challenge, all at once.

Claire turned away and closed her eyes, the pain in her heart overwhelming, fully expecting Bernard to succumb under the onslaught. But it wasn't Bernard who screamed in anguish.

She had to look, and could hardly believe what her mind said couldn't be true. Yet another of her father's men, Theo, lay on the ground, not moving.

Bernard toyed with Roger and Louis, herding them back up the road to Durleigh. Claire let out the breath she'd been holding.

Sweet mercy, Bernard was a sight to behold. He moved with the grace of a cat, his scimitar flashing here, a quick slash there. No strain showed on his face, only intense concentration as he fended off one sword thrust after the other.

Then Roger went down, stripped of his weapon, bleeding from a large gash under his knee.

"What say you, Louis?" Bernard said to the fourth soldier, stepping back. "Must you bleed, too?"

The point of Louis's sword lowered. He glanced about at his three comrades on the ground. "Nay," he said.

Just when Claire thought Louis would surrender his sword, he turned and ran—straight for her.

"Cabal! To me!" Bernard shouted.

Cabal's muscles bunched. The horse lurched forward. Claire held tight to fistfuls of black mane as Cabal broke into a run. Tied with a long rope to Bernard's pack, the poor mule had no choice but to follow. The well-trained courser circled around the men lying in the road and came to a halt at Bernard's side.

"Dammit, Louis! Must I kill one of you to make this fight look good for Setton?" Bernard asked. "Are not three wounded enough to satisfy him that you tried to do your duty?"

Claire glanced at Theo, who lay facedown in the road and hadn't yet moved. He wasn't dead?

"And failed!" Henry yelled angrily, having gotten to his feet, still clutching his arm. "Do you think Setton cares if we die or not? He will know only that four of us fought one man and lost."

"Fine. Beat each other senseless if you think it will help. Bleed to death if you want. My fight, however, is not with you, but with Setton. I would rather not kill any of you unless you insist!"

Louis made a move toward Bernard as if to insist.

Bernard pointed his scimitar at the only unwounded soldier. "Do not be a fool," he warned Louis, his tone low and dangerous.

Louis looked down and stared at his sword, then spat out a foul word and tossed the weapon onto the road.

"Wise man. See if you can wake Theo," Bernard said, then turned his attention to the soldier with the wounded leg. "Can you stand, Roger?"

"Hmpf. Mayhap, if it is bound."

"Why bother?" Henry complained, sinking back to the ground. "I believe I will take your suggestion, Bernard, and sit here and bleed to death. Where did you learn to fight like that? Gads, I barely saw where the strokes were coming from!"

Bernard smiled. "Recognize the name Hugh of Halewell?"

"A tournament fighter, is he not?"

"Aye. The best. Served with him in the Holy Land. I have a towel in my pack. We must bind up those wounds."

Claire glanced from one man to the next in disbelief. Henry and Roger were wounded. Louis helped Theo—who held his head in his hands and sported a large bruise on his forehead—to sit up. Not a few moments ago the guards had hacked away at Bernard, and him at them, with sharp swords. Now they chatted like friends.

Of course, these men were old friends, or at least comrades. Bernard knew the four guards, probably better than she did, from having served with them at Dasset. Together they'd stood guard duty. Played at dice. Guzzled ale. Crossed swords in the practice yard.

Bernard had known the soldiers' fighting styles and each of their strengths and weaknesses. They'd thought they knew Bernard's, too, but couldn't have guessed his skill had improved by so great a degree.

"You can come down now, if you wish," Bernard told her, holding a large square of linen he'd fetched from his pack.

Though his sable hair was tossed in disarray, he didn't sweat. Nor did he gloat over his show of unparalleled sword play, though he did seem pleased the fight ended with no one dead or dying.

Claire let go of Cabal's mane and brushed away the strands she'd pulled loose from the horse's head. Bernard leaned his scimitar against Cabal. She reached for Bernard's wide, steady shoulders. He put his hands at her waist. She fair floated down to the ground, supported by the strength she always marveled at.

"Ware Louis," he said, taking up his weapon again.

Claire took the towel from Bernard's hand, ripped it in two and gave him back a piece. "I will see to Henry."

The soldier had gone pale and was obviously in pain.

"We failed you, my lady," Henry said. "When we saw Bernard halt we thought surely we would have you away from him within a trice."

She knelt down next to the wounded guard. "Do not be too harsh with yourself, Henry. I think Bernard surprised us all. Take your hand from your wound so I might wrap it."

The gash on his upper arm was both long and deep, but would heal with proper care. "When you go back into Durleigh, have this stitched."

"Are you all right, my lady?" he asked.

"I am unharmed," she assured him, and wrapped the strip of towel around his arm.

She pulled the knot tight, tucked in the loose ends, and then helped Henry to stand. They walked over to where Bernard and Theo watched Louis wrap Roger's leg. Once done, Bernard gave a satisfied nod.

"Now we can go about this in a more civilized fashion," he said, and sheathed his scimitar. "I care not how you explain our encounter to Setton. Tell him whatever you must to keep your heads on your shoulders."

"He will not be so merciful," Louis declared. "Likely, we will end up in the dungeon with Edgar."

With a sense of dread, Claire asked, "Why is Edgar in the dungeon?"

"Setton is angry with him for not locking Bernard's manacle as he should, thus allowing the escape. Edgar maintains he secured the manacle, but—"

"Edgar *did* lock Bernard's manacle," Claire said, angry that her father had manacled one of his own guards for something he'd had no part in. She felt the blood drain from her face. "Father did not put Edgar to the rack, did he?"

Bernard put his hand on her shoulder. "Easy, Claire," he said, then asked Louis, "Is Edgar all right?"

"For now," Louis said. "Edgar is not happy to be locked into the manacle you abandoned, but is otherwise fine. My lady? You released Bernard?"

Relieved beyond words, Claire could only nod.

"Most of us suspected as much," Henry said. "No one dared suggest the possibility to Setton, however, after he laid the blame on Edgar. We thought it best, for your sake."

Claire crossed her arms. "Father knows who arranged for Bernard's escape, make no mistake. Why he chooses to blame Edgar is beyond me."

"You suspected Claire?" Bernard asked of Henry.

Henry nodded. "In Julius's absence, Lady Claire often assumes the task of countering her father's... excesses. The people of Dasset admire her for sometimes defying Setton on their behalf."

A blush flowered on Claire's cheeks, and laid one of Bernard's doubts to rest. He now knew for certain that she hadn't conspired with her father about his escape. She'd released him out of compassion, or a sense of duty. Whichever was fine by him.

Bernard shook her shoulder. "Hear that, Claire? You are the hero, not I."

At the reminder of their conversation in the tunnel Claire's blush deepened. Bernard fought the impulse to gather her into a hug.

Henry ran a hand through his hair. "Hero she may be to some, but not to Setton." He shook his head. "Lady Claire, you should not have stopped me from bashing Bernard's head a second time. If he had been unable to leave, none of this would have happened."

Louis took the conjecture a step further. "If Bernard

had not made that ridiculous demand of Setton, none of this would have happened.''

All four soldiers looked to be of like mind.

''I demanded nothing of Setton that he did not promise to me, whether you believe it or no. And did we not just cross swords over Claire's return to Dasset? If you had won, would you not have taken her back to face her father, knowing it ill-advised for her to do so?''

Henry nodded. ''Having you to toss at Setton's feet would have gone far to distract him. He might take his anger out on you and leave Claire alone.''

The soldiers had been willing to sacrifice him to Setton to aid Claire, still were if they could figure out how to go about it.

''All this conjecture does not help Edgar,'' Claire stated. ''I could not bear it if Father decides to put him to the rack.''

Edgar need not face torture, not if Henry and the others would go along with the plan forming in Bernard's head. He suspected they would, most eagerly.

''Henry, can you arrange an escape for Edgar?'' he asked.

''Aye, but then Setton will blame someone for Edgar's escape and—''

''Not if Setton thinks I snuck into Dasset and let Edgar loose. I have an old helmet in my pack. Leave it in the dungeon in Edgar's place. If I remember aright, he has a sister who lives near London. Mayhap it is time he paid her a long visit.''

''Setton will know the helmet is yours?''

Setton would know it, and be most amazed and furious to have it appear in his dungeon. Bernard almost wished he could be there to see the old lord's face.

''He will know it. 'Tis one of Setton's. He gave me

the battered old thing on the day he sent me off on Crusade. This seems as good a way to return his property as any. Better than most.''

Henry thought it over, then said, ''Your plan just might work, but is unnecessary if you turn Lady Claire over to us. You have your freedom. Let us take her home.''

''Claire stays with me. When you men return to Dasset, tell Setton I am holding Claire for ransom against the reward he denied me.''

''Ye gods, Bernard!'' Henry swore. ''Have you not caused enough trouble already? I strongly protest.''

''You already did—'' he pointed to Henry's bandaged arm ''—and lost.''

Louis scoffed. '''Tis hard to believe Setton would reward a mere squire with land and his daughter.''

''Well, he did. If Bishop Thurstan had lived to bear me witness, I would now own several hides of land and be settled there with Claire as my wife.'' A question popped into Bernard's head. ''Claire, was your betrothal sealed before or after the bishop's death?''

Claire's jewel-toned eyes narrowed. ''After. Father had been bargaining with Marshall for several months. Two days after Bishop Thurstan's burial, he packed Mother and I up and hauled us south to Huntingdon.''

Bernard wasn't surprised. If he'd returned to Dasset straightway, while Bishop Thurstan yet lived, he would now have his land and be married to Claire. Damn Setton.

''Henry, tell Setton I demand Claire's weight in gold as her ransom. Tell him to put it in two sacks and deliver it to me at the chime of nonce in Durleigh's Market Square on…the fifteenth of August. I get my gold, he gets Claire. 'Tis far less than I am due.''

The four soldiers looked from one to the other.

Louis waved a hand at Claire. "Before we agree to any of this, we need some assurance of Lady Claire's well-being. A fortnight is a long time to keep her hidden and cared for properly."

Bernard had to admire the soldiers. If they thought Claire might come to harm, they might take up their arms and attack him all over again.

"I will take very good care of Claire. I give you my oath that she will come to no harm while in my care."

Louis wasn't convinced. "My lady, you have said little on this whole affair. At a word from you, we will tell Bernard to go straight to the devil."

Claire bowed her head and took a deep breath. Bernard held his while she struggled with her decision. Her chin came up.

"Give my father Bernard's message. And free Edgar."

Henry proclaimed, "'Twill be a miracle indeed if we can manage both and still keep our heads."

After handing Henry the old helmet, Bernard kept Claire behind him as the soldiers retrieved their weapons and headed back up the road to Durleigh.

"Can they do it?" Claire asked.

"They can," Bernard said. "By this time on the morrow Edgar should be free, and your father scrambling to find enough gold to pay your ransom."

"And where will we be?"

Good question. He wished he had a good answer.

"Hiding," he said, and helped her back up onto Cabal.

Odo Setton flung the helmet across the dungeon. It bounced off the rack and flew through the gaping doorway to the tunnel.

Edgar was gone, freed by the same bastard who now demanded Claire's weight in gold—a king's ransom—for her return.

If not for his alliance to Marshall, he'd let Fitzgibbons keep her, by God.

For the past three days his soldiers had searched Dasset land, then Durleigh, and gone all the way into York. Except for the one encounter outside of Durleigh with Henry and the others, no one had seen Fitzgibbons or Claire. Both of his wounded soldiers were now confined to their cots in the armory, suffering with fever, with Louis and Theo taking turns hovering over them.

He still didn't know how much of the soldiers' story to credit. Roger was all but witless, blubbering about a demon from hell who'd tried to cut off his leg with a giant scimitar. Henry's mind was clearer, though Setton wondered if the man remembered the amount demanded for Claire's ransom correctly.

Probably not. No woman was worth her weight in gold. Especially not Claire, particularly after she'd defied him and let Fitzgibbons go free.

He could, therefore, assume Henry remembered wrongly and Fitzgibbons had demanded only half that amount. Not that it mattered. Fitzgibbons wasn't getting anything.

Oh, he would meet Fitzgibbons at the Market Square in Durleigh. But not with gold in hand.

Setton walked over to the tunnel's entrance and retrieved the helmet. Damn, he'd never thought to see Fitzgibbons again, much less this helmet. Why couldn't the wretch have stayed dead?

Last fall, when news had come of Fitzgibbons' death,

he'd been delighted to be freed of that regrettable promise made in Bishop Thurstan's presence. He'd immediately begun the search for a husband for Claire, knowing he couldn't be fussy about his choice for a daughter of advanced age.

Quite by accident, he'd learned that Eustace Marshall coveted a hide of forest land on Dasset's northern border—good hunting grounds that marched alongside other of Marshall's lands.

Eustace Marshall maintained a knightly court at his splendid castle in Huntingdon in the south of England, held a high office in the royal court, hawked and hunted often, and was counted among the best jousters in all of England.

A man like that could select a wife of much higher rank and a worthier dowry—much too good for Claire.

Once married, she was Marshall's problem. Her husband could do with the meddlesome chit as he wished. Glad the day when Claire no longer meddled in Dasset's affairs.

Best of all, Odo Setton gained a son-by-marriage who had access to the king, whose high standing would bring favor, and eventually material reward, to the house of Setton.

Then the message had come from York that Fitzgibbons was alive and coming home. All the bargaining with Marshall might have come to naught if Bishop Thurstan hadn't succumbed to poisoning. The bishop's murderer had done Setton a great favor in a most timely manner.

'Twas now his word against Fitzgibbons that any reward had been granted, and Setton couldn't see why he must settle for a lowly knight as son-by-marriage when he could have a great lord.

Setton pushed the lever to close the tunnel door.

If Fitzgibbons had freed Edgar, then he might still be in the area. It ranked that the vermin had been so close all along and not found. Where had Claire been while Fitzgibbons snuck through the tunnels and into the dungeon? 'Twould be just like his contrary daughter to have helped her own kidnapper.

A shuffle of feet from near the stairway reminded Setton of the guards who'd discovered Edgar missing, and that he should send out men to search the immediate area once more. To what point? His men were exhausted and Fitzgibbons was likely long gone.

Setton gave a brief thought to hiring mercenaries to run down Fitzgibbons, but dismissed the notion. Mercenaries commanded high fees, and he'd learned in sorry fashion that they didn't always follow orders as they should.

Nor would he alert the sheriff. Best to take care of Fitzgibbons himself without the interference of a man who might take sympathy with a fellow Knight of the Black Rose.

Besides, Setton knew exactly where to find Bernard and Claire on the fifteenth of August. He'd have Claire back in plenty of time to marry Marshall, and Bernard's head on a pike before that sorry day was through.

Chapter Ten

Claire cringed as Bernard made another trip across the manor's massive support beam, which sagged and creaked each time he hauled a load of branches. One of these times Bernard was going to fall through the hole in the roof he was attempting to repair, she was sure of it.

They'd returned to Faxton—Bernard refused to call it Fallenwood—two days ago. While Claire still wasn't sure that hiding under her father's nose was a good idea, Bernard seemed to think no more patrols would come this way. So far he'd been right.

He'd also been content to spend his days in less dangerous pursuits, like getting the well to work, or snaring rabbits, or weeding his mother's roses. Last night's storm, and the resulting waterfall in the manor, had him up on the roof this morning.

A sharp, loud crack above her head sent her running for the door and out of the manor. The man would surely kill himself, and her with him, if he didn't cease this foolishness.

"Bernard!"

"Up here!" he called, as if she didn't know.

Claire glanced over the roof and spotted one of his legs near the center. He straddled the beam and was reaching for something on the back side of the roof.

"Bernard, that beam is ready to give way. Come down."

"What?" he yelled, and sat up.

Claire's mouth went dry. Bernard had removed his tunic.

Bits of thatch from the roof clung to his sweat-sheened chest of smooth, beautifully sculpted muscles. Her fingers itched to remove the bits of thatch, one by one. Slowly. 'Twas good he was up on the roof so she couldn't give in to the temptation to skim her hands over his sleek chest.

Sweet mercy, but he was magnificent to look upon. Bernard's rich, thick sable hair framed a ruggedly handsome face. He possessed the body of a warrior, big and powerful. Yet for all his size, he moved with a courtier's grace. For all his strength, he had yet to touch her with other than gentle hands. Firmly, aye, but never hurtful.

This hero of the Crusades compared much too favorably to the heroes of the troubadours' romantic tales. This one could slay a dragon in the morning, rout a band of outlaws after nooning, and still thoroughly satisfy his lady at night.

She'd stopped blushing when wondering about his prowess in a bedchamber. The heat that flamed within her now burned deep and bedeviled her woman's places. She'd known Bernard most of her life, but never truly noticed him until he'd returned to claim her. Now he tortured her body with desire and teased her imagination with sinful thoughts.

She knew about fornication from Father Robert's many sermons on the subject. Mother had given her the briefest of lectures on submitting to a man. She'd learned the most about rutting, however, when she'd caught her brother Julius in the castle garden with his breeches down and a dairymaid's skirts up.

The dairymaid hadn't worried about sinning, nor had she seemed to submit. The girl had enjoyed herself thoroughly, her legs wide spread, her hips rising in rhythm to his thrusts. And when done, she'd begged Julius to do it again.

More than once over the past few days Claire had been tempted to push down Bernard's breeches and toss up her skirts.

She was far past the age when a woman usually coupled with a man her first time. Most women married and bore several children long before their twentieth summer. In only a few weeks she would marry Eustace, become his wife and share his bed. But there was no fire in her betrothed. His kiss didn't thrill her to her very core as Bernard's did. To Eustace, she would submit. With Bernard, she would know the ecstasy of the dairymaid.

But more, she was growing very fond of Bernard, who could make her smile, who took such pains to make sure she ate well and slept comfortably. Did he know how badly she wanted to pull him down onto the pallet of straw and blankets he'd fashioned as her bed? Would he allow her to pull?

She wasn't beautiful, but she wasn't ugly. She wasn't reed slender, but she curved in all of the places a woman should curve, if amply. Bernard didn't find her repulsive. He *had* kissed and caressed her, if only the once. Could she seduce him into an embrace again? From an embrace, to shucking his breeches?

Unfortunately, she hadn't the least notion of how to

go about seducing Bernard without making a fool of herself. Nor had she figured out how to explain her lack of virginity should she be successful and Eustace called her on it.

Whether her father had promised her to Bernard or not, the marriage to Eustace Marshall would take place. Her betrothal was binding, the bargaining done. Once the ransom was paid, Bernard would hand her over and go on with his life. She wouldn't see him again. She would marry Marshall, bear his children, run his household—all in the name of duty.

Was it wrong of her to want to experience more than dutiful kisses and submissive beddings? To crave fire and ecstasy from the man who might have been her husband if he'd only returned home sooner? From the man who should truly be her betrothed?

"Claire?"

How lovely her name sounded from his lips. Would he shout it as he united his body with hers? Or would he whisper it softly when drained and unable speak?

Harlot, her mind accused. *So be it,* her heart answered.

"You are a knight, Bernard, not a carpenter or a thatcher. That beam creaks as if to break. Come down."

Come to me.

He smiled. "I imagine it sounds much worse from underneath than from up here." He got to his feet and bounced on the beam. "See? 'Tis sturdy."

Claire put a hand over her thudding heart. "Nor are you a rope walker. Please, if you must have that hole covered, get another to do it."

He waved an arm in a large sweep of the surrounding woodlands. "See you anyone else about? If I want it done, then I must do the deed. For myself, I would not bother. But I did promise to have a care for your well-being. Should we get another storm like last night, and you get wet, your sniffles are likely to return. You have not coughed in two days, and I prefer the silence.''

Claire thought the sentiment rather sweet of him, but not at the cost of his own safety.

''And if you fall and break your leg again, or more likely your head, who will see to my well-being then?''

Carefully, he lowered himself to sit on the beam. ''I have given that some thought,'' he said. ''The skirmish with your father's men-at-arms reminded me that I could be injured or killed and unable to see my plan through.''

Claire shivered. ''You defended yourself rather well.''

He shrugged a shoulder. ''I have seen many a man fall prey to a swifter sword or keener attack. I am good, but not invincible. If something untoward should happen to me, I worry about what might become of you.'' He tilted his head. ''Could you find your way to Huntingdon from here?''

He would have her go to Marshall for protection. Claire tried to make light of his concern and preference, and of the fear that gripped her innards at the thought of Bernard injured or ill, or dead.

''Nothing untoward will happen to you. Unless, of course, you fall off of the roof.''

''Be serious, Claire. 'Tis a possibility you must consider.''

Claire sighed inwardly. Bernard wouldn't let the subject drop until she gave him an answer.

''If I tried to make my way to Huntingdon, I might end up in Scotland,'' she said, drawing a smile from Bernard over how hopelessly lost she might become. ''Besides, Marshall is likely even now on his way to Dasset. He has a long way north to come, and travels with an impossibly large and lumbering retinue, and will probably stop at Westminster to see the king for a day or two along his journey. We expect him to arrive at Dasset…'' Claire smiled at the coincidence ''…the day after the ransom exchange.''

''He comes several days before your wedding, then?''

Claire didn't want to talk about Marshall or her wedding or the ransom. She wanted him off that roof, beside her, where she could get her hands on him and more if she could manage it.

''Bernard, if we must talk, come down. My neck is getting sore from looking up at you.''

''Then we will talk later. I am nearly done.''

Stubborn man. Once he set his mind on a course, 'twas nigh impossible to put him off it. He would finish the repair no matter what. She could probably strip naked right here in the yard and he'd tell her to wait until the last branch was in place. Would he even notice?

Aye, he'd notice. He was a man, after all. A healthy one, with a male's base urges. There had been times when riding in front of him on Cabal when she'd felt the physical evidence of his male arousal on her backside.

She wasn't bold enough for so obvious a ploy to get his attention. There had to be a more subtle way to entice him off the roof.

Claire pulled the netting from her hair, remembering he'd removed it when she'd tried to escape him and he'd kissed her, touched her. She ran her fingers through the long tresses to take out the worst of the snarls, then shook her head. Her hair spread out and fell in disarray around her shoulders, most of it falling forward to cover her breasts.

He noticed. He sat very still on the beam, watching.

She nearly laughed in giddy delight that so small an action produced a much desired result.

Then he looked up, out over across the treetops, and stared with greater intensity than he'd watched her antics.

He pointed up the road. "Smoke," he said, and scrambled down off the roof.

Bernard's heart beat faster. If he guessed aright, the thick, black smoke billowed up from nearby Lillian's cottage. He tossed on his tunic even as he unwrapped Cabal's reins from around the tree where the horse had been left to graze.

He pulled the horse to the front of the manor and handed the reins to Claire. "Hold these," he told her, then backed up, took a few running steps, and vaulted onto the horse's bare back.

He reached for the reins. Claire put her arms up.

"You stay here," he ordered.

"Either take me up with you or I run up the road after you."

"Ever ridden bareback? 'Tisn't easy."

"There must be a first time for everything. Take me up."

Only a moment ago, he'd been wondering if there might be a first time for them. The two of them together on a pallet, alone in the manor, Claire's long hair draped enticingly over her bare breasts. His lust still hadn't cooled.

If not for spotting the smoke...

He reached down, Claire jumped, and she was soon settled between his welcoming thighs and pressed hard against his aching arousal. She couldn't help but know what he'd been thinking while up on the roof watching her take her hair down. Was still thinking, and reluctant to set aside.

"Press your legs together, hard," he said, wishing beyond sense he was beneath her. He damn near lost his mind when she obeyed, wiggling slightly to get a better grip on Cabal's back.

"Like so?" she asked, her voice husky.

"Just like so," he whispered in her ear, wrapping his arm around her, just under her breasts. The pleasant roundness of her female form rested lightly against his forearm.

Ah, hell.

With a push of his knees he ordered Cabal forward. Cabal's smooth gait sped them up the road. Within minutes they reached Lillian's cottage.

He found Lillian standing outside, waving her arms at the kettle at her feet. The kettle smoked, but the wisps rising into the air were now white, not black. Relieved that her cottage hadn't caught fire with Lillian in it, Bernard dismounted and helped Claire down.

Lillian smiled. "Just like in the old days. A Fitzgibbons comes to my aid."

"What did you do?" he asked.

"Oh, I got the cook fire a bit too hot, and careless with an old rag. Then the oil caught flame and—well, I managed to get it hauled out before everything caught up."

Crashing in the bushes alerted Bernard's instincts. He reached for his scimitar. Not there. Damn. Still, he put himself between the women and the woodland.

Two men rushed out of the woods—and stopped dead when they saw him.

The older man crossed himself. "Holy Mother of God," he said his eyes going wide. "You were right,

Lillian. A branch grown straight and true from the trunk.''

Memories flooded Bernard's head, all good, of this man and his son. Of Wat, who'd tended Faxton's fish pond, and the boy, Garth, a childhood companion.

Garth's smile warmed Bernard clear through. '''Tis good to see you again, my lord. Welcome back to Faxton.''

My lord?

Granville Fitzgibbons had been the lord here. 'Twas natural, Bernard supposed, for Garth to make the mistake.

''Not lord,'' Bernard said, extending his hand. Garth came forward, followed by Wat, and clasped hold of Bernard's forearm. '''Tis yet Bernard, my old friend. How goes the fish pool?''

Wat answered with a hint of distaste. ''Full of eels instead of perch, but puts food on the table.'' He elbowed his son's ribs and bowed to Claire. Garth followed his father's lead. ''Lady Claire, 'tis an honor.''

Claire's head bobbed in royal fashion, but her smile for Wat and Garth held warmth.

Another crashing through the bushes. Hob and his wife, Mary, came at a run. Within the space of a few minutes ten people stood around him. Most he knew, some he didn't, but all greeted him warmly and with a hint of awe. Each bowed or curtseyed to Claire, who greeted them with warmth and interest in Lillian's explanations of who each of them was and how they served Faxton, and thus Dasset.

Obviously, they'd all seen or smelled the smoke and put aside their own chores to rush to Lillian's aid. 'Twas as it should be on a small holding, one neighbor helping the other in time of need. His father's people had always done so, even on a night fourteen years ago. They'd come, but not in time. There hadn't been time.

Even as he enjoyed seeing some of his father's tenants again, he wondered if he had best leave the manor. Too many people now knew where he was, and word of his whereabouts could easily get back to Dasset.

Bernard wandered back to Claire's side, hearing the tenants ask after each other and admonish Lillian to be more careful. Then, with no more excuse to linger, the people made their farewells and returned to what they'd been doing before Lillian's smoking kettle had drawn them away.

Wat and Garth remained behind.

"Did the fire do your hearth any damage?" Garth asked of Lillian.

"I think not," she said.

"Mayhap I will have a look to be sure before I go," he said, then ducked into the cottage.

"I should be on my way, too," Wat said. "Will you stay in the manor a while, Bernard?"

Bernard wondered how much Faxton's people knew of what had happened at Dasset and of Claire's kidnaping. He had to assume Setton's soldiers had talked to all of them, not just Lillian. Too, from Wat's reaction upon first seeing him, he knew the two of them had discussed his previous visit with her.

"I wish I could stay," he said honestly. "But I must keep Claire hidden away for a while yet. Too many people now know we are here to keep our whereabouts secret. Nor do I want to put any of Faxton's people in danger. 'Tis best we leave."

"'Tis safe to stay," Wat argued. "Not one of these people will give away your whereabouts. Most of us would hide you in our own homes if the need arose.

Indeed, if you decide to claim Faxton as your own, we would stand with you."

"That is what I tried to tell him," Lillian injected.

Touched by their loyalty, Bernard shook his head. "I thank you for the offer, but I could not ask it of any of you. If Setton's soldiers should happen upon us—"

"They will not. Setton has halted the search."

Bernard had thought he would. By sending his soldiers out day after day, Setton left Dasset Castle too vulnerable. These might be times of peace, but no lord could deplete his defensive force or exhaust his guards for long.

"Did Setton reopen Dasset's gate?"

"Yesterday," Wat said, then laughed. "When I heard the news, I took in two barrels of eels. The place is abuzz with gossip over how you escaped and are holding Claire for ransom. The guards you ambushed near Durleigh are said to tremble at the sound of your name. And with Edgar's sudden and unexplained disappearance...well, I must tell you, you are becoming something of a legendary figure, Bernard."

"Nonsense."

"To the contrary. Even Old Peter admires you, somewhat. He is unhappy to have lost the stable, but is most grateful that you had the good sense to loose the horses before you burned it down."

"A regular hero," Claire said, amused.

"Well said, my lady," Lillian agreed.

Wat nodded. "Amen."

"Face it, Bernard," Garth chimed in from the cottage doorway. "You have defied Setton as no one has in recent memory, not even Lord Julius or Lady Claire, here. Many thought you daft, at first, but now many hope you win your battle."

"Aye, the last to butt heads so hard with his lordship was our own Granville," Wat said. "He was well loved, your father. More than Faxton's people would have followed him to the inner rings of hell if he had asked, as they would you, should you decide to claim your rightful place."

The lump in Bernard's throat nearly choked him. "Again, I wish I could. But once I collect Claire's ransom, I will have no choice but to leave. Even if I purchased the rights to Faxton from the bishop of Durleigh, Setton would never leave me in peace."

Wat tilted his head. "Aye, just like your father. He talked of doing the same, before…"

Before he died. Before the outlaws had come and killed him, stealing away all of their lives.

"I did not know he wanted to purchase the right."

"I know he talked to the bishop," Lillian said. "Your mother told me so."

"Granville talked to Setton, too," Wat added. "His lordship was less than pleased. Then your folks were killed, and you went off to Dasset, and no more was said. Always did bother me, Setton taking you off like that, but there was not a thing any of us could do about it. So we buried your folks in the church and hoped for the best for all of us."

Bernard knew Granville and Alice Fitzgibbons had been laid to rest beside the altar of St. Michael's church, where they'd been married, attended Mass and had their son baptized. Setton had told him when assuring him the outlaws had been caught and hanged for their evil deed. Bernard hadn't yet gone to visit the graves. Maybe it was time he did.

"I suppose I should be grateful the outlaws did not escape justice. I owe thanks to Setton for that, at least."

Silence. Lillian and Wat exchanged questioning looks. A chill ran down Bernard's spine.

"You did see them hang, did you not?"

"Far as I know, they were never caught," Lillian said.

Bernard's outrage swelled and threatened to overcome his senses. He fought to hold it in. Venting his anger before anyone but Setton for the lie served no purpose.

His voice hoarse, he said, "Setton told me he had not only caught the outlaws but hung them in front of the people of Faxton, so you all might know justice had been served. He lied to me."

Wat ran a hand through his hair. "I fear he may have done more, Bernard, but I have no proof. Nor should I make wrongful accusations before her ladyship."

"Lady Claire knows her father is no saint," Lillian told Wat, "and Bernard should know what you suspect."

Wat looked to Claire.

"Please, Wat, say whatever it is you need to say," she said softly.

"All right, then. So much happened on the night your folks were killed, that not until days later did several things seem strange to me. If outlaws had attacked the manor, why did they not take anything except your folks' lives? They stole nothing, not even your father's chest of coins, which Setton took possession of, by the by. Stranger still, Setton rode up with several of his guards shortly after the attack happened. No one from here ever went to fetch him. 'Twas as if he knew the manor would be attacked. He fair swooped in here, gathered up your folks' valuables and their most prized possession, you."

Bernard wanted to scream a denial at Wat. What he was suggesting was too horrifying to be true. "Are you saying you believe Setton ordered the murder of my parents?''

Wat shook his head. "Nay. I do not think Setton wanted them dead, only taught a lesson for your father's defiance. I have come to believe the outlaws were mercenaries, hired to harry your father. Something went wrong and your father and mother were killed. But as I said, I have no proof.''

Claire had gone white. "Could it be the mercenaries acted on their own? That my father learned of their intention and came after them?''

"To what purpose, my lady? Mercenaries fight only for coin. They would not have attacked if not already paid. And I do know that after that day, no mercenary was ever again hired at Dasset.''

"Sweet mercy," Claire whispered, and turned away.

Bernard noted Claire's distress, which nearly matched his own. If Wat was right, Setton's faithlessness toward his underling was unforgivable.

"Wat, do you know why my father sought to serve the bishop of Durleigh directly?''

"Granville did not see eye to eye with Setton on many things, but mostly your father wanted assurance you would inherit Faxton after him. Setton would not agree to it. The bishop did.''

Chapter Eleven

The small, stone church of St. Michael boasted a sweet-toned bell in its square, Norman-style bell tower. Light filtered into the church through two stained glass windows, both gifts from Granville Fitzgibbons—one at his marriage to Alice, the other upon the birth of his son.

A man-sized bronze plaque marked the final resting place of Granville Fitzgibbons, Lord of Faxton, and his wife Alice.

They'd been buried together beside the altar where they'd taken marriage vows. Bernard thought it fitting.

He ran his fingers over the raised lettering of their names, hoping they rested peacefully, knowing he wouldn't find peace until he learned the truth about how they died. Unfortunately, the only people who knew the truth lay beneath the plaque—and Odo Setton.

"Wat could be mistaken," Claire said from behind him.

Bernard doubted it, and doubted Claire believed it either. She was as horrified by Wat's suspicions as he, though for different reasons. She grappled for answers, too.

She knelt down beside him, not touching him, not speaking—just there. Staring down at the bronze plaque.

He tried to pray but it was a useless effort. Nor was a church the place to be plotting revenge.

"We should go back to the manor," he said.

She nodded, but didn't move until some time later, when he finally found the will to get up.

They were almost back to the manor when she asked, "How do we learn the truth? Who else but my father might know?"

"Bishop Thurstan, perhaps." But he was dead, too.

"That leaves the outlaws or mercenaries," she said, then took a long breath. "And possibly you."

He couldn't believe what he heard. *"Me?"*

She shifted in front of him. "You were there. I am sorry, Bernard, for all that has happened and for how you must hurt. But you *were* there, and may know of some small, telling sign that you have not thought of since that night."

He hated that she might be right. He'd buried those memories deep and in great haste. As a lad, they'd hurt far too much to remain at the fore of his mind. So he'd pushed them down to depths beyond his dreams, much less his waking hours.

The memories were old and likely tarnished by time. He doubted he remembered small details. He could hardly bear to dwell on the prominent events.

Was there a clue within those details a boy hadn't thought important, but a man would find enlightening? Or maybe a woman listening to his rambling might catch a hint of something not quite right.

He'd never told the whole of it to anyone. Not even to the knights he considered more brothers than friends. Bits and pieces had come out, especially on a night of boredom and too much wine when they'd sat in the desert and compared stories of how they'd managed to get caught up in the Crusade.

They'd never pressed him for more of the tale. There hadn't been a reason for it, as there was now.

"This is not going to be easy," he confessed.

She rubbed at his arm clasped around her midriff. "I know. I wish I knew of a way to make the telling less painful for you."

'Twould be painful for her, too. While he'd be searching for a reason to run her father through, she'd be hoping for a reason to hold Setton blameless. She knew her father for the harsh man he was, but no child wanted to think of a parent as ruthlessly cruel.

If he found that reason, he'd tell her. She'd given him her cooperation and honesty. He could give her back no less.

The faster done the better over.

He nudged Cabal to a faster speed.

"Claire, how much of your father's lands are held of the bishop of Durleigh?"

She was silent for a moment. "Nearly half."

"Those lands are held with the right to will them to his heir?"

"I believe so."

"Does your father grant the right to any of his landed knights?"

"Nay."

So Granville Fitzgibbons had been the rebel. If he'd won out, then others in Setton's service might apply to the bishop, and Setton would lose control over much land and many fees.

Enough to kill for? Maybe.

He refrained from posing the question to Claire.

Once back at the manor, Bernard returned Cabal to where he'd been grazing. Determined to get the tale over with, he circled round to the back of the manor where it seemed easiest to begin. Claire followed.

He waved at the blackened stone marring the corner of the manor. "They started a fire here. We had been abed for some time when Father woke to the smell of smoke. He roused Mother and me. We tossed on clothes, grabbed up buckets and ran for the well."

Bernard envisioned the fire, heard the crackle of flame devouring wood. "The pile was not large, but the wood was dry and the flames leapt high. Mother drew water for us while Father and I ran back and forth. He feared most that the thatch would ignite. I remember him heaving his first bucketful upward to wet the roof down some. My first bucketful went toward the highest flame."

The heat had been tremendous, keeping him back. He'd been lucky to get any water into the middle of the fire on that first toss.

"'Twas obvious someone had set it burning apurpose. I knew it. Father did, too. All the while we worked to put the fire out, he kept looking around, searching for whoever had set it and might be watching."

Bernard felt the burn of exertion in his arms, his legs. He couldn't now remember how many buckets full of water he'd carried. His father had carried more.

"We were all sore and worn by the time we were done. My feet and legs were wet and black with soot. Father burned his hand trying to pull the pile of wood apart and drag it away from the manor. He sent me for another bucket of water to douse the last embers. I walked, thinking the worst of the danger over."

Claire's hand slipped into his, a link to the present.

He held tight as the past closed around him, the worst of the tale yet to come.

"With the fire out, the night returned to dark and silence. There was just enough starlight to see my way back to the well. I handed Mother my bucket. 'Only one more,' I told her. She ruffled my hair and said that was good because her arms were about to give out. Then she laughed and said she would draw another for Father and me to wash off with so we did not blacken our blankets."

Bernard turned toward the well, but set his gaze on the spot where the attackers rode out of the woods. The sound of thudding hooves rang in his ears. The terror of a young boy squeezed his heart.

"I was halfway back to my father when I heard them coming. Four huge, black shadows charged out of the woods. I was so stunned I could not move, not even when one came straight for me and hauled me up. Then Mother screamed."

High and shrill she'd screamed his name, seeking his help. Her distress had pierced his terror and set him into motion. Too late. Far too late.

"I kicked and flailed like one gone mad. I think I connected with his jaw, but he held tight, told me to be still and I would not be hurt. I did not listen, but fought, knowing I had to get to my mother."

He'd never made it back to her side, hadn't been able to help her. He swallowed the lump forming in his throat. Fourteen years had passed since he'd failed her. Nothing he could say or do now would change his reactions of that night. Now, perhaps, he could give her justice.

"I fell, along with the man who held me. Father had pulled both of us off the horse. I went rolling in the grass. I heard them scuffle. Next thing I knew Father set me on my feet and told me to run for help. The last I saw of him, he had pulled my captor's sword from its scabbard and was running toward my mother.''

"Oh, Bernard," Claire whispered, and slipped under his arm, wrapping him in an embrace.

He buried his face in her hair, drawing in the sweet scent of her while he fought back tears. If he gave in to them, he'd never finish. He blinked and cleared his throat.

"I ran to St. Michael's and rang the bell. Three rings, a pause, three rings, a pause...over and over. The tenants knew the meaning of the signal. They rushed to the manor, but too late. By the time I returned, the men and horses were gone. People milled about. Women cried. I ran for the well.''

He'd known his parents were dead before he got near the well. They lay on the ground, too still. He could smell the blood. Feel Wat's hands on his shoulders, holding him back.

"My father had reached my mother. You could see where he dragged himself through her flowers. Their hands were touching.''

"No more," she said on a sob. "No more.''

Her hands slid up his chest then around his neck. Her soft cheek, wet with tears, pressed against his. He pulled Claire up hard against him, turned slightly and found her lips, right there, waiting for him.

He drank her in, full and thoroughly. Her lush, moist mouth was flavored of salty tears mingled with dark honey. As though he drank sweet wine, the heady taste of her shot to his head, muddling his mind.

Did he give comfort or take it? His numbed mind

didn't care. Then the tenor of the kiss changed, from soothing to passionate.

Claire clung to him and returned his kiss with ardor. She breathed in short, desperate pants. If he put his hand to her heart, he would feel it pounding. He could have her, right here and now, in the grass behind the manor. So her body told him.

He knew a woman's signs of desire. Did Claire? Did she truly know what her kiss and body were begging for? Or had her emotions led her astray?

Did she want him out of desire, or did she seek to comfort the teller of a sad tale?

He broke the kiss.

"I neither want nor need your pity, Claire."

"Then pity me," she said. "Take the hurt away, Bernard. Take us both to where there is no pain, only mindless pleasure."

She didn't know that in pleasure there was also pain, but a pain so exquisite to drive them both beyond reason. He could take her there, but only for the right reasons.

He gently pulled on a strand of her long hair, remembering when and how she'd taken it down.

"This morning. You let loose your hair. Why?"

He expected a blush and got glimmering eyes.

"'Twas my feeble attempt to seduce you off the roof."

He'd damn near fallen off the roof.

"And if you had succeeded?"

She took a resolving breath, but didn't look away. "Then I was going to drag you into the manor and onto my pallet."

So much for pity. Her utter directness stunned him. If he hadn't seen the smoke from Lillian's, and instead answered Claire's siren's call, he'd have been with her already.

Ah, fate. What strange turns it took.

The turmoil fed by his tale had begun to ebb. Visions of fire and blood were fading. The pain eased. By losing himself in Claire, would it all vanish?

Selfish of him, he knew, but Claire seemed willing and he needed her so damn badly.

He kissed her brow, her temple, under her ear. "Your pallet, hmm? Had you sleep in mind?"

"Oh, nay," she said, becoming breathless again, her neck arching to give him better access. "At least not until after I pushed your breeches down and tossed my skirts up."

The vision hit his brain and clung. Now he knew she'd been imagining him naked, as he'd imagined her—beneath him, joined in bliss.

He couldn't stand it. He picked her up and strode into the manor. He would take her to that mindless place she craved, slowly and gently. Bring her to pleasure. Just as she asked for. As he needed.

Bernard fell onto the pallet, bringing Claire down atop him.

He kissed her until he went witless. Ran his hands over her until he couldn't tolerate the feel of silk, but craved the touch of warm skin. Claire's warm skin.

The lacing on her gown gave way to his tugs. He rolled her onto her side, sliding his hand under the loosened neckline to expose her shoulder. Her skin was the color of cream and tasted as rich. Her lips were swollen from his kisses, her eyes bright with desire. A wanton in a lady's disguise.

"And when your skirts are up and my breeches down, what then, my lady?"

He teased, but Claire heard the need beneath his question. She knew what male part went where. If she hadn't witnessed it in the castle garden, she'd have known *something* had to reach the ache within her and give it ease. From the length of the bulge in Bernard's breeches, she knew he would relieve her ache with rod to spare. She didn't think Bernard would mind at all showing her the way it was done.

"I know what is done, but not the way of it," she said, noting the light in his eyes dim somewhat. "I am depending upon you to teach me what I do not know."

He pushed her hair back from her face, contemplating her confession of ignorance. "Ah, Claire, I should not. We violate our pact."

She wouldn't escape him; he would protect her. She'd promised not to seduce him; he vowed not to touch her.

"Then we make a new pact. For as long as we are together, I will not escape, and you will take care of me. And we will be lovers. Make love to me, Bernard."

"Sweet, sweet Claire. I want you so much I could expire from desire. Are you sure? Do you know—"

She put fingertips to his lips. "I know what we do will have consequences. But if you do not soon join your body to mine I may, too, expire."

He was quiet for a moment, then his mood shifted again, and Claire thrilled to the knowledge that he'd given in.

"Hmm. If I allow you to expire, I could be accused of not taking care of you. We cannot have that, can we?"

"I should say not."

She felt the tug at her skirts. Then his hand on her calf. She closed her eyes as his fingers skimmed her knee.

"Ready to learn?" he asked, his voice gone husky.

"Most eager," she answered, her body tensing as he caressed her thigh.

She spread her legs, willing him to keep going. He did. And when he touched that hot, wet spot at the juncture of her thighs, her body rose of its own volition, seeking more of his touch. She thought she'd expire when he granted her wish, and cried out in protest when he took his hand away.

"Greedy wench," he accused.

"Is that bad?"

"Oh, nay. For I can be greedy, too. Come up."

He pulled her to her knees, then made quick work of removing her gown. Covered only by a thin chemise, she felt exposed and vulnerable—and powerful. No one had ever looked at her with awe, as Bernard did now, as if she were exquisitely beautiful. A much desired treasure. In that moment, Claire felt a Venus, a goddess.

"Look at you," Bernard said, thinking there had never been a woman more flawlessly formed than Claire.

From the slope of her delicate shoulders, down to the rosy circles at the tips of her breasts, to the dark thatch of hair where he'd already played, Claire was perfection in every way.

The nubs of her nipples stood proud, pushing at the gossamer veil of her chemise, begging his touch. He skimmed his palms over the tips of her breasts, the barest hint of what he would do to her later. She shivered at the wisp of a touch. So responsive. So rare.

He removed her chemise inch by slow inch, sliding his hands along the swell of her hips, the dip of her waist, along the sides of her breasts, kissing her all the while.

She was far less patient with his tunic. She flipped up

the hem to get her hands underneath, and with an ago-
nizing glide up his chest, had it up and off him in sec-
onds. When she reached for the belt of his breeches, he
grabbed hold of her hands.

"Not yet," he said.

She looked confused, a sign of her innocence, reminding him to take the greatest care of her, as he'd
promised.

"If you are to reach your pleasure, I must hold back
mine a bit," he explained.

"Oh," she said, then smiled. "When you tell me it
is time for your pleasure, you will let me remove them."

Not a request, more of a command. One he would
gladly obey. Later.

Skin to skin, mouth to mouth, Bernard lowered Claire
to the pallet and worshiped her. He took his time learning where and how she liked to be touched. He savored
each kiss, each caress of her tentative, exploring fingers.

She learned quickly, and the heat of his passion rose
swiftly, unerringly upward. Deep within he smoldered
until holding himself from her became nigh impossible.

Claire loved the sound of his groans. Each time she
slid her hand over the smooth, hard plane of his chest,
he let her know he liked it. If she ran a fingernail down
the sculpted sinew of his arm, his muscle twitched.
When her fingers skimmed the flat of his stomach, he
quivered.

Whenever she came close to the ties of his breeches,
he backed away. He moved less far from her each time.

What he did to her was unbelievable. This huge, male
animal possessed the strength of a bear and the gentleness of a lamb. Those long-fingered hands that gripped
a scimitar with surety played on her skin with delicacy,
as if strumming a harp.

Without doubt, he'd done this before. She could hardly fault him, for now she benefitted from his knowledge. He knew exactly where to touch and what to push. His mouth knew where to kiss and how to suckle.

As if hearing her thoughts, he lowered his head to her breast and drew her into his mouth. His tongue lapped at the tip, driving her mad.

She ached. Gad, she ached in places she hadn't known existed before Bernard had brought them to agony. Once more, she reached for the rope belt. He didn't move. 'Twas time.

"Come up," she whispered, and drew them both to their knees.

The bulge in his breeches strained the seams. Her hands shook as she undid the knot of his belt and pulled it apart. She eased open the waist, and finally, pushed down his breeches.

"Magnificent," she said, staring at that part of him which she hoped fitted into her.

"Think you?" he asked.

"Oh, aye. Never doubt."

Long and thick, he was. Longer than the hand she placed beneath him. Thicker than her closed fingers could wrap around. Like iron, covered in smooth, silk-slick skin.

He hissed. "Easy, Claire."

"Does it hurt?"

"'Tis a good hurt," he assured her.

Like her lovely aches.

In a flurry he rid himself of boots and breeches, removed her shoes and stockings, then took her down to the pallet and swept her once more into a witless stupor.

She gloried in his tenderness. His gentleness. Even as he made love to her with an almost reckless abandon.

With the focused determination that he went about most things, he established his male strength and prowess beyond doubt.

The combination of fierce warrior and gentle courtier proved irresistible. Intoxicating.

She gave him all she knew how to give. With caresses and kisses, she matched his physical ministrations. When he loomed over her, his eyes filled with hunger, his body taut with need, she opened to the joining of their bodies without a qualm in heart or head.

This was right and good. Joyful.

Bernard eased into Claire's velvet haven with all the control he could muster. He'd never taken this much time and care to prepare a woman in his life. Only for the woman beneath him, welcoming him into her untried depths, would he be so patient.

Only for Claire.

Deeper he slid, watching her eyes close and lips part as she took him in. Deeper still—until he butted up against the barrier he'd always known would be there but hadn't given much thought to.

He could withdraw now. Leave her whole. There were other ways to take her to bliss, to gain his own release. Claire took the decision from him with an upward arch of back and thrust of hips. A sharp intake of breath. A small smile.

She was his.

With long strokes he pleasured her, deeply and thoroughly. He watched her face, her wonder, her rising tension. On the verge of her ecstasy he thrust with his all and hovered tight, holding her on the very brink.

"Bernard," she cried out.

With his name still on her lips, he took her up and over, and lost himself.

The ripples of her release mingled with the throb of his. Perfect. Magnificent. Only with Claire.

He nuzzled in her neck, feeling her heart pound against his chest, enjoying the massage of her fingers in his hair. He'd been vanquished by the wanton lady he hadn't the least wish to withdraw from.

Resigned to rolling off so she could breathe, he raised up. She pulled him back down.

"Can we do it again?"

To his amazement, his loins stirred to the slight plea as if it was a command brooking no denial.

"Greedy wench," he said, growing hard and determined all over again.

"Hmm. You, too," she said, and he had to agree.

Her hips rose and fell in rhythm to his increasingly invigorated thrusts. This second time seethed with lust. He took her fast and hard, more rough than gentle. More rutting than loving. All singly-focused sensation of male joined to female.

This time she screamed his name. This time he conquered.

Even as he reveled in the power of it, his heart flipped in his chest. The woman who'd pleaded for a second bout then matched him thrust for thrust didn't look vanquished but joyful.

In that moment Bernard knew he'd never find another woman as perfect and wanton and beautiful as Claire. No one else could bring him the peace or excitement or joy she did.

With Claire, he could share his deepest, darkest memories, then find fulfillment beyond his brightest, most vivid dreams.

She should be his wife.

He'd asked for the wrong reward. He should have demanded the marriage to Claire.

Chapter Twelve

"**I** need to get up," Claire said, not moving.

"Stay there," he told her, unwinding his body from around hers and getting to his feet. Naked. Glorious.

All that stirred was her stomach.

"But I am hungry," Claire protested, utterly famished.

"Still hungry?" he asked.

Mischief, and the promise to pleasure her again if she asked, played in his eyes.

"For food, man, food."

He laughed lightly. "I know. I heard your stomach insist."

His ear had been very close to her stomach when it growled. She'd thought he'd been too occupied to hear. What he'd been doing had been too delicious to call to a halt for mere food.

She pushed the hair out of her eyes but didn't bother covering up. Bernard liked to look at her, and heaven help her, she adored the appreciative gleam in his eyes.

They were lovers now. If this afternoon were any indication, she would need energy to keep up with him. She needed food.

"I think there is a meat pie left," she said.

He turned, and Claire did some appreciating of her own.

Bernard had the most adorable, dimpled bottom. Each muscle of him was beautifully molded, and became rock-hard when put to use. Even his bottom. She'd felt the tightening under her hands as he thrust within her, and now watched the graceful play of muscle as he walked to the other end of the room.

Bernard belonged at Faxton. He moved about the manor, even bare-arsed, with the ease and surety of lordship. If her father hadn't been so tightfisted with his father—she pushed further thoughts of both men away.

Today's upheavals yet hovered in the back of her mind. Wat's suspicions and Bernard's horrifying tale—both black storm clouds rumbling in the distance, threatening to drench her current peace and flood Bernard with pain again.

For the moment, Bernard seemed content. For herself, she was so sated as to be languid. For a little while more, maybe they could keep the storm at bay.

He returned with the meat pie, a tin cup and an open bottle of wine. She stared at the bottle.

"Where did that come from?"

"France," he said, as if he'd bought it there.

"You have not had that in your pack all this while. I would have noticed."

"Bought it in Durleigh. I thought to save it for a special occasion. Now is as good as any occasion will ever get."

She hadn't seen him buy it. But then, she'd been trying to hide her face and keep a watch for her father's men-at-arms. He handed her the wine and cup, then sat on the pallet next to her, cross-legged.

"What occasion?"

He kissed her lightly. "You."

"Oh."

Flustered, but pleased, she poured the wine then set both bottle and cup down near his knee. He broke off a small chunk of the pie and handed the biggest share to her. The savory, pastry-wrapped pork defied accolades, but Bernard merely nibbled at his piece.

Claire found it hard to believe he wasn't hungry. He hadn't eaten since this morning either. After this afternoon's exertion, his stomach should be empty, too.

"Not hungry?"

"Not very."

"You are not ill, are you? Mayhap you caught my sniffles."

"Just not hungry."

Then either he took his responsibility for taking care of her much too seriously, or he was upset. The storm clouds were rumbling.

Claire dreaded thinking about his past anymore, was almost sorry she'd asked for the tale in the first place. Almost. Bernard needed to lay his parents to rest once and for good, and she needed to know what part her father had played in their deaths.

She knew her father capable of harsh measures, his usual methods of punishment being the rack or whipping. The whip was a particular favorite when he wanted to make an example of someone. Had the possibility of losing Faxton pushed him to extremes? Had he ordered murder over the loss of a knight's fee and twenty barrels of fish?

More than the loss of Faxton had been involved. If Granville Fitzgibbons had succeeded in his attempt to hold his land directly of the bishop of Durleigh, other of Dasset's landed knights might have applied to the bishop for the same privilege. With Dasset's resources depleted, Dasset itself would be at risk.

She could see her father's reasoning for wanting to hold on to Faxton. His methods, however, left her cold.

Claire licked the last juices of meat pie from her fingers and looked for the cup of wine. Bernard was refilling it. He may not be eating, but he was making hearty progress on the wine.

"Does it help?" she asked, pointing to the half-empty bottle.

"Not much."

He lay down on his back, his forearm across his brow, his knees raised.

She hated to do it, but she must get him talking again. He'd held his dark memories in for too long. Since he was but twelve. Fourteen long, lonely years.

Claire lay down on her side next to him, propped on an elbow. She laid her other arm across his chest.

"You came back to the manor and realized your parents were dead. What then?"

He sighed. "Ah, Claire. My head hurts."

"'Tis all those nasty memories rattling around inside your skull. Let them out."

He shifted his head to look at her. "There really is not much more to tell. A few of the men tried to follow the horses' tracks, to no avail. The women took care of my parents. I could do no more than cling to Lillian. 'Twas near dawn when your father arrived."

"Wat said no one summoned him. Did Father say how he came to be there?"

"Not that I remember. He and several soldiers were just…there."

"Could he have heard the summons of the bell? Or

perhaps someone from between Faxton and Dasset heard and alerted my father.''

Bernard thought about the possibilities for a moment. ''Too far for anyone at Dasset to have heard. As for the other, 'tis possible. I would think Wat would have learned of it later, though, if it were true.''

Likely. The funeral for the Lord and Lady of Faxton must have been well attended. Whoever had summoned their overlord would have told someone and the information would have spread. For what other reason could her father have been out near dawn than he'd known the attack would happen and wanted to be at Faxton shortly afterwards?

''Then Father brought you to Dasset,'' she prompted him to go on.

''Setton decided 'twas best for all if I were raised at the castle. Lillian offered to keep me, but Setton was adamant. So off I went.''

Not to return until fourteen years later.

''I remember the day you came. I was with Mother and my brothers and sister. We were in the bailey, on our way to break fast in the hall after morning Mass. You were riding on the tail of a cart.'' Which struck her as strange. ''I wonder why Father took a cart with him?''

''You remember the first time you saw me?''

The question took her by surprise. ''I remember.'' His mouth curved upward. ''Do not let it go to your head. I was always curious about new people at Dasset, and a lone child on the back of a cart drew my interest.''

She refrained from confessing he'd also drawn her sympathy because he looked so sad. He'd see it as pity.

''I remember the first time I saw you, too,'' he said, still smiling. '''Twas the next day. Your mother had dressed all of you in your finest and lined you up in order—Julius, Geoffrey, Jeanne, Claire—on the castle steps to be presented to some noble visitor. I thought you looked regal for one so young. Then you ruined the impression when you lifted your skirt to make a curtsey. You were bare-footed. Your poor mother about fainted.''

Claire recalled the incident though the memory was hazy. She had no idea how her bare feet had escaped anyone's notice—especially her mother's—until too late.

''My shoes were too small and hurt my feet. Father had promised to bring me a new pair from Durleigh, but he—'' Claire forgot about explaining her bare feet. ''Bernard, that is why Father had a cart. He had gone into Durleigh for supplies. He forgot my shoes.''

Bernard sat up and took another sip of wine, a long one. ''I never knew your father to visit the markets. He always had supplies shipped into Dasset.''

''Aye, usually. But for some reason he went into town. Mayhap he had other business there, too, and decided to bring the supplies home himself. 'Tis possible he could have been on his way back to Dasset and for some reason stopped by Faxton.''

He scoffed. '''Twas just after dawn, Claire. He would have had to leave Durleigh in the middle of the night. Makes one wonder what kind of business he might have had in town, does it not? It gave him the perfect opportunity to hire a band of mercenaries to kill my parents, then pass by on his way back to Dasset to ensure the deed done.''

True enough. Claire gave up looking for excuses for her father's behavior. Each time she suggested an innocent reason for his presence, Bernard could discredit it with a reason that suggested his guilt.

''Whenever Father goes into Durleigh, he stays at the

Royal Oak. If we could talk to the owners, they might be able to tell us why he was there and whom he talked to. But that would involve going back into town. We might not be as fortunate to escape next time."

"I was thinking to go back anyway. Maybe it is time to see Simon."

Claire cringed at the thought of involving the sheriff.

"I know he is your friend, but he might feel obligated to arrest you. Then you lose everything you have fought for—the ransom, your freedom."

"The ransom holds less and less appeal."

Claire realized Bernard might forgo the gold if he could prove her father guilty of murder. Indeed, if Odo Setton was guilty of causing Bernard's parents' deaths, then he deserved punishment. But there was no proof. 'Twould likely come down to Bernard's accusations against her father's denial—just like Bernard's reward.

She could almost hear her father gloat.

Nor did she want to go back to Dasset before either Eustace Marshall arrived or her brother Julius came home. She needed one of them to act as a buffer between her and her irate father. A selfish reason, to be sure. Still, 'twas in Bernard's best interests to see his original plan through.

"You should collect the ransom first," she said. "Then if you choose to press the other matter, you will have the funds and your freedom to do so."

"I wish I had more answers than questions."

Claire reached for him, and he eased back down with little prodding on her part.

"Think on it another day or two. There is time yet."

Time for us.

She put her head on his shoulder, his arms came around her.

"Aye. There is time yet," he said with less resignation than she'd hoped for.

She might yet have to convince him to wait. And wouldn't her father be horrified if he learned she'd been the one to convince Bernard to hold out for the gold.

Her whole life she'd sought to win her father's approval. Nothing worked, so she'd given up, like her brother Julius. Then, like Julius, she'd sought to counter Father's excesses. She'd paid a price for the times he caught her in her machinations, but she managed to ease others' suffering. 'Twas worth a bruise or two.

These past months, since her betrothal, had been nigh on heavenly. He finally thought her worth the cost of her keep, and his mood had been so good he'd not been too badly tempered.

Until Bernard returned and demanded his reward.

She fully believed Bernard in that regard. He'd trusted Odo Setton to keep his word, probably because Bishop Thurstan could bear witness. With the bishop dead, Setton felt no obligation to give Bernard a sou. Considering what her father may have done, he owed Bernard far more than Bernard requested for her ransom.

He should have Faxton. He should have the gold.

He should have me, too.

"I will be fine, Bernard. While you and Garth catch our supper, Lillian and I will visit," Claire said to his unwillingness to leave her at Lillian's cottage.

"I would rather you come with us," he said.

"I hate fishing. You catch and clean them and I will cook them, but waiting around for one to take the bait is not my idea of a fine time. Truly, there is no reason for you to worry."

"We will go into the cottage and clean herbs and talk

of women's things,'' Lillian said, then made a shooing motion with her hands. ''Go on with you.''

Bernard looked at Garth, who shrugged his shoulders.

''They should be safe enough for a short while, especially if my father is right about Setton's ending the search,'' Garth said.

Bernard looked at her as if wondering if she would stay put. She would, but wouldn't say so. He either trusted her or he didn't.

''All right,'' Bernard said, yielding, though Claire noted the resistance in his words. ''Be sure to keep an ear tuned to the outside for trouble. I will be able to hear you if you call out loudly.''

''Nothing will happen,'' she said.

''I wish I were so sure.'' He raised a hand slightly, as if to touch her, then closed his fingers in his fist. ''Take care. We will not be far away or gone long.''

Claire waited until Bernard and Garth were several steps down the road before she let out a relieved breath.

''For a moment there I though he would change his mind,'' she told Lillian. ''He needs this time with Garth.''

'''Twill do them both good.'' Lillian turned and went into the cottage. Claire followed. ''I gather Garth found his way up to the manor this morn.''

Claire sat on a stool next to Lillian's worktable. She smiled. ''Garth invited Bernard to go fishing. Bernard insisted he had to fix the roof, then could not think of a way to refuse Garth's offer to help. You should have seen them. They looked like two little boys trying to get their chores done so they could go play.''

Lillian chuckled. ''The two of them did the same often enough as boys.''

''I thought so, but I could not talk Bernard into leaving me at the manor. My thanks, Lillian, for being out of doors when we passed by and inviting me to stay.''

''My reason was selfish, I fear. You were here and gone so fast last time, and I am dying to hear the whole of how you two got into this mess.''

Claire chuckled. '''Tis little enough payment for your timely rescue, I suppose, though I can hardly remember what I told you and what I did not.''

''Then begin again and tell all.''

Claire thought back to the very beginning, when she'd come down the stairway into the hall, hearing her father's loud laughter. Bernard's back had been to her. She'd known him only by the black-and-red trimmed tabard he wore.

He'd stood tall and stiff, his hands clenching then letting loose.

''You know about the reward Bernard demanded of my father?'' Claire asked.

Lillian had picked up her pestle and mortar. The scent of rosemary filled the air. ''I heard he demanded land and you, and your father denied making such a bargain.''

''Aye, land and me. Bernard was willing to give up a portion of the reward, me, but stood firm on his demand for land.''

''Tsk. Just like a man. Land, always land.''

Almost Claire's thought, exactly, when Bernard had said he'd be willing to give up the marriage. She'd made a noise, drawing his attention. For a moment his eyes had held sadness, then hardened. He'd turned back to her father and restated his demand for the land.

''In Bernard's defense, at the time he thought me a married woman. Had my father not told him about Eustace, Bernard might have pressed for the entire reward.''

"Most likely. So your father tossed him in the dungeon."

Claire related the rest of the argument and Henry's knock on Bernard's head. She recalled Bernard lying so still on the dais, the back of his head bleeding.

"I warned Father he had best have a care toward a hero of the faith," she said, becoming angry all over again at her father's stubborn refusal to heed her warning. "I tried to reason with them both. Neither listened, of course. 'Twas like dealing with two rams intent on butting heads."

"Only your father had the advantage."

"Too much of an advantage. With Bernard locked in the dungeon, Father could do whatever he pleased whenever he chose. I feared Father would go too far. So I unlocked Bernard's manacle and told him to ride fast and far. Well, he went fast," she said looking about her, "but as you can see, not far."

He'd brought her home.

Watching Bernard and Garth work in concert on the roof, hearing them laugh together, only confirmed her belief that Bernard belonged at Faxton. Even if he collected the ransom and bought land elsewhere, she doubted he'd be as happy anywhere else than here. Unfortunately, so long as her father lived, Bernard wouldn't be able to stay.

Lillian put her grinding aside and moved to the hearth. She swung the kettle out to check on whatever bubbled within. Satisfied with what she saw, she grabbed a thickly folded cloth and lifted the kettle from the hook.

Claire noted the easy way the woman handled herself. She might be getting old but her movements were neither stiff nor awkward. Her herbs were lined on her worktable in neat bunches. Even though she had the distraction of another person in her cottage, she went about her work as if her attention weren't divided.

Becoming suspicious of yesterday's mishap, Claire crossed her arms. "Lillian, how was it you managed to burn up a kettle yesterday, creating enough smoke to bring all of the neighbors running?"

The woman blushed. "Told you. I got a bit clumsy—"

"You did not. You did it apurpose. Sending up a cloud of black smoke was akin to ringing the church bell. You wanted Bernard and everyone else to gather."

Lillian huffed and put the kettle on the worktable. "You make too much of it, Lady Claire."

Claire smiled. "Do I? Somehow you knew Bernard and I had returned to Faxton. You wanted him to meet up with his father's tenants again, mostly Wat and Garth. So you brought them together in the fastest way you knew how." She grasped hold of the disgruntled woman's hand. "Lillian, I believe you want what is best for Bernard. He now knows he still has friends here, but you must know he cannot stay and take his father's place in the manor. Once he collects the ransom, he must leave."

"Not if he purchases the right to it from the bishop."

Claire shook her head. "I doubt the bishop will do so, not when the payment for it was gained as the result of a crime. All Father need do is have Bernard declared an outlaw for kidnaping me and every man from here to York and beyond will be honor-bound to turn him in to the sheriff."

"Mayhap Bernard should go to the sheriff and have him look into the matter of Granville Fitzgibbons' death."

Since they'd talked yesterday about the possibility of

Bernard going to his friend the sheriff, the subject hadn't come up again. She'd avoided reminding him of it.

"Mayhap. But without proof of my father's involvement, whether he meant Granville harm or not, the sheriff can do nothing."

"There must be some way for Bernard to regain his rightful place," Lillian insisted. "He belongs at Faxton."

"I agree." Claire let go of Lillian's hand and picked up a bunch of parsley. She began separating the heads from the harder stems. "Unfortunately, my father does not."

"Would Julius agree?"

Claire stopped plucking. "He might," she said. Her brother's sense of fairness far exceeded her father's. "He is supposed to return for my wedding. I can ask Julius to intercede, but he may not be able to soften my father's ire any better than I did. And by then, it may be too late anyway. Bernard will be gone."

"And you will be married. A shame, that. You should be the lady of Faxton."

Claire pursed her lips to keep from agreeing to that sentiment, too. She'd realized it while lying in Bernard's arms and then pushed the thought away. She wouldn't be the lady of Faxton, but of Huntingdon.

Truly, she admired Eustace Marshall's magnificent castle, where wax candles in gold sconces glowed against rich, shiny marble. Huge, vividly colored tapestries hung on the walls, their themes ranging from biblical stories to bloody battles.

Those who peopled his court dressed in the finest of fabrics, cut in the latest styles. They enjoyed poetry and music, and held lively discussions on the politics of the day.

Troubadours were welcomed. Wine flowed. Feasts were common. All were encouraged to gaiety and polite discourse.

She'd been overwhelmed during her one visit, knowing she would reign over all as the lady of the castle. Many in Marshall's court must wonder at his choice of a bride. He could have chosen a woman of much higher rank.

She'd wondered, too, but hadn't questioned his willingness to marry her in return for several hides of woodland. She'd looked on as her father and Eustace had agreed to the terms of the betrothal, then she'd shared a quick, polite kiss with her newly betrothed and considered herself fortunate. This had been her dream, and she could hardly believe it was coming to be.

While she'd dreamed of marble-lined castles, Bernard had dreamed of a cozy manor—and Claire Setton.

How odd, she now realized, she could be just as happy in a small manor as in a huge castle. 'Twas the man, not the residence, that made the difference.

All things being equal, if Bernard and Marshall were stood side-by-side and she was asked to choose, she would choose Bernard. She would choose the man she loved over the man she must wed.

Claire took a deep breath, wondering how she'd let that happen. How, in a bit over a week, she'd fallen in love with a man she couldn't have? Before now, she'd admitted fondness. Had she loved Bernard all the while and simply buried the knowledge knowing how much it would hurt when the truth won out?

If given the choice…but she had no choice.

From somewhere, she found her voice.

"I cannot be the lady of Faxton, Lillian. No matter what else happens, I must marry Eustace Marshall. If this kidnaping interferes with my wedding and the alliance with Marshall, Father will go mad. He will hunt Bernard down if it takes every soldier at his disposal and every coin in his treasury.''

Chapter Thirteen

Garth gave him a shove. Bernard slipped on the pond's slick bottom. If he was going under, he wasn't going alone. On his way down into the cool water, he caught hold of Garth's arm and dragged him along.

He came up sputtering, then laughed at Garth's vow to remember Bernard's longer reach next time. The water felt good, the laughter cleansing.

Garth had grown up tall and lanky, and incredibly strong. One had to be, Bernard supposed, to handle the nets used to haul in enough eels to fill barrels. He still lived with his father and two sisters in the cottage halfway up the hill overlooking the pond. His mother had died two years ago, Garth had said.

Bernard splashed out of the water and headed toward where they'd left a bucket of eels, their tunics and boots, and Bernard's scimitar. He tossed on his tunic and peeled off his wet breeches.

"Remember when we used to do this naked?" Garth asked.

"Aye, but that was before your sisters were old enough to know what they were looking at."

"True. I wish they would find husbands and move out soon. Both are a trial."

The last time he'd seen Garth's sisters, they'd been little more than infants. So much time had passed.

Bernard shook the water from his hair. "Ah, my. The last time I took a dunking like that was in the Nile. Felt good that day, too."

"Hot?"

"Like you have never felt. So hot the sand blisters your feet right through your boots."

"This time I know you jest."

Bernard chuckled and didn't tell Garth one way or the other. Each time he'd told his friend a story of his travels and battles, Garth looked at him skeptically, then judged. He was rarely wrong. The boy grown to man could still read a friend's tales correctly. 'Twas good some things hadn't changed.

He pulled on his boots and buckled on his scabbard.

Of the four eels in the bucket, three were Bernard's. Never in his youth had he caught more fish than Garth. Odd that the feat should feel so good.

"Want to take yours up to the cottage?" Bernard asked.

"Nay, keep it. I know where I can get more."

"Too bad they are not perch," Bernard said, reminding Garth of the fish pond's stock in earlier days. Bernard scrunched his nose. "Why did Setton want eels when he could have perch?"

Garth laughed lightly. "I heard Bishop Thurstan had a particular liking for eels."

"So Setton did his best to please Bishop Thurstan."

"Many did. 'Tis said the bishop's palace contains wealth beyond description, all due to men who sought to please the bishop."

"I have been in the bishop's palace," he told Garth. "Everywhere one looks, one sees wealth. The furniture, the tapestries, the works of art hanging on walls and sculptures sitting on tables. Bishop Walter strikes me as a man used to a humbler existence. I imagine most of the treasures were collected by Thurstan."

"'Tis the manner of collection which fuels the gossips. Many believe Thurstan used the sins told him in the confessional to extract material goods from wealthy sinners."

"He used the same method to gather men for the Knights of the Black Rose."

Bernard wondered how many, besides himself, had joined the Crusade as a direct result of Thurstan's manipulation. Hugh of Halewell, for one. Thurstan had insisted on Hugh taking the cross to atone for the death of an opponent in the lists. Hugh hadn't meant to kill the man, but when jousting, even with blunted lances, much could go wrong.

Bernard picked up the bucket, anxious to return to Lillian's and collect Claire. He'd been gone longer than planned, letting himself enjoy the solitude of the pond and Garth's company. At least he'd solved the problem of tonight's evening meal. One eel would suffice for tonight. The others could be set out to dry to provide meals for other days. He hoped Claire liked eel. She'd never said.

"Before we go back, I want to talk to you about this ransom business," Garth said. "You know enough not to trust Setton to simply hand you the gold in exchange for Claire, do you not?"

He knew. He'd just tried very hard not to think about it.

"I intend to be watchful."

''You have no eyes in your back, which is where Setton will strike. I am not good with a sword, but can see. Let me go into Durleigh with you when you collect the ransom.''

Bernard didn't have to think about his answer. ''Nay, Garth. I appreciate the offer, but cannot accept.''

''Why the hell not?''

''Because I will not put anyone but myself at risk.''

At the rising ire in Garth's eyes, Bernard shook his friend's shoulder. ''Do not argue, Garth. I need you well out of harm's way because I have a task for you, if you are willing.''

Garth took a deep breath and crossed his arms. ''The day Setton took you away, I watched you climb into that cart and could not figure out a way to pull you out. I felt…helpless. You have only to name the task, Bernard.''

Helpless. Bernard knew the feeling well. He put the bucket back down.

''I want you to be at Dasset on that day. I am hoping Setton returns with Claire and without his gold. In that event, you need do nothing but come back here.''

''Where will you be?''

''That depends on whether I am free, captured or dead, does it not?''

Garth wagged a finger at him. ''Do not jest about dying, Bernard.''

He cuffed Garth on the shoulder. ''All right. I have some relics I need you to take care of for me if I am…unable to do so myself. Have you time to come back to the manor with me and take charge of them?''

''Sure. Lead on. But I still think you should let me go with you into Durleigh.''

Bernard tossed his wet breeches over his shoulder,

picked up the bucket of eels and headed down the path toward Lillian's.

"This really is the more important task," he assured Garth. "I highly doubt Setton intends to kill me on the spot. He would much prefer to haul me back to Dasset and take his sweet time about it. Mayhap the fates will be kind and he will make the exchange without incident."

"Do not count on it. Setton will try something. If he feels you slipping from his grasp, he may let loose his soldiers on you, even in the middle of Market Square."

'Twas what Bernard feared most, that once he put Claire down the soldiers would rush him. Claire or innocent town folk could be hurt. He may have chosen a bad spot for the exchange.

At the time he'd given Henry the ransom demand, Market Square had seemed a good place—out in the open with many streets flowing out of it, all potential escape routes. Too, he hoped Setton wouldn't create a disturbance where the sheriff might become involved. He hadn't taken into account that at that point, Setton might not care who became involved or who might be hurt.

Bernard sighed. "You know, this all seemed so easy and straightforward when I took Claire from Dasset. I figured that since Setton denied my reward, I would simply ransom Claire for the coin due me. The whole thing is more complicated now than I expected it to be."

"How so?"

How not so? From the time Claire had released him from the dungeon, most everything had gone awry.

"At first I only wanted my reward. Then I came here and learned of Wat's suspicions. Now I want justice for my parents if it is warranted—and it seems to be. Claire and I have discussed several possibilities, but it all comes back to Setton wanting to keep Faxton so badly he would go to extreme measures.''

"What about Claire?"

Bernard pulled up short. "Meaning?"

"Claire seems a willing victim in this, is all."

Bernard thought back to the first night, when Claire tried to kick him in the jaw. And the next day, when she attempted an escape—and he'd gotten his first taste of her on the forest floor.

"She was not willing at all, at first. Then we made a pact. In return for her cooperation, I would take care of her and make sure she returned to Dasset in time for her…wedding.''

The word came out hard.

Garth shook his head. "Seems a shame you have to let her go. She was to be part of your reward, was she not?"

Bernard could only nod, knowing now she was the part of the reward he should have demanded. Not that Setton would have agreed. He had other plans for Claire, plans Claire wasn't averse to.

Garth went on. "I am not the only one to have noticed how well the two of you deal together. Having the two of you in the manor has seemed right somehow. Many wish the arrangement was permanent.''

"It cannot be."

"I know. You gave Claire your word, and you will keep it. That is why most of us wish you were the lord here. Your word can be trusted, as was your father's. I guess if Claire wants to marry Marshall and hie off to Huntingdon, then she is entitled to it. No one will begrudge her whatever happiness she can find.''

"Claire is well liked by her father's people, is she not?"

"Aye. Very much so. And she is probably wondering what has become of us."

As it turned out, Bernard doubted Claire had missed him or even noted the passage of time. He heard giggling as he approached the open door of Lillian's cottage. Both women looked his way when he stepped inside. Garth followed him in.

"Back already?" Claire asked, grabbing a towel from the worktable to wipe her hands. "Catch anything?"

Her smile and good mood were infectious. He put his own dour thoughts aside.

"You doubt my abilities with line and hook?"

Her smile widened. "I gather we eat, then."

"Naturally. I even caught more eels than Garth."

"Then Garth let you," Lillian chimed in. "That boy knows where each fish sleeps in the pond, I swear. Let us see what you have there."

Suspecting Lillian might be right, Bernard put the bucket on the work table and looked over his shoulder at Garth. Garth shrugged and tried not to smile. Bernard sighed inwardly. So much for his amazing feat.

"Oh, good-sized ones. These will bake up nicely. Well-done, Bernard," Claire said.

He puffed up with pride all over again at the simple praise from Claire. The woman could turn him inside out with a word, set his world to spinning with a touch. Break his heart with a single tear. Make him feel bold and brave, able to conquer the world single-handedly when she made love to him.

The only woman who'd ever made him feel that way reached into the bucket and pulled out an eel.

"How does something so ugly taste so good?" she asked.

Lillian laughed. "Baked with a few wild onions stuffed inside and he turns beautiful."

"Oh," Claire said with a look of ecstasy. "Are there onions near the manor?"

"Aye. Bernard can show you."

Claire looked to him for confirmation. He could only nod. 'Twould be beyond foolish to tell her there wasn't a thing he wouldn't do for her if she asked. If it was onions she wanted, onions she would have.

Claire traded Lillian an eel for a bunch of parsley, and on the way back to the manor, Bernard and Garth picked onions. With the cook fire lit and fish cleaned, Bernard asked Claire to fetch water. When she was out of the manor, he pulled out the relics.

As Garth looked on, Bernard opened each leather pouch and ornate chest in turn, explaining what each contained. He saved the biggest and most valuable for last.

Bernard unwrapped the reliquary from the protective oilcloth.

"Holy Mother of God," Garth said, then whistled through his teeth. "That must be worth a sou or two."

Bernard put the gold and silver, jewel-studded reliquary on the table. "'Tis said to contain the arm bone of St. Babylas, a Syrian bishop-martyr. I won it in a game of dice, so have no idea what it might be worth."

Garth stared at it for a moment, then looked up. "So what do you want me to do with them?"

"For now, hide them away. If all goes well, then I will be back to collect them. If the worst happens, or Setton manages to drag me back to Dasset, take the relics to Simon Blackstone. He will know who best to sell them to and bring me the coin I need for fees and fines…and such.''

"Hold a moment. You believe the sheriff of Durleigh will spring you from Setton's dungeon if need be? This assumes, of course, that Setton does not put a rope around your neck the moment you reach Dasset."

"Setton likes to toy with his victims. He will want to play with his whips and such first. Which is why you must be quick to alert the sheriff. And, aye, Simon will come for me, just as he knows I would come for him."

Garth tossed up his hands. "If you say so. Let us hope all goes well and the sheriff's aid is unnecessary."

Bernard began wrapping up the relics. "We can hope," he said, but knew better than to trust to fate alone.

Indeed, the eel had turned beautiful, baked to flaky perfection. Bernard worked the bones from his piece, thinking eel had never tasted quite so good. But then, he'd never eaten it while sitting across from the lovely woman who was responsible for the feast.

"It wants for salt," she said with a slight frown.

A seasoning found only at a wealthy man's table— like her father's, or Marshall's. Bernard had lost the taste for salt while in Egypt.

"It wants for nothing. 'Tis delicious the way it is."

"You like it, then?"

Fishing for compliments, was she?

"'Tis perfect. A true feast. Flaky but not dry, with a hint of onion and a sprinkle of parsley. Magnificent. Fit for a king's table. Why, were I to describe the truly delectable—"

"All right, Bernard. Enough," she said with an embarrassed laugh. He could tell she was actually pleased, and it pleased him to please her.

"I like the eel," he said, sending her into another round of laughter.

"So you said. 'Tis one of your favorites, I gather."

"Oh, no. I much prefer perch."

"Hmm. If I remember aright, you also like pork in pepper sauce."

Bernard remembered the food she'd brought him while in the dungeon. She'd come to feed him and convince him to demand less of a reward from Setton.

"The pork tasted so good because I had not had a slice of pork in years. In Egypt, we ate a lot of goat. Too much goat," he said, then laughed. "There was one particular goat we wanted to eat and did not dare. Hugh would have had our hides."

"Hugh of Halewell. You have mentioned him before. And Simon Blackstone, of course. Were there not six of you who returned?"

"Aye, only six, and then we were fortunate to escape with our lives."

Claire had pushed aside her food. She sat across from him with one elbow on the table, chin in her hand, waiting for him to go on. So he did.

"During one of the last battles of the Crusade, Hugh was captured by the Saracens. We learned that he'd been taken to a prison. Five of us went to rescue him. We learned later that the final, decisive battle of the Crusade was fought in our absence, and that the Knights of the Black Rose no longer existed except for we six."

"That is why you were reported dead, then."

"Aye. We had permission from our commanders to attempt to rescue Hugh, but apparently they had not mentioned our absence to those in higher authority.

Truly, they would have no reason to. So when the entire unit fell, we were assumed among the dead. The treaties were signed and the rest of England's Crusaders came home during the fall passage, and must have sent word to Bishop Thurstan that his knights were not coming home.''

''Aye. Bishop Thurstan sent word to Dasset. He also said a special Mass for all of you in the cathedral. 'Twas quite a shock, I must say, when we received your message that you were alive and in York.''

Laid up in an abbey with a crotchety old monk for a nurse. Then he'd gone on to Hendry Hall in answer to Nicholas's call for help. If he'd come to Dasset first, while Thurstan was still alive to verify his claim for the reward, he would now have several hides of land to call his own and Claire would be his wife.

Even knowing he would have to fight for his reward, he'd have gone to help Nicholas rescue his Beatrice.

''''Twas a shock to many that we still lived. Nicholas told me his mother fainted dead away when she first saw him.''

''Nicholas?''

''Nicholas Hendry. You would like him. I have not yet met a woman, with one exception, who does not swoon at his feet, and he does have a way with the ladies.''

''A rogue, then,'' she declared.

''A tamed rogue, now. He married the woman who slapped him hard on first sight instead of swooning. But make no mistake, rogue or no, one could not have a better man at one's back in a fight.''

She smiled. ''Can they all wield a sword as well as you wield a scimitar?''

"Almost," he said, not bothering to hide his pride.
"All but Hugh. No one is as good as Hugh."

She looked skeptical. "If so, then how was it Hugh
managed to get captured?"

"Unfortunately, Hugh *knows* he is the most highly
skilled. He is also given to impulse. We rode into battle
together, the six of us, as we always did. The next thing
I know, Hugh gives out with a roar, wheels his horse
and charges at a full gallop into a Saracen company
haunting our flank. We tried to get to him, but by then
we had engaged the main force and the Saracen ranks
closed around us. After the battle ended, we searched for
him among the injured, then learned he had been captured and taken away. So we went to rescue him."

Claire's eyes went wide. "You rescued Hugh from a
Saracen prison?"

Bernard nodded, remembering every detail. "Guy,
who is half-Arab and knows the language and Saracen
ways, got us into the city by the prison. We brought
Hugh and little Maud out and—"

"Little Maud?"

"An infant given to Hugh by an Englishwoman who
died in the prison. Darling little girl. We brought her
back to England with us."

Bernard had to admit he liked the way Claire stared
at him, as if he were the most skilled troubadour in the
kingdom. Her father believed troubadours to be thieves
and vagabonds of the worst sort, so allowed very few
within Dasset's gates. Even as a young girl, Claire had
listened with rapt attention to the troubadours' every
song and tale.

'Twas likely the strangeness of the tale he told, and
not his telling of it, that held her enthralled, however.
Still, he went on.

"Once beyond the prison walls, we heard the guards call out. Guards swarmed off the walls. Arrows fell like rain. Hugh was so weak he could not run and was hit."

She gasped. He smiled.

"We chanced upon a woman who heard little Maudie's cries, and seeing us as knights and her being Christian, she bid us enter her home. She saved our lives that day."

"You stayed with her?"

Bernard shook his head. "Too dangerous, for both her and us. We stayed only long enough for Gervase to pull the arrow out of Hugh and bandage him up. Then Guy kept us moving from place to place. We hid in some of the most vile abodes this side of hell. Six knights and horses, one adorable infant, and the orneriest goat in Egypt. Odetta. I swear we would have eaten her had Maud not needed the milk."

"How awful!"

"Some of it was too awful to describe. But we had each other and were determined to return to England. The following spring we caught a ship home."

Claire leaned back. "I understand now why you went to Nicholas's aid when he asked, and why you are so sure Simon will come to yours if needed. Do you know where the other knights are?"

"Simon and Nicholas you know of. Last I heard, Gervase was headed home to Palgrave, in the far north. Guy had gone off to London looking for the man his mother claims is his father. And Hugh—he was headed for his brother's estate to give Maud over to his brother's care, then rest for a while before traveling the tournaments again."

Claire's eyebrows curved into the adorable arches that said she was pondering. "Your Hugh. I do believe he has been invited to Dasset for the tournament my father is giving to celebrate my marriage. How strange that a friend of yours will attend.''

"Strange indeed." Bernard echoed her words, not liking the idea of his friend attending Claire's wedding to Eustace Marshall and joining in the festivities to follow.

Claire patted his arm, a smile on her face. "You tell a good story, Bernard. I would love to hear more of your adventures, but first I have to set out the rest of the eel to dry."

She got up and bustled over to the hearth. He watched her work, humming as she skinned the baked eels to expose the meat.

For a woman who'd grown up in a castle, she'd not complained about the lack of amenities. Except for sharing the manor with Cabal and the mule—understandable. The lack of salt hadn't truly been a complaint, more of an observation.

Claire was living little better than a peasant—hauling water, doing the cooking, sleeping on a thin pallet of straw and blankets. No servants. No change of gown.

She wore a soft smile as her natural expression. The roses from near the well provided her only adornment. A far cry from the regal daughter of a wealthy lord. A far cry from the victim of kidnaping.

She should be his wife.

That insidious thought had plagued him more than once today, and each time it came to the fore, 'twas harder to set aside.

He was living his dream of him and Claire in a stone manor sharing a quiet meal and conversation. Of him and Claire sharing a pallet and love play during the night.

They would make love again tonight. He knew it even

as he knew his own name. Rough or tender, playful or in earnest. He needed to be more careful with her. In less than a fortnight she would marry another. He'd not get her with child.

Gads, he should let her go before they became more attached, before he began dreaming more impossible dreams.

'Twas his dream he lived, but Claire had dreams of her own, always had, and was on the brink of getting everything she'd ever wanted.

At Huntingdon, she could be like Eleanor of Aquitaine and preside over a grand court. Spend hours in the company of poets and musicians. Never go without a change of gown or salt on her food.

If he thought for a moment he could give Claire the life she'd always craved, he would ask her to marry him and move the heavens to make it come about. He'd press his claim to her on the grounds of first right and find a way to get Setton to yield.

He'd do it all for Claire, if she'd have him.

He'd do it all for the woman he'd fallen hard in love with when he hadn't been looking and let down his defenses.

Letting Claire go, knowing she would marry another, was the hardest thing he would ever do. He'd do it, for Claire.

Then what was he going to do without her?

Chapter Fourteen

Claire set the manor to rights.

She scrubbed the kettle and put it beside the hearth, then scraped out the ashes as best she could and spread them among the flowers near the well.

On the table she placed the last of the dried eel and a loaf of brown bread Lillian had baked for them. On the morn, she and Bernard would break fast, take the mule to Lillian's, then head for Durleigh.

Tomorrow she would begin the journey home, and heaven help her, she didn't want to go.

Bernard burst through the doorway. "Claire, have you seen Cabal's brush?"

"Beside your pack," she said and crossed the room to fetch it for him.

"I could have sworn I left it out near the well."

"You did. I thought you had mislaid it and brought it in to pack. Sorry."

Claire glanced at the open pack that contained most of Bernard's belongings, and noted it was nearly empty. She knew immediately what was missing.

"Where are your relics? Shall I pack them for you?"

Bernard took the brush from her hand. "Garth has

them. I did not want to take them into Durleigh with us, so I asked Garth to hide them until I could come fetch them.''

Claire supposed it made sense to leave his valuable possessions with a trusted friend.

"You will come back to Faxton?"

"For a short while only, and not until I am sure your father no longer searches for me." He rubbed his brow. "I should not be telling you this. Best you do not know of my plans for after the ransom is paid."

It hurt that he didn't trust her not to reveal his plans. But then, what good would it do her to know where he was and what he was doing? After tomorrow, they would go separate ways, not to meet again.

"You could come back on the day of my wedding," she suggested. "Everyone at Dasset will be otherwise occupied."

He smiled wryly. "Or the day after when everyone is recovering from the festivities." He glanced at the pack. "Do you think the pack big enough to hold all of the gold?"

Her weight in gold. His ransom. 'Twas the reason he'd taken her from Dasset and would tomorrow take her to Durleigh.

"I do not know. Perhaps," she managed to say.

He shrugged a shoulder. "No matter. I will find a way to carry it." He tossed the brush in the air, caught it. "After I give Cabal and the mule a final brush, I will bring them in. Is there aught else we need do tonight?"

Be together. Talk. Laugh. Make love.

"Not that I can think of."

"Good. This should not take me long."

He left in a great hurry, not looking back.

She needed something to do. A task to occupy her

hands and take her mind off of tomorrow. Sweet mercy, she did not want to think about tomorrow. Claire glanced about the manor—over the hearth, the table, the floor. All neat and tidy. She purposely avoided looking at the pallet she would share with Bernard one last night.

She could go out and putter with the flowers, but then all she would do is watch Bernard groom Cabal and wish he were paying sweet attention to her and not his horse.

Claire spotted Bernard's chain mail where it lay in a heap in the corner. It wanted polishing. Delighted, she hefted the heavy mail shirt and took it to the table where there was more light. She fetched a rag from Bernard's pack and lost herself in the welcome, tedious task of removing tarnish from silver links.

Since the only time she'd seen him wear his mail, he'd also worn his tabard to cover it, Claire decided to start with the sleeves because they would show. She pulled one from the heap and plied the rag. Link after meshed link, Claire rubbed at the silver. The chain mail was far too old to shine. The best she could do was bring up a burnished glow.

Some of the links didn't fit together right, as if they'd been replaced over the years. It happened. Links weakened and a knight took his chain mail to an armorer and had them replaced. A mail shirt was terribly expensive, and could last a long time if properly cared for. Only this armorer hadn't done a proper job of making repairs.

At the niggling feeling of something amiss, Claire put the rag aside and spread the mail on the table. She ran her fingers over the front. As on the sleeve, links had been replaced. They held together, but the repairs were crudely done. The coif seemed to be in one piece. The fastenings on the flap that covered the throat and upper chest would need work soon.

Then she turned the shirt over, and gasped. Holes. Six of them. Not large, but they shouldn't be there. Claire suspected the links missing from the back had been used to repair the front and sleeve. No armorer worthy of the title would have robbed the back.

At Dasset, a suit like this would be deemed unfit for use, the links from it used to repair others. Sometimes squires would wear the old shirts to become used to the weight of mail while swinging a sword in the practice yard.

Or it could be taken on Crusade by a squire who, lacking the rank of knight, wasn't entitled to a new shirt or more than an ancient helmet or battered shield. Not even a horse that could withstand the rigors of the road.

At least Bishop Thurstan had replaced Bernard's horse with one of high quality. She could still hear her father complaining over the coin the bishop had demanded in repayment.

Claire sat on the bench and put her face in her hands.

Bernard had every right to hate Odo Setton for sending him off so ill-equipped and unprepared. 'Twas a miracle Bernard had survived.

His friends had helped him, she realized. Those men he'd told her about over a dinner of eel and wine. Nicholas was a good man to have at his back, Bernard had said. She'd thought it a turn of speech. He'd meant it most literally.

Then her father had denied Bernard's reward. 'Twas more than possible her father had been responsible for the death of Bernard's parents.

Why hadn't Bernard turned bitter and vicious? Why didn't hate rule his actions instead of a desire for justice? He'd tried talking to her father to no avail, but been willing to wait for Julius to return to discuss the matter further. He'd started one carefully controlled fire instead of flinging torches into the hay. True, he held her for ransom, but had taken such pains to keep her well and comfortable she'd forgotten she was his captive.

How could she not do everything in her power to ensure Bernard received everything from Odo Setton that he deserved?

Blessed be, there had best be two heavy sacks of gold at her father's side tomorrow or she would raise such a hue and cry her tirade would be heard in York.

The light was fading fast. Bernard would come in soon. Claire picked up the chain mail and put it back down in a heap. She grabbed a sleeve and took up where she'd left off, rubbing at the chain mail until her fingers tingled and numbed.

Bernard came in, leading the mule. "What are you doing?"

"Polishing."

"Why bother? It no longer holds a shine."

No, but the ill-kept mail had held Bernard safe for many years and deserved to glow.

"Something to do."

By the time Bernard finished bringing in and settling Cabal, she'd finished both sleeves, the coif and the flap. 'Twould look good when covered by his tabard.

Bernard tugged off his boots and lay down on the pallet. Unlike other nights when he stripped down to bare skin, tonight he left his garments on. Claire put aside the rag and joined him. He'd been reminding her all day, in subtle ways, that their time together was over. Severing their intimacy was his final withdrawal.

She refused to cry. She'd known all along this day would come, and now that it was here, she couldn't protest. He'd taken care of her for a fortnight. Given her joy beyond the heavens and asked for little in return.

'Twas her turn to take care of him.

Claire stretched out beside Bernard. Unwilling to give him up completely yet, she lifted his arm and snuggled next his side. To her relief, he didn't protest. Deep into the night, Claire fell asleep with her head on Bernard's shoulder.

Morning came too fast and too bright. He'd barely slept, trying hard not to move and wake Claire. When she woke, she would leave him, and his dream would come to an end.

Bernard knew Claire cared for him or she wouldn't have lain with him. However, she didn't care enough to say she would miss him or to protest going back to Dasset. Lord knew, he'd given her plenty of chances to do so.

At a word from Claire, he would wrap her in his arms and not let her go. Coward that he was, he hadn't asked her to state her preference outright, afraid she would laugh.

Nay, Claire wouldn't laugh. Being Claire, she would gently but firmly put him in his place. Unworthy of her. Nothing to offer. No permanent roof above her head. Not even the surety of another meal. No new gowns or wax candles or troubadour's tales.

No troubadour he. He could tell a story, but his only adventures had been those of war. Women didn't want to hear of blood and gore, but of flowers and love. Chivalrous love. Of some poor knight pining for his lady fair from afar, describing her eyes and hair in poetic phrases to the strains of a harp.

He couldn't play a harp. Or describe Claire's eyes

other than jewels of amber or her hair other than light brown. So much for poetic phrases.

He'd not make a good courtier, either. The thought of keeping company with men of learning and political shrewdness scared him far more than facing a company of Saracens alone. He'd not know what to say to them.

Nay, he'd not have a place in her dream.

Claire stirred against his side, her hand rising from his chest to brush the hair from her face.

Best not make the parting any more difficult. Best to get it done. When he returned Claire to her father, he would wish her a good life and get on with his own.

"Another bright day," she said. "This stretch of decent weather cannot last."

"Why not?"

"This is England," she said, amused. "'Tis good today is fine, though. We need not travel in the rain, so I need not face my father looking like a drowned urchin. How much time have we before we leave?"

"Oh, midmorn should do it."

She sat up and ran her fingers through her hair. "Good. 'Twill probably take hours to make myself presentable."

Claire looked divine.

"Best hurry, then. We slept overlong."

She rose and went to the window. "Oh, dear, we did." She glanced down at her gown and pursed her lips. "You intend to leave the mule at Lillian's, do you not?"

Bernard tried to make a connection and failed. "Aye."

Claire rushed over to the table and broke off a chunk of the brown bread. She then grabbed her cloak and headed for the door.

"Fetch me at Lillian's," she said, and was gone.

Bernard lay on the pallet until his confusion cleared. For some reason she needed to go to Lillian's to make herself presentable. He got up. With the rest of the bread in hand, he went about getting the mule and horse readied.

Bernard chuckled as he shrugged into his overtight chain mail. Claire had done her best to ensure he was presentable, too, and he had to admit that what his tabard didn't cover looked better than before. One would think them going to a feast or fair, not on their way to a ransom exchange.

Dressed and packed, with the animals waiting without, Bernard took a last look around the manor. He wouldn't say farewell to his home, not yet. He would be back to collect his relics. Time enough then.

Claire brushed the last of the mud from the hem of her emerald silk gown. She'd worn it for two full, hard weeks, and but for some fraying about the hem and where her bottom scraped against Cabal's hide, it had held up well.

Mother would likely faint when she saw it. The gown had been made up recently and deemed suitable for Claire's wedding. She'd been wearing it the day Bernard returned and events spun beyond her control. She hadn't planned to ruin the dress, just as she hadn't planned to be kidnaped.

"'Twill have to do," she said, and gave her skirts a final smoothing.

"You appear the grand lady, you do," Lillian said, and handed over the small cap that matched the gown.

Claire put it on over the crispinette that again bound her hair up. "Cleaned up, anyway. My thanks, Lillian, for the use of your soap and brushes."

The clop of horses' hooves on dirt road entered the cottage.

"Bernard comes," Claire said, quite unnecessarily.

Lillian opened her arms. "Come here, child."

Claire stepped into the old woman's embrace and squeezed her eyes shut. "I will be back," she whispered, and wondered why she'd said it.

Lillian's arms eased from around her. "Will you?"

There must be some reason to come to visit the herbalist before she married and left for Huntingdon.

"You once told me there are herbs I should not have, so I must know which ones, so I do not become ill on an ill-mixed potion."

Lillian smiled, though her eyes glistened. "Your mother can tell you which herbs to shun."

"Aye, but you can show me, which is the better way."

"As you wish, my lady." Lillian reached into her pocket. She drew out a small, wax-sealed jar. "Your unguent. Have a care."

Claire took a deep breath and accepted the cream made especially for her, to ease pain and fade bruises, praying she wouldn't have need of it.

"I will," she promised.

Claire put the jar into the pocket of her cloak—and felt the veil. The scarlet, gossamer veil Bernard had gifted her with and she'd forgotten about.

Sweet mercy, what a fool she'd been last night. If she'd gone to Bernard in nothing but her chemise and the veil—or better, just the veil—he wouldn't have been able to ignore her. Ah, well. Maybe it was better she hadn't thought of it. If she'd worked up the courage to be so brazen, and he *had* ignored her, she would have been devastated, and she'd been upset enough as it was.

Still, she regretted the missed opportunity. She could only wear the veil for one man, Bernard. And in a few hours…

Nay, she wouldn't go all morose and weepy again. With only a few hours left to spend in Bernard's company, she would enjoy those hours without regret or tears.

Claire set a smile to her mouth and went out the door.

Bernard had dismounted and was handing the mule's lead to Garth. They appeared deep in quiet discourse.

"Oh, Bernard shines!" Lillian said from behind her.

Claire laughed and allowed herself a moment's pride that Bernard, indeed, shone. Sunlight glinted off his chain mail, now a proper companion for his cherished tabard.

With sable hair skimming his shoulders, the hilt of his scimitar gleaming above the scabbard, Bernard appeared the proper *chevalier.*

While Lillian fussed over Bernard, Claire said farewell to Garth. She tossed her cloak over her shoulders to stave off most of the road dust. In moments, they were once again on Cabal, riding for Durleigh.

Claire leaned back against Bernard and tilted her face upward. A beautiful day should be enjoyed. A pleasant ride savored.

"I image you will be glad to return home," Bernard said.

In several ways she would. She desperately needed a bath. A long soak in hot, rose-scented water. Too, she missed her mother, though she hadn't thought about her much lately. The poor woman must be near her wit's end by now.

"Mother must be in a frantic state. In my absence,

the last of the wedding and tournament preparations fell to her.''

''What preparations? Order extra ale and food set out, strike a few tents for visitors, and ensure the priest is sober to perform the rite.'' She felt him shrug. ''What more is there?''

She laughed. ''That is why these things are best left in a woman's hands.''

''I suppose so. Truly, I have only witnessed one large wedding, your sister Jeanne's. About all I remember is the vast amount of food and ale, the tents set up in the fields for guests who could not be housed in the castle, and Edgar following Father Robert around to keep him sober.''

''Mostly I remember Mother's dismay that Jeanne was marrying so young. And Jeanne's upset over her gown. The embroidery along the edge of the sleeves wasn't done to her liking. Oh, and the cook's tirade over the shortage of white flour. Dear me, that was…eleven years ago. You and Jeanne are of an age, are you not?''

''Aye. How does she?''

''Last I saw her, she seemed content. She has two little girls she dotes on.'' Two nieces Claire doubted she would now recognize. ''I have not seen Jeanne in an age. Her husband and Father had a falling out some years ago. I am hoping they come for my wedding.''

''What was the argument?''

Over something senseless, in Claire's opinion, but enough to so irritate Jeanne's husband that he no longer allowed his wife and children to come to Dasset.

''Father was incensed that Jeanne had not given her husband sons and told her so. Then William told Father to keep his nose out of what was none of his affair. Father declared the matter was his affair because he did not want his daughter divorced over the matter and sent back to Dasset. William then informed Father he would not give his most ill-favored hound over to Father's care, much less his wife. 'Twas quite a row.''

"That must have happened after I left."

"Shortly after. I remember because Father was beginning to recover from his illness when it happened."

Claire couldn't help thinking her father would have done all of his children a great favor if he hadn't recovered. A terribly unchristian thought, but not a new one.

"What of your brothers? Did Geoffrey ever take vows?"

As the second son, Geoffrey was to have gone to the Church. For years he'd studied and prepared under Bishop Thurstan, then under the tutelage of the archbishop of York. He'd reveled in the education he received, but chafed at taking vows.

Claire shook her head. "Nay, nor will he. Father tried to force Geoffrey to take vows, so he left England and went to Paris. He is studying at the university there. I have no idea how Geoffrey is paying his way, but he must be because Father refuses to send funds."

She doubted Geoffrey would come for the wedding either, for fear their father might try to force him to go back to the abbey to stay.

"And Julius is in Italy," Bernard stated with a tone that said he was still unhappy over her eldest brother's absence. So was she.

"Last spring, Julius went to the fair in York, supposedly to bargain for horses. When he came home, he announced he was going on a pilgrimage to the shrines in Italy. Father was livid. He refused permission, saying that as heir to Dasset Julius should see to his duties at

home and not be trotting off to Italy. Julius said he had
no choice, and left.''

''No choice?''

''That is the part I find confusing. 'Twas so sudden,
and Julius was in earnest. I suspected he had little interest in shrines, but would not explain, even privately.
He told me he had to go, that I should take care, and if
I should need to reach him to send a message to the
archbishop of York.''

''Hmm.''

''Aye, mysterious, but there you have it. When my
wedding date was set, I sent a messenger to the archbishop, who promised to relay the message. St. Chris-
topher only knows if Julius got it, and in time.''

They rode in silence while Claire opened the brooch
on her cloak and let it slide back off her shoulders. No
sense baking just to keep a bit of dust from her dress.

''Claire, why did Julius tell you to have a care?''

Father perceived each of his children as failures.
Jeanne for not having sons. Geoffrey for not taking
vows. Julius for not taking his responsibility as heir seriously. Claire for not being as meek and self-effacing
as her mother.

As children, they'd all suffered an occasional slap or
sting of the rod. Not until after Geoffrey's leaving had
Father closed his fist. She'd been the only one to suffer
a severe beating.

''Father has never been one to spare the rod, and Julius knew Father would be bad tempered for a while. He
told me to stay out of Father's way until his fury cooled.
So I faked illness and hid under my blanket for several
days.''

Then she'd heard her father was considering disown-
ing Julius and had come out of hiding. She probably

shouldn't have left the safety of her pallet to plead her brother's cause. Servants had carried her back to her pallet afterward, but something in her argument had broken through Father's outrage. Julius was still heir to Dasset.

Bernard reined Cabal off the road and into the woods for no reason Claire could discern.

"Something wrong?"

"That is what I need to find out." Once out of sight of the road, he halted.

As always, she sat quietly, listening for sounds of pursuit. She heard nothing untoward—not the plop of a horse's hooves or jangle of tack, or the sound of someone's voice.

Before she could tell Bernard, much to her surprise he lifted her high up. "Turn," he said.

Claire swung a leg over and landed sideways on his lap.

Bernard wore a deep frown. "What happens when you get home? Will you need to hide from your father?"

His concern touched her deeply. "Likely."

"I do not like this, Claire. By giving you over to your father, do I place you in danger?"

"Even before I unlocked your manacle, I knew Father would punish me for the deed in some way. Despite publicly blaming Edgar, I am sure he knows who is truly responsible for letting you loose. I accepted then that I would pay a price. Nothing has changed except I have had a reprieve of over a fortnight."

His frown deepened. "He will strike you."

Claire could almost feel the blow land. She suppressed a shiver. "He may. As my father he has the right."

Bernard cursed. Claire took it as an affirmation that

he cared. 'Twas nice to know he would protect her from her father's wrath if he could. But he couldn't.

"Bernard, you must remember I am important to my father right now. He needs me well and steady in order to stand before the priest and exchange vows with Marshall. Too, Marshall will arrive tomorrow, which affords me some protection. Believe me, I will remind my father that Marshall may object to a bruised bride. Father will do nothing he thinks might offend Marshall."

Claire wondered briefly who she was trying to convince, Bernard or herself.

"There are too many uncertainties in your beliefs, Claire."

She rested her cheek against the black rose stitched on his tabard, certain only that she loved the chivalrous, handsome, brave knight who wore the symbol with pride and honor.

"I thank you for your concern," she said. "However, you should be far more concerned for your own hide. Father may be angry with me, but he is likely furious with you. This ransom exchange may not go as smoothly as you hope."

"Aye, well, I have more reason than most to mistrust your father. One of the reasons I chose Market Square for the exchange was the many ways in and out. At the first sign of treachery, we get out." With a finger under her chin, he tilted her head up. His expression softened. "Which means we will need to find another way to go about this, and you might not get home for another few days. Would that upset you overmuch?"

She smiled. Another few days within Bernard's tender care would be no hardship at all. "Not overmuch."

His kiss merely brushed her lips, sweet and too brief.

"Then let us go see what your father has waiting for us, shall we?"

Chapter Fifteen

Bernard chose not to enter Durleigh until the time came for the exchange. 'Twas easiest to avoid capture from without the town walls than within. So, for nearly an hour, he and Claire hid in a wooded area near the gate, observing the comings and goings of guild members and peasants, priests from the great cathedral and merchants from far-off places.

He should have given Claire more time at Lillian's, because now he had too much time to waste. Too much time to ponder over what could go wrong.

Bernard had never doubted that Setton would be eager for this meeting. Setton wanted Claire, more because of the desired alliance with Eustace Marshall than out of paternal concern. He also wanted Bernard, for daring to defy him so blatantly and then demanding a hefty amount of gold in return.

All Bernard wanted was justice. The gold served as the reward promised and then denied. That he would now rather have Claire made no difference. He'd proposed a bargain to Setton, and would keep his word. If he didn't take Claire to her father as promised, then he'd be no better a man than Setton.

Fears of what Setton might do to Claire sat heavy on his mind. Her assurances had eased his concern, but not banished it. He hated the thought of her being struck, even if it was a father's right. Bernard would give her back, but was still afraid for her.

"Nearly time," Claire said softly from behind him.

By now, Setton likely stood in Market Square.

"Nearly," he said, wishing he had hours left, not minutes.

Claire stood near Cabal. She'd dusted off her gown and fastened her cloak around her shoulders. Neat and tidy. Chin high and back straight. Ready for whatever came next.

"Once we get inside the gate," he told her, "I will circle the outer streets and cross the river at the western bridge. That way we will come into Market Square on Highgate."

"You do not want to approach through the center of town."

"Not particularly. Highgate is wider and straighter than most streets. I should be able to see Market Square from several blocks off, and have room to turn Cabal if I must."

She nodded her understanding.

He put his hands on her shoulders. "The cathedral will be behind us and the sheriff's quarters before us. Do you know where Simon's office is?"

"On Highgate, near Thief Lane," she said with a small smile. "I always thought it appropriate."

"So it is," he said, appreciating the irony but more grateful she knew where to find Simon.

He squeezed her shoulders. "Claire, the most dangerous moments will be those during the exchange. Once I set you down, I may not be able to reach you if there is trouble. Swear to me, if fighting breaks out, you will run to the bishop or to the sheriff. Either will shelter you until the danger is past.''

She put her hand in the middle of his chest, over the red Crusaders' cross that covered his heart. ''You have my oath. Now you must swear you will then come for me and we will find another way to get your ransom.''

How could he make such an oath? ''Claire, I may not—''

She shook her head vehemently. ''Swear, Bernard. Above all else, you will keep yourself safe and not be hurt!'' Tears sprung into her eyes. ''I will not run, will not leave you to fight alone if you do not swear!''

How was it he could face a Saracen army with nary a tremble to his hands, yet this woman's tears could bring him to his knees?

Bernard gathered her in his arms and held her close.

''I swear, if I must face more than six, I will not make a stand. Satisfied?''

''Six!''

''If I am on horseback and they are afoot, then aye, six is about right.''

He felt her deep breath. ''You make light of my worry.''

''Never. Seven would be a strain, but not six.''

His arrogance was not to be borne, but Claire remembered the ease with which he'd taken on four of her father's soldiers, then sent them off to deliver the ransom message. Maybe six was no idle boast.

'Twas near time to go, and here she was watering the rose on his tabard. She should be bidding him a farewell, but the words stuck in her throat.

''Come, let us go,'' he said. ''The sooner done the better over.''

She didn't want an ending, but a beginning. She didn't want to go home, but remain with Bernard. Neither was to be. She snaked her arms around his neck and hugged him hard.

"I shall miss you," she whispered, then backed away and headed for Cabal.

I shall miss you.

Bernard looked down at his hands and wondered how he'd let her slip through them.

Fool. She'd not declared love, only said she would miss him. How much? For how long?

The cathedral bell peeled, calling the priests to mid-afternoon prayer, telling Bernard to hurry.

If only she had told him sooner.

Bernard swung up onto Cabal, and for what might be the last time, lifted Claire up to sit before him. He clamped her firmly around the middle, then headed for the town's gate to the chime of cathedral bells and the thud of his racing heart.

"You will miss me?" he asked, desperately sorting his thoughts.

"Very much," she said, her voice no stronger than before.

Once past the town wall, on the edge of his vision, Bernard saw a man race directly north up Michelgate. A lookout for Setton? Likely. After the man was out of sight, Bernard turned left, intending to wind through the streets to reach the bridge on the far west side of the town.

Accustomed to all manner of visitors come to buy goods made by the craftsmen of Durleigh's many guilds, the townspeople made way for a knight on a warhorse as a matter of course. Bernard attributed the few stares they received to Claire.

"I will miss you, too," he ventured.

Claire didn't answer, merely rubbed at his arm. He could barely feel it through the sleeve of his chain mail.

His attention was too divided. 'Twas nigh impossible to concentrate on watching for trickery from Setton with his mind filled with Claire.

"I think I will most miss your smile," he said. "'Tis your most natural and enchanting expression, I vow."

"My thanks," she answered, patting his hand.

This wasn't going well. He crossed the bridge. Ahead loomed the great cathedral.

Claire drew the hood of her cloak over her head. She pressed back against him, as if bracing for the worst.

He wished he were half as good with words as he was with a scimitar. As the last note of the bell's song faded away, he turned onto Blake Street, where he'd bought bread and treated Claire to a pastry.

"I will miss you so much I am sore tempted to keep you."

She went very still. "Are you?"

"I know now that when I stood before your father and made my demands, I was willing to settle for the wrong part of the reward. I should have insisted on the marriage to you. You are, by far, the more valuable part of it."

"Am I?"

He leaned very close to her ear. "Had I to do everything over again, I would forget the land, forgo the ransom, and keep you. I love you, Claire."

Claire took hold of Cabal's reins and pulled hard. To Bernard's amazement, the horse obeyed. In a swift, impossible move, she turned sideways in the saddle.

Claire couldn't believe she'd heard him aright, and if she had, her heart would surely break in two.

"Truly?"

"Marry me. Be my wife. Share my food, my bed, my life. I have no right to ask you to give up your dream for mine, but I swear to you, no man will ever love you better or care for you with more diligence."

He was earnest. She was betrothed. Her heart split asunder, flying apart in sharp little shards.

Claire leaned against him. "I love you, too. If it were my choice, I would choose you above all others. But there is my father. And Eustace. And..." She tossed up a frustrated hand. Why list the obstacles? He already knew of every one.

He wrapped her in an encompassing embrace. Safe. Warm. Loving. Impossible to break away from and hopeless to stay within.

"We still have a week," he said. "Do not despair yet."

A week until her wedding day. To the wrong groom.

Bernard nudged Cabal forward and made the turn onto Highgate. Toward Market Square where her father waited.

"Have you a plan?" she asked.

"Not much of one. But I do know that from this time forward, I must do things from within the law of the land and the Lord. I have the right of first claim to you. Somehow, we must force your father to both acknowledge and honor it."

'Twould never happen.

"How?"

He chuckled. "I wish I knew, but there must be a way, and I will find it."

How could he laugh when she was again on the verge of tears? Claire looked up into his wide grin and the utter confidence in his eyes. How could she doubt? How could she help? The last time she'd tried to make peace between her father and Bernard she'd failed utterly.

"There he is," Bernard said.

Claire straightened and looked toward Market Square. From the high vantage point of atop Cabal, she spotted her father. Oblivious to the cries of the vendors and the people who wandered from stall to stall, he paced the middle of the square. A few steps only, not moving far from a large flour sack lying in the dirt.

Father wasn't alone. Two guards flanked him, both holding lances, guarding the sack Claire very much feared contained flour, not gold.

"Now what?" she asked Bernard, praying he'd found the words to make her father see reason.

"As much as I hate to do it, in order to assert my claim to you, I must first let you go."

"Nay!"

"We need to wipe the slate clean and begin over, which means you must go back to Dasset. I will come for you, I swear. I will talk to the bishop and to Simon. There *must* be a way to force your father's hand. Trust me, Claire. I know I ask a lot of you, but trust me."

One of the guards spotted them, and pointed. Her father's head spun round. His anger reached out to her from nearly two blocks distance. Her stomach roiled and her head spun. She listened to the whisper of her heart.

"When will you come?" she asked.

"I will send word. Through Garth or Wat."

"And if there is no way to press your claim?"

"Then I will just have to kidnap you all over again."

Her stomach settled, some. "What of the ransom?"

"Your father gives me no credit for intelligence at all. Look closely at the sack. Do you see a bump or bulge anywhere to suggest it filled with gold and not flour? He did not even go to the trouble to make the bait tempting. I think I will let him keep it.''

Setton made a beckoning motion to his right. Two more guards with swords drawn ran to their lord's side. Two swordsmen, two lancers—not bad odds, Bernard thought. Were there more? Probably.

He glanced among the crowd, which had begun to take closer notice of the happenings in the middle of the square. He saw no more men he knew to be Setton's, but that didn't mean others weren't about and ready to spring.

His hand itched to draw his scimitar, but he left it alone. He'd not incite anyone to begin a fight, especially not with Claire so close.

Letting her go would be the hardest part. He saw no choice. He had to return what he'd stolen before he could make her his by rights.

Bernard reined in a fair distance from where Setton stood. The cries of the vendors had ceased. The townspeople halted where they were and edged up to the buildings. Claire sat up straight, looking down at her father.

Setton gave Claire the merest glance, then sneered at Bernard.

''Think to sell her back to me, do you?''

''Setton, were I to ask for Claire's true worth, you could not meet my price, not even if you sold your soul to the devil—if you have one.''

''Watch your tongue, Fitzgibbons. You do not have your ransom yet.''

''Nay, but neither do you have your daughter.'' He waved a hand at the flour sack. ''Full of gold, is it?''

Setton nodded. '''Tis what you asked for as nearly as I could guess. You will have to make do with what I could stuff in the sack.'' He stepped back. His guards did likewise. ''Put Claire down and the gold is yours.''

'Twas far too obvious a trap to be borne. The moment he got off Cabal, the guards would attack him.

Bernard sighed mightily. ''Ah, 'tis a temptation, I admit. But I come not for your gold, Setton, but to give your daughter back into your care.''

Setton's eyes narrowed. ''What foolishness is this? You demanded her weight in gold as ransom and now refuse it?''

''I do. All I ask is your solemn oath, on your honor as a knight, before your own guards and the good people of Durleigh, that Claire comes to no harm after I release her.''

Setton pointed at the sack. ''This is your payment for Claire, as you asked. I give it to you. 'Tis all the payment you will receive for the chit!''

Claire whispered, ''To your right, hiding behind the pie vendor. Archers. Two of them.''

He dared not look. Dear God in heaven. If the lancers and swordsmen missed their mark, Setton would order the archers to fire. In Market Square. Innocent people could fall to satisfy Setton's desire for revenge.

Bernard's fury flared as he looked down the wide, straight street, choosing his escape route.

''Hold tight, Claire. We are leaving.''

''So I prayed.''

Bernard drew his scimitar and shouted at Setton. ''Stand aside! I wish to see this *ransom* you offer me.''

He put heels to horse. Cabal responded instantly—to a full charge, straight ahead. The guards leapt aside. Setton barely got out of the way before Bernard leaned over and slit open the flour sack as he swept by. Cabal's hind foot kicked it upward, spewing brown flour over guards and ground and Setton. Bernard wheeled the horse around.

Setton was on his hands and knees.

"While you are down there, Setton, pray that God has mercy on you, because I no longer will."

Bernard lifted his scimitar high in the air and reared Cabal high off the ground. "For the rose!"

The crowd cheered. Claire hung on, her fingers entwined in the horse's mane. Cabal no more than landed when Bernard wheeled again.

"Beware! Archers!" he shouted to the crowd, then leaned over Claire and kicked Cabal to a full gallop down Highgate. "Clear the way! Clear the—"

Pain stabbed through him, jolting his body forward. Stars danced before his eyes. The groan he heard must be his own.

"Bernard!"

Through the worst pain he'd ever known, he realized he couldn't hold himself upright and control Cabal, too.

"Get to…Simon. The reins."

"Sweet mercy," she said, and took control. "Clear the way!" she screamed. "Clear the way!"

Bernard hung on to both his senses and Claire as she raced down the street. He thought to look behind him to see if anyone gave chase, then decided he would fall of if he tried. Best to concentrate on getting to Simon before passing out.

Nearly to the edge of town, at a building near Thief Lane, Claire reined in hard, nearly throwing him off.

"Bernard?" Fear edged his name.

"Sorry, Claire…thought we…could outrun them."

A crowd began to gather. Several men ran out of the building with a tall, dark-haired man at their lead. Bernard knew himself in brotherly, capable hands.

"I told you to stay out of trouble," Simon scolded.

"Greetings, my friend."

Simon eased the scimitar from Bernard's fingers and handed it to one of his men. "Let us get you down before you bleed all over my street."

As Simon reached up, Cabal sidestepped and snorted.

"Hush," Claire said. "You have done your part, you great beast. Now let the men do theirs. Hush, now."

Simon gave Claire an approving smile before he reached his arms upward again. "Gently, men. Ware the arrow. Come, Bernard. Give us what help you can."

Guided by Simon, Bernard slowly slid off the horse. His arms draped over Simon's shoulders and those of another burly fellow, he retained his senses, though the arrow stabbed anew with each step into the building.

He caught snatches of shouted orders. Aid the lady. Care for the horse. Fetch a physician.

Going down the stairway nearly did him in for good.

"Claire," he managed to breathe.

"Your lady follows. She is fine."

Upon Simon's reassurance, Bernard passed out.

He woke to gentle fingers combing through his hair, and opened his eyes to stare into Claire's. Jewels of amber.

"Heaven," he said.

She smiled. "Nay, you are on a cot in a cell. Far from heaven."

He lay facedown, bare above the waist save for a wide, white bandage encircling him, on a too short cot not high above the dirt floor. Claire had chosen to sit on the floor to watch over him and wait for him to wake.

"You are here. 'Tis heaven enough."

He raised a hand to touch her angel's face. She stopped him.

"You are not to move," she said. "The arrow is out, but the physician says you are to lie still for a few hours."

His back hurt, but not like before. He decided not to test it, or Claire's patience, by moving, however. "I think I could sleep the day round."

She laughed lightly. "I must admit it has been a most interesting day."

"Cabal?"

Claire turned scarlet. "That horse of yours is impossible. It took me forever to convince him to go with the sheriff's man."

"Convince?"

"'Twas absurd. While the sheriff and his men carried you in here, I was out on the road reassuring your horse that a physician was on his way to care for you and that you would be fine once the arrow was removed and the wound stitched. 'Twas a ridiculous display, but it worked."

He wished he'd seen for himself. Cabal was getting so used to carrying the two of them that he now obeyed Claire's commands and responded to her voice. A warhorse shouldn't, but he'd been glad of Cabal's willingness when he'd handed Claire the reins.

"Simon?"

"Upstairs. Waiting for you to wake. If he hears our voices…ah, there, on the stairway."

"He will not be happy with me. He *did* warn me to stay out of trouble."

Simon walked into the cell. "Would that you had listened."

"I did, for all of two days. Anyone in the square hurt?"

Simon's face lit with a smile. "Not anyone of any import. Lady Claire, might I fetch you a chair? You should not be sitting in the dirt."

Claire waved the offer away. "I am comfortable, my lord sheriff. Do go on."

Simon eased down next to Claire. "Well, Bernard, it seems you were both the entertainment and the hero of the day. By the time I got to Market Square, the people of Durleigh were near to rioting. To hear them tell it, a brave, wondrous knight and a beautiful lady rode into the square on a spectacular horse."

"Who might that be?" Bernard asked wryly.

"Hush, Bernard. This is my story to tell."

"You embellish."

Simon shook his head. "Not I. As I was saying, this knight proposed to ransom the beautiful lady back to her father, for her weight in gold. Now, said knight refuses the wealth and demands only the fair treatment of the beautiful lady from the ignoble lord—with pardon, Lady Claire. The lord not only refuses to give the oath, but the gold turns out to be flour. To add insult, when the knight takes umbrage—and justly so—the ignoble lord tries to kill the knight, with no regard to the safety of the beautiful lady or the innocent citizens of Durleigh. Correct?"

Bernard sighed. "I still say you overstate the matter, but aye."

"I simply repeat what was told to me."

"What of Setton?"

Simon chuckled. "Had I not arrived when I did, the mob might have hung him. As it is, two of his guards suffered broken bones, others are bruised, and the bows are in splinters.''

Startled, Bernard asked, ''Why would the people go after Setton?''

''Ah. The answer is twofold. The tabard. They recognized you as a Knight of the Black Rose. In this town, if nowhere else, we are considered true heroes.'' Simon tilted his head. ''Then there was that feat of horsemanship and knightly prowess you put on with Cabal. Hooves waving high in the air, scimitar flashing bright in the sun, the fair maid beaming with pride—''

''I was frightened out of my skull!'' Claire declared.

''I imagine you were, my lady. I have seen Bernard perform that trick with Cabal. 'Tis impressive, and sealed Bernard's fate. The town lays at your feet, my friend.''

''Not after they hear the whole of the story.''

Simon's smile faded. ''I advised Setton to leave the city, for his own protection, then provided escort to the gate. He told me his tale of how this ransom came to pass. He tells it ugly, Bernard.''

''I doubt I can pretty it up much.''

''Up to telling it now?''

''Since I cannot move until Claire allows, why not? But I hardly know where to begin.''

Simon leaned forward. ''From the day you joined the Knights of the Black Rose, you often spoke of the prize awaiting you on your return. Marriage to Lord Setton's daughter, Lady Claire, and lands on which to settle. When I last saw you at Hendry Hall, you seemed confident of collecting your reward. What happened?''

''I do not suppose Lord Setton's tale included his denying me the reward.''

''Nary a word.''

Bernard wasn't surprised. He reached for Claire's hand, and with her fingers entwined with his, told Simon of riding into Dasset with his hopes high.

"I left my belongings and scimitar in a stall with Cabal," he said, so beginning a tale of betrayal and quest for justice.

The minutes sped by. His mouth went dry. Claire carried the tale at times. Little by little Bernard managed to raise himself until he was sitting.

All the while Simon leaned back on his hands and listened. Bernard knew the mind of this man, a leader of intelligence and courage and compassion. So he left nothing out, except for those hours he and Claire had spent intimately entwined.

Bernard grew weary, knew he was weak from the loss of blood and the jolt to his body. Yet he finished.

"I knew the archers had to take their best aim at me, so I kicked Cabal into a gallop down Highgate. The arrow hit. I handed the reins to Claire and told her to find you. The rest you know."

The silence was long and deep.

"Incredible," Simon finally pronounced the tale.

"Aye. So now the question is, where do we go from here?"

Simon rose to his feet and brushed the dirt from his breeches. He held out a hand to Claire to help her up.

"The Royal Oak Tavern," he said. "You need food and sleep. I need time to think. And my lovely wife would never forgive me if she missed the chance to meet you."

Bernard accepted Simon's help up off the cot. Right now an ale sounded so very good.

"By the by," Simon said, "the teller of the tale in

Market Square sends his greetings and your relics. Garth said to tell you he knew your back needed guarding. Unfortunately, he could only knock down one of the archers before they fired.''

Chapter Sixteen

Claire sat back in her chair and half-listened to Bernard and Simon indulge in recalling old times and old friends. Simon's wife, Linnet, appeared fascinated, so Claire needn't keep up her end of any conversation.

The Royal Oak Tavern hadn't changed. The main room was cozy, the stew and bread delicious, and Mistress Selwyn as pleasant and efficient as ever.

The hours following Bernard's wounding had been a severe strain. She'd kept calm during the wild ride down Highgate. Managed to help Simon remove Bernard's blood-soaked tabard. Stood by while an armorer pried open the links up the back of Bernard's chain mail. Not until they'd gotten him out of his chain mail and gambeson could the physician begin his work.

She'd held Bernard's head as the physician pulled the arrow out, her fingers hovering over his temples to ensure his heart beat through it all. The physician assured her the arrow had come out cleanly and hit nothing vital.

After everyone had left the cell, alone with Bernard, she'd trembled and cried into his tabard. Thankfully, she'd regained her composure by the time he awakened.

Bernard would heal. Even now his color improved.

He didn't seem in severe pain. Every so often his hand wandered over to rub at the tightly wrapped bandaging under his tunic. The stitching could come out in a few days, leaving behind a scar to remind him of the wound.

A scar by which to remember Odo Setton's treachery.

"Simon, we must leave now," Linnet told her husband. "These two look ready to fall facedown into their stew."

"That they do," Simon agreed, and rose from his chair.

Everyone got up but Bernard. "Before you leave— have you thought over all I told you?"

"A bit. Morn is time enough to go over it all again. We will need to see Bishop Walter, I believe. Let us hope he has time to see us tomorrow."

Bernard nodded, his reluctance to wait even that long apparent.

Linnet grasped Claire's hands. The woman ran an apothecary filled with curing herbs, oils and fusions. Her grasp was both firm and comforting, as soothing as the potions she mixed and sold.

"My shop is directly behind the Royal Oak," Linnet told Claire quietly. "You have only to slip out the back and pound on my door if you need us."

Claire had heard stories of how Linnet had been suspected of poisoning Bishop Thurstan and of Simon proving the woman's innocence and catching the true killer. Anyone with sense could see, after only a few moments in Linnet's company, that the woman wasn't capable of murder.

With a wry smile, Linnet continued. "I would take you and Bernard home with me if I thought I could sneak you past Mistress Selwyn. She is adamant you grace her with your presence tonight, however."

"I wish she would not insist on giving up her and her husband's private sleeping chamber."

"Oh, my dear, cots in the common rooms would never do! She is both honored and delighted to have you. Indulge her."

After hugs and farewells all around, the Blackstones left. Bernard put his hands on the table and pushed up from his chair. Beads of sweat formed on his brow.

Master Selwyn, owner of the Royal Oak, appeared, his wife at his heels.

"I have more ale, cheese and bread waiting for you in the room," Selwyn told Bernard. "If there is aught else you require, you have but to ask."

Mistress Selwyn nodded. "I scrubbed up your tabard. It hangs over a chair in the room to dry. On the morn, I will mend the hole and make it good as new."

Claire pursed her lips to keep from smiling at Bernard's amazed confusion at the deference. He wasn't used to having people willing to attend his every whim.

"My thanks. You have been most gracious," he finally said, kindling the spread of wide grins.

Claire slipped under Bernard's arm and led him to the private bower of the thoughtful Selwyns. Indeed, the room was cozy. A bed with a thick mattress dominated the room. The promised refreshments sat on a table. Bernard's tabard was draped over the back of a chair, drying. Her cloak hung on a peg near the door.

Bernard glanced around. His gaze landed on the traveling pack in the corner, once again filled with his relics.

"I may have Garth's head once all this is done," he said.

"Whatever for? He did you a good turn today."

"I asked him to go into Dasset to learn what happened

here, not to come into town. Your father will not appreciate having one of his tenants turn on him so.''

''I doubt Father recognized Garth. Garth is the son of the man who delivers eels to Dasset on occasion. My guess is Father would have a hard time putting a name to Wat, much less his son.''

''I dearly hope so.'' Once more, he inspected the room. ''What happened to my chain mail?''

''The armorer who pried you out of it took it with him, along with your gambeson. He will repair them as best he can, but advises you replace the mail before another arrow finds another hole.''

''A suit of mail costs far more than the coin I possess. The repairs alone will be hard to cover.''

Claire walked him over to the bed, her ire rising. She waited until he eased down to sit on the edge before expressing her thoughts on the matter of his chain mail.

''If your armor had been repaired properly, today's mishap could have been avoided. True, Father likely gave it to you in disrepair, but to leave your back vulnerable was foolhardy. Then, to make matters worse, you deliberately turned your back to an arrow and made yourself a target.'' When tears threatened to gather, she looked for some chore to do. ''Give me your foot.''

He obeyed. She tugged at his boot.

''Better me than you or one of the townspeople,'' he said. ''No innocent should suffer because of a situation I helped create.''

She tossed the boot in the corner. ''Naturally, no one should take any risk on your account. Not me, not Garth. Only you. 'Tis a wonder you survived the Crusade.''

''Now, Claire—''

''You think yourself invulnerable.'' The second boot followed the first, landing harder. ''Well, today proves you are not. You are flesh and blood and bone, just like the rest of us. Put your arms up.''

He raised his arms. She tugged his tunic over his head, uncovering the white bandage wrapped tightly around his ribs.

She continued. ''Outside the gates, you swore to me you would not take undue risks. I consider making your back an archer's target an undue risk. If you persist in this nonsense, you will get yourself killed. And I shall never forgive you, Bernard. Hear me? Never!''

He smiled. ''I hear you, Claire. I love you, too.''

It knocked the wind right out of her. She reached for her anger and came up empty. She tossed her hands in the air.

''What am I going to do with you?''

''Come to bed with me. Love me.''

She easily understood the spark that lit his eyes and crossed her arms.

''I undress you to sleep, Bernard, no more.''

''Truly?'' Mischief rang in the taunt. ''We will see about sleep once we have my breeches and your gown off.''

''What about your wound? You will open your stitches.''

He reached for her, caught her round the hips. ''Today the woman I love gave me her heart. Tonight I want her body, if she will have me.''

She quickened, her woman's places quite willing to accept his intimate attention. Her common sense balked.

''You are wounded. You need rest.''

''I need you.''

''I will sleep right beside you.''

''We can sleep later.''

Her common sense was fading. She ran her fingers

through his hair, needing to touch him. She'd almost lost Bernard today. Then she'd be grieving now, not arguing with him.

"Your stitches."

He pulled her close, his face nuzzling in the valley between her breasts. "They will hold if we go easy. Come love me, Claire. My beautiful, precious Claire."

He turned his head and nipped at her breast, making her ache for more.

"We should not," she said, grasping at the last threads of her wits.

"We can. I will show you how."

She surrendered. "I love you, Bernard."

"Sweet words. Sweet woman. Sweet, sweet heaven."

Garments melted away. Bernard lay back on the soft mattress and gave over control. Claire knew where on his body to caress, where to stroke and rouse him to mindlessness. Without hardly moving, he roused her, too. What he couldn't reach without stretching, she brought to him. When the time came for coupling he showed her how to straddle him, and take him into her, and set the pace.

She watched his face twist with agony, knowing the pain didn't come from his wound. Then the ecstasy of his release, so hard and deep, pushed her over the edge of heaven and beyond.

Afterward, Claire lay snuggled into his side and listened to him sleep, fingering the bandage around his chest. He'd taken an arrow, and all for naught. All the problems were yet there, and possibly worse. The sheriff was now involved, and tomorrow so would the bishop.

No matter their love and desire to marry, despite the help of others, if her father remained firm, she could still lose Bernard.

* * *

Once more Bernard told his tale, this time to Simon and Bishop Walter, gathered around the ornate writing table in the bishop's private apartment.

The reliquary of St. Babylas sat on the corner of the table. Bishop Walter was anxious to purchase it, but wished to consult with a monk more experienced in the value of relics before offering a price. Bernard was willing to leave it in the bishop's care. He'd carried the valuable relic far too long, and trusted the bishop to offer a fair price.

Trusting Bishop Walter came easily, both because he'd been welcoming and fair the first time they'd met, and the man had helped Simon through his ordeal. If Simon, whose trust wasn't easily gained, thought the man reliable, Bernard could do no less.

The bishop was also easy to talk to, as a holy man should be, Bernard supposed. Or maybe the telling had been easier because this time he hadn't simply listed events, but included the people along the way, and realized he hadn't been so alone as he'd thought. Claire was right. He'd held everyone at arm's length to prevent them from becoming involved. Even Claire, to an extent.

So Bernard revealed everything, even his intimacy with Claire, which he probably wouldn't have done if Claire had insisted on coming along.

Claire had agreed to stay behind—much too quickly, in his opinion—with Linnet in her apothecary.

The bishop's face reflected his reactions to the tale, which were much as Bernard expected. At the end, the bishop leaned forward and glanced from Bernard to Simon and back again.

"I cannot wait to meet the other Knights of the Black Rose," he said. "Do you all share the same talent for getting yourselves in deep trouble with both the law and the Church?''

''I surely hope not, Your Eminence,'' Bernard said. ''Certes, Simon and I managed. Nicholas was only almost arrested for murder. Of the other three...'' He shrugged.

''Murder?''

''A misunderstanding. Right, Simon?''

Simon nodded and smiled. ''Correct. 'Twas one arrest I was grateful I did not have to make.''

''Am I going to end up back in a cell?''

''I surely hope not,'' he said, then redirected the conversation. ''Let us take Lord Setton's grievances against you and examine them closely.''

For the next while they discussed Setton's accusations.

There were several witnesses who could verify that while he'd been angry and taken a step toward Setton when denied the reward, Bernard hadn't reached out to throttle Setton or drawn a weapon.

As for the fire, Simon could testify from their experiences in the Holy Land that if Bernard had wanted to burn Dasset to ashes he knew how and would have gone about setting the fire differently. To Bernard's chagrin, he agreed he probably owed Setton recompense for lumber and labor to build a new stable.

Bernard's only part in Edgar's release from the dungeon had been to lend the use of a battered helmet to throw Setton off guard. Henry and the other soldiers had gotten Edgar out.

They saved his worst offense for last—kidnaping Claire.

''Not the wisest move you have ever made,'' Simon commented

"Perhaps not, but I would be hard pressed to say I am sorry for it."

Bishop Walter leaned forward. "You have no remorse for removing an innocent young woman, who had only tried to help you, from the safety of her home?"

Bernard remembered tossing Claire over his shoulder and taking her up on Cabal.

"At the time I did not think her so innocent. I feared she and her father had concocted a scheme to do away with me. I fully expected the guards at the gates to be armed with crossbows, waiting. So I took her hostage, knowing the guards would not fire at her. Only afterward did I realize my mistake."

Simon picked up his line of reasoning. "So now you are out of Dasset and have decided to hold Claire hostage against a portion of your reward, the land. Then you reason you cannot live on land over which Setton is the lord, so you demand a ransom of gold with which to buy land elsewhere, leading to yesterday's mishap in Market Square."

Bernard nodded.

"Might we back up a moment?" the bishop asked. "I am not clear on the granting of the reward, Bernard. How did it come about?"

As if it had happened yesterday, Bernard saw himself standing in Setton's private chamber.

"Setton was abed, dying, or so we all thought. Bishop Thurstan had come to hear Setton's final confession. I was summoned to the chamber and told I was being done a great honor. As part of Setton's penance, Bishop Thurstan required a man from Dasset to serve in the Crusade. Setton had chosen me.

"I balked. I knew I was inept. My lack of eagerness must have shown. The bishop looked down at Setton and said, 'Tell him of the reward.' That was when Setton said that upon my return, I would have Claire's hand in marriage and lands upon which to settle. 'Twas too generous a reward to turn down."

"Then the two of them had discussed your being chosen and the reward beforehand."

"Apparently."

The bishop sat back in his chair. "I am given to wonder why Setton chose you, and why such a large reward."

"I was not told," Bernard said. "Nor did I have the presence of mind to ask. I have since wondered, but…"

"Hmm. The other thing I wonder over is why Bishop Thurstan was sent for. There is a priest at Dasset, is there not, who might have heard Setton's confession?"

"Aye. Father Robert. I did not give the bishop's presence a second thought. He often visited Dasset."

"That may be, but when a man is dying and fears taking his last breath unshriven, any handy priest will do. Unless…unless Setton felt he could not reveal the sin to Father Robert." The bishop paused a moment, then went on. "Or the sin was so great he thought only a bishop could absolve it. Too, when a priest gives a penance, 'tis suited to the sin committed. In this instance, I am led to believe Setton's sin was against you, and the reward granted a reparation for that sin."

Bernard went cold as ice. "Murder. My parents."

The bishop hesitated before he said, "Possibly. Remember, Bernard, I merely speculate."

Bernard got up, his wound sore and body stiff, his head spinning and heart hurting. He walked over to the window that looked out over the gardens. Wanting badly to shout and curse, he stared at the roses below.

"Your speculation makes sense," he said, desperately

holding on to his temper. "If Setton had ordered my parents killed, he might not wish anyone at Dasset, including Father Robert, to know of his villainy. So he sends for the bishop, and Thurstan demands reparation. I am granted land and Claire, which satisfies Thurstan, and which Setton believes he will never have to give me. Imagine his joy when he hears I am dead, just as he had believed all the while would happen."

"That mistaken report affected many lives," the bishop said. "For Setton, it meant he could search for a husband for Claire."

"He found Eustace Marshall. The betrothal is about to be realized when Setton gets my message, informing him I am alive and in York, my leg broken. With Thurstan alive to bear witness to my claim, Setton must honor it. But when Thurstan dies, then the matter of the reward comes down to Setton's word against mine. He agrees to the betrothal terms between Claire and Eustace Marshall believing he can deny me and I can do nothing about it."

Bernard turned to look at Simon. "There is no way to prove any of this, is there? 'Tis all, as the bishop says, speculation."

"To be honest, 'twould be near impossible to prove Setton's involvement with your parents' deaths," Simon stated. "I could ask questions at Faxton and here in Durleigh. But even if someone could identify the men, 'tis doubtful we would find them. As for Setton, if he has already confessed to Bishop Thurstan, and been absolved, he will not feel obliged to confess a second time."

Bernard looked for a ray of hope. "Is Setton absolved if his penance is not fulfilled?"

The bishop nodded. "I would think Thurstan gave

absolution the moment you left the chamber. But God knows the penance is not resolved, so Setton's place in heaven is not as secure as he might like. A reminder might be in order.''

''Humph. Setton may not care until he is at the point of death again. The earthly prize of a powerful son-by-marriage is too great. As much as I would like to bring Setton to the point of death again, if I held a blade to his throat 'twould give him an excuse to hang me sure.''

Bernard turned back to the window. He found no answers among the flowers and shrubs in the garden.

''How do I make it right? Start over? I would give most anything to begin again, from the moment I rode into Dasset.''

''What could you have done differently?'' Simon asked.

Bernard shrugged. ''I do not know. I have gone over it all in my head. Each time I get to the point where Setton tells me Claire is beyond my reach, I lose my temper all over again.'' He spun around. ''Claire is mine. By rights, she is my betrothed, not Marshall's. She was to be my wife, not his.''

''Except for Marshall's betrothal agreement with Setton! Powerful family, the Marshalls.''

''Rich. Lots of influence at court,'' the bishop added. ''I wonder what he thinks of all this.''

Bernard doubted Setton had informed Marshall his bride was missing. ''The man may not know. He is supposed to arrive at Dasset sometime today. Setton may have a time of explaining Claire's absence.''

''Marshall will not likely take the news well,'' the bishop commented. ''He may even try to find Lady Claire, especially if he thinks she is wandering about by herself. If nothing else, the Marshalls take their commitment to the code of chivalry quite seriously. Their courts are among the most respected and well attended in the kingdom.''

Bernard sat back down in the chair facing the bishop. ''An honorable man, then,'' he said, his thoughts whirling and hopes rising.

''The family is well known for observing a strict code of honor. I do not know Eustace, but I assume he is cut of the same cloth as the rest of the family. Naturally, there is always the black sheep of any clan, but—''

''If he heard my story, might he give it credence?''

''Possibly, but after hearing Setton's tale first—''

''True. But if I entered Dasset and talked to him, knight to knight—''

''Slow down, Bernard,'' Simon warned. ''First, you may have a problem getting into Dasset. You may not get past the gate before being seized and tossed back in the dungeon. And if you do get so far, remember Setton and Marshall will have already talked lord to lord.''

Bernard put up his hands in surrender. ''All right, Simon. I hear what you are saying. But consider, if I go into Dasset and restate my claim to my reward before Setton and Marshall, as a matter of honor to a fellow knight, Marshall will at least hear me out—I hope. To what outcome?''

Bernard counted off on his fingers and answered his own question. ''They could both laugh in my face and I am tossed back into the dungeon or hung on the spot. Or Marshall believes me and backs out of the betrothal and leaves Claire free to marry me. Or, most likely, I will have to somehow prove I am telling the truth and Setton is lying.''

Simon scoffed. ''Setton is not about have an attack of guilt and admit he lied.''

Bernard shook his head. "Nay, he will not. Which leaves only one way to prove myself in the right. The tournament."

The bishop clapped his hands together. "Oh, well-done!"

Simon groaned and rubbed his hands over his face. "You cannot be serious."

"Why not? I should have thought of it before. It makes perfect sense."

"Bernard, you are a master of the scimitar. No one can question your superior skill. Your horse is superb, none better. However, you have a faulty suit of chain mail, no helmet, and are wounded." Simon lowered his voice. "And if I remember aright, not only have you not touched a lance in three years or so, you don't possess one. How can you issue a challenge for Claire's hand?"

"How can I not? I cannot prove Setton was responsible for my parents' deaths, whether he ordered them harassed or murdered. I cannot prove he granted my reward. 'Tis his word against mine. A lord's against a knight's. What other choice have I but to challenge Setton in the one way I might win? By the strength of my arm and the rightness of my cause."

During the ensuing silence, Bernard wondered if Simon wasn't right. He would need a helmet, lance and shield...

"I can go to Hugh," he realized with no little relief. "Halewell is but a few hours south of Durleigh. Certes, Hugh would have a spare lance or two, if he is not off using them himself. Hugh might well be at Halewell if he plans to attend the tournament at Dasset."

Simon still looked uncertain. "That makes me feel a bit better, but can you hold the weight of a lance steady with your wound?"

"I have five days to heal. 'Twill have to do."

The bishop rose from his chair. "What about Lady Claire?"

"I will take her with me, I suppose."

"Nay, that I cannot allow. The lady has been through quite enough, and though you may consider her yours, the church does not."

Bernard chafed at the bishop's subtle admonishment for having lain with Claire, but supposed it was to be expected from a priest.

"Claire is welcome to stay with Linnet and me," Simon offered.

The bishop nodded. "That will do, for now. As a show of Bernard's good intentions, however, she should return to Dasset."

"I hate the thought of sending her back to her father," Bernard voiced his immediate reaction. "Setton's anger toward her will have increased after what happened yesterday. I fear he will harm her."

"Your fears are likely well-founded. I believe I have a solution. When you were here last, you asked about purchasing rights to church-held land. The question made me curious, so I did some hunting in the records. I found that Setton holds a good deal of land from the Bishop of Durleigh, and I have seen Odo Setton but once since I became bishop, on the day he came to do me homage for the lands he holds of me. 'Tis truly a shame that I cannot defend my vassal for lack of firsthand knowledge of the man." The bishop smiled wryly. "'Tis also a shame he did not invite me to his daughter's wedding, but if I arrive at his gates, I doubt he would turn me away. So what say I take Lady Claire home, under my protection."

"I say that would ease my mind greatly, and will agree if Claire does."

Yesterday he'd taken an arrow in the back, and now he was excited about crossing lances in the lists. The most likely to take up his challenge was Eustace Marshall.

Claire stood near the herb garden behind Linnet's apothecary, wrapped in Bernard's arms, while he explained this new plan of his. Liking none of it. Knowing she couldn't prevent it.

The bishop's presence might afford her some protection from her father. So might Eustace Marshall's. Better if her brother Julius had come home, but she couldn't count on him being there.

Not that it mattered. Whatever punishment she faced she could deal with. What she couldn't bear was the thought of Bernard getting himself killed.

Deaths didn't happen often in the lists. The knights used blunted lances, and contests were normally limited to either first blood or simply being unhorsed. Still, too much could go wrong. Bernard was already wounded. Five days was not enough time for the wound to heal. He would go in at a distinct disadvantage.

"You can stay with Simon and Linnet," he was saying, "then on the day after tomorrow Bishop Walter will take you home. We will be apart for three whole days, then never again."

Unless he lost.

"You leave for Halewell tomorrow?"

"Aye, I need to check on my chain mail and gambeson, and get one more day's rest."

He needed more.

He cupped her face and tilted her head back. "I miss you already."

Her bottom lip trembled. "Bernard, what if—"

"None of that," he ordered. His thumb stroked her mouth to still the quiver. "More than anything, I need you to believe in me. I can do this, Claire. I can win. I *will* win. I must."

Bernard's confidence and determination showed on his face. No longer the squire of old, but the warrior who had returned from the Crusade. She loved him. Trusted him. Into whose better hands could she place her fate?

Not that she wouldn't try to give fate a nudge.

"Fine. You go play with your lances. I will be waiting for you at Dasset. But this time when we leave together, could we do so in less spectacular fashion?"

Chapter Seventeen

Riding Cabal without Claire before him felt strange. He'd become used to her warm, pliant body pressed against him, his arm around her middle. The scent of her hair wafting over from beside his cheek. He missed her sometimes endless questions and the frequent companionable silences.

Leaving Claire this morning had been wrenching. He'd left her in Simon's care, knowing she would be safe and with good companions. Bishop Walter would take her to Dasset on the morrow, and who better to entrust her than a bishop? He could trust both men, yet leaving Claire to the protection of anyone other than himself troubled him.

Claire was far from helpless. Her mind was quick, her senses keen. At times she'd been aware of dangers before him and gave warning. If not for their pact, she would have escaped him.

She could be both lioness and kitten, and Bernard couldn't say which nature of the woman bewitched him more. All he knew was his empty arms ached and the ache wouldn't go away until he held Claire again.

He'd held her long and hard before leaving her, wondering if it might be the last time. They'd both put a good face on their parting. Claire's tear-touched smile had nearly broken his heart. He'd done his best to reassure her that all would turn out well, but deep in his heart lingered a shard of doubt.

The last time he'd held a lance, nigh on three years ago, he'd made a decent showing, but not a spectacular triumph.

A stretch of boredom had led one group of knights to challenge another group to a friendly contest. With blunted lances and wagers made all around, they'd marked off a piece of the Egyptian desert and had their fun.

On his first pass he'd been lucky to unhorse his opponent, and Hugh had told him in very blunt terms just how fortunate he'd been. With his ears ringing from the scolding, he'd changed the set of his shield and the grip on his lance.

His second opponent had gone down cleanly, and still Hugh hadn't been satisfied.

Bernard had lost his temper, and thus his vigilance, and his third opponent had taken quick advantage.

Hugh had shrugged one of those broad shoulders of his. "You got angry," he said, then went on to win the tournament.

Hugh had done it apurpose, of course, and Bernard took the lesson to heart. He hadn't drawn a weapon in anger against an opponent since, but learned to channel his anger into cold calm.

Holding his anger in tight rein at Dasset might prove impossible. Just the sight of Odo Setton could make his blood run hot.

Bernard knew his opponent wouldn't be Setton. The man would choose a younger, stronger, more able champion. Likely Eustace Marshall, whom Bernard refused to think of anymore as Claire's betrothed. Marshall might even demand the right to cross lances, either because he truly wanted Claire as his wife or merely to uphold his honor.

Bernard broke from the woodland into the expanse of cleared ground surrounding Halewell, a looming, squared keep of old stone circled by a moat and a single curtain wall. Hugh's brother Roger ruled as lord, and Bernard hoped that if Hugh weren't here, Lord Roger knew of his brother's whereabouts.

He urged Cabal to a quicker pace, anxious to once more heft a lance, find the perfect balance and take aim at a quintain.

A single guard at the wall spotted him and turned to call out to someone in the bailey. Bernard wasn't stopped, but waved through. He slowed. Not far within the enclosure stood Hugh—big, blond, genial Hugh. The shock on Hugh's face sparked Bernard's grin.

Bernard leapt down from his horse and braced his feet. Hugh hadn't changed in the least. A bear of a man, he greeted Bernard with a suffocating hug and a hearty slap on the back.

Bernard nearly doubled over. "Ye gods, Hugh. Have a care with we lesser men."

Hugh's laugh rumbled over him. "Shorter, mayhap, but not lesser." As Hugh released him, his hand skimmed over the bandaging wrapped around the wound. "Here, what is this?" he asked, suddenly all concerned. "Wounded?"

And now very sore. Bernard waved away his friend's worry.

"An arrow wound. Not deep and healing well. How fares little Maudie?"

A soft smile touched the huge warrior's face. "A little angel to tug at this old devil's heart. She walks steady now, and tries out a few words. 'Tis the most fascinating thing, to watch a wee one explore her world, see how far up she can reach or how fast she can get from one place to another. But come, you can see for yourself."

Bernard wanted to. Filling his arms with the little girl he adored might help ease the emptiness. But he'd come to Hugh for a purpose.

"I shall, but first I need to ask for a great favor."

Hugh looked at him for a moment. "This is not merely a visit to an old friend, then?"

Bernard shook his head. "Nay. I wish I could say it was, but I have an urgent matter before me and need your help."

"Name it."

Ah, just like Hugh. What was his was yours. Bernard hoped he didn't take sore advantage.

"In four days time I must challenge another in the lists. I need a lance or two, some practice, and your voice shouting at me to ware what I am about."

"A challenge?"

Bernard took a deep breath before admitting, "The reward I was promised was denied me, so now I must challenge another for the right to marry Claire."

"Your homecoming did not work out as planned then?"

"Nay, nor did Simon's—who sends his greetings by-the-by—nor did Nicky's. 'Tis good to see your plans fell into place."

Hugh shook his head. "My brother died, and Elena...well, you shall meet Elena. Anyway, I am now the lord of Halewell."

Bernard thought he caught a hint of dissatisfaction,

but then Hugh would be. He'd planned to stay at Hale-well only long enough to rest and then resume the rounds of tournaments.

"Have you plans to attend the tournament at Dasset?"

Hugh's smile returned. "I have heard of it, but nay, I do not attend. Is Dasset where you make your challenge?" To Bernard's nod, he continued. "Then let us see if you have a prayer of winning."

Through the afternoon Hugh sent Bernard through drills that only an experienced soldier could complete and only a tough, determined man—or utter fool—could survive. By the time they broke for evening meal, Bernard remembered the heavy weight of a lance, the bone-jarring blow of a misstruck quintain, and the sting of Hugh's disapproval.

Bernard removed the borrowed helmet and shook the sweat from his hair. Hugh caught him off guard with a cuff to the shoulder.

"Like old times," Hugh said, his grin wide.

"Ha! Almost. I am not angry with you. Yet."

Hugh ran a hand over Cabal's flank. "At least this fellow is in fine shape. The same cannot be said for his master. You list to the right."

"I know." A fire had burned from his wound since he'd hefted the first lance. He'd trained through the pain, hoping the stitches yet held.

"We will get Cabal settled, and your wound cared for, then have supper. The heaviest thing you need to hold now is Maudie."

Bernard allowed Hugh to help him rub down Cabal because he didn't have the energy to argue otherwise. The climb up the stairs to the keep's entry nearly did him in, but he entered the guardroom under his own power.

Bernard stripped off his tunic and gambeson—his chain mail remained with the armorer in Durleigh. Hugh flipped open a small chest on the floor near the doorway. Bernard looked about the room, noted the few pallets lining the wall, and thought each of them looked as good as a soft mattress.

"Lean against the wall," Hugh commanded. Bernard braced his hands against the stone while Hugh cut away the bandage. "You bled some."

"Not surprised," he said, then hissed when Hugh poked at the wound.

"Stitches seem tight."

"Good."

Hugh rubbed the wound with an ointment, then began wrapping him with a fresh bandage.

"Hugh, I *do* have to breathe."

All the admonishment brought was a low chuckle. Bernard reminded himself that Hugh was his friend, as dear as a brother, and knew what he was about.

"Done. You will find a basin and towel over there," Hugh said, pointing to the far end of the guardroom. "Then we can go up to see what Elena intends to feed us for supper."

Food. Ale. Rest. All that would make the evening complete would be for Claire to be here to share it with him.

Bernard tossed on his tunic. Right about now Claire would be sitting down to table with Simon and Linnet, either in the living quarters at Linnet's shop or over at the Royal Oak.

Did she miss him, too?

He dragged his weary body to the basin, splashed water on his face and plied the towel.

Tonight, when she slept alone, would she dream of him as he would surely dream of her?

Bernard followed Hugh up the stairs into the keep's hall. Modest, he thought of the large room, noting the hangings on the white-washed walls. A few trestle tables had been set up for evening meal. A short, dark-haired woman directed the servants. Once Bernard spotted Maud, he couldn't drag his attention from the lovely little imp who seemed determined to crawl up onto one of the tables.

"Maud!" Hugh's voice boomed through the room and echoed from the high ceiling. "Look who I have brought to see you."

She scrambled down from the bench and waddled across the rush-covered floor.

"This cannot be Maud. Look at how big she is, and how well she walks. Aye, that is Maudie. Look at her smile." Bernard ignored the pain in his back and swept the tyke up into a hug. "Ah, little one, I have missed you."

Maud giggled. Hugh was laughing, but Bernard didn't care. How good it felt to hold a wee one again.

"I want one of these, Hugh," he said, the admission not surprising. His dreams had often featured Claire with a babe or two in her arms.

"So win Claire and sire a dozen."

Bernard's heart flipped. They'd never talked of children or the future, only spoke of what was to happen day to day. They'd centered so hard on the present, thinking only as far ahead as the tournament. Had he already sired a child of his own with Claire? 'Twas more than possible.

Suddenly his back didn't hurt quite so much. The room seemed brighter, his steps less heavy.

The meal was of plain but hearty fair, served efficiently by the dark-haired woman he now knew as Elena, the daughter of Halewell's steward, and who seemed to be acting as Hugh's chatelaine. Maud sat contentedly on Hugh's lap, ate tidbits from his trencher, and eventually fell asleep. The ale went down smoothly as he told Hugh what he knew of their fellow knights and a bit of his own situation.

"What of you?" he asked Hugh. "Are you content to play lord of Halewell?"

Hugh glanced at Elena before saying, "'Tis a different life than I expected, but not so bad once I became accustomed to it." Hugh burst into a long listing of what he'd done to improve Halewell since becoming lord. Bernard felt his eyes droop. "I must say I am doing quite well, have all in hand," he boasted.

Was it his imagination, or had Elena's eyes rolled in disbelief? He was too tired to know for sure.

He quaffed the last of his ale, set the tankard on the table and pushed his body up. "I refuse to insult the lady for this excellent meal by falling face forward into my trencher. If I might be excused, I intend to be asleep within moments."

Elena bowed her head graciously then shot a smug look at Hugh. "My thanks, Sir Bernard. 'Tis lovely to be appreciated. I have a pallet prepared for you upstairs."

Bernard looked at the steep spiraling stairway. "Nay, my lady, not up. A pallet down in the guardroom will do me fine."

Hugh grinned. "Take whatever pallet you fall on first. The guards will work around you. On the morn we will break fast, then go another round with the quintain." His smile widened. "Then you take a turn with me."

* * *

Traveling in Bishop Walter's company would have been a pleasure had not her destination been Dasset. The dainty palfrey given over to her use moved with delightful grace and spirit. The bishop, garbed in the full regalia of his office kept up a lively conversation. His troops, acting as escort, marched in the orderly fashion of soldiers trained in a high lord's household.

Still, she missed Bernard so badly she'd nearly burst into tears each time the bishop mentioned his name. She knew Bernard wouldn't come to Dasset until sometime on the morrow, yet she looked for him around each bend of the road.

Simon seemed to think that with the training Bernard would receive from Hugh, Bernard was capable of winning any contest of arms. Bishop Walter believed Bernard's story, and declared the Lord favored a righteous cause.

All very well and good, if the knight in question didn't have an arrow wound in his back that might affect his ability to hold a lance in the correct position.

As Dasset came into view, Claire knew she had to stop worrying over Bernard, at least for the moment. She had her father to deal with, and dealing with Odo Setton was never easy.

Father was probably frantic, she mused, noting the number of brightly colored tents that had sprouted up in the surrounding fields. Already the knights who intended to participate in the tournament had begun to arrive. She wondered briefly how her father had explained the missing bride to the guests—and to Marshall.

Eustace Marshall—her betrothed, and truly innocent in all this.

"Steady now, my lady," Bishop Walter said. "All will be well, with the grace of the Lord."

She had to smile. "Your Eminence, the last time I passed through these gates, I begged the intercession of the Blessed Mother. I believe I shall trust to her again."

As order of rank dictated, Claire rode behind the bishop across the drawbridge and through the gate. A quick perusal of the bailey showed her nothing had changed, except for the stable, which had been rebuilt. As Wat had said, the fire hadn't spread farther.

Naturally, the approaching entourage had been spotted and the necessary preparations made to greet the arriving party. The bailey had been cleared between the gate and the castle's steps. Stable lads rushed forward to take away the horses as soon as the party dismounted. Miles, her father's steward, looked harried as he rushed down the stairs.

As was entirely proper, Miles first bowed to the bishop. "Your Eminence. We did not expect you, but we welcome you warmly to Dasset Castle. And Lady Claire, his lordship is *most* anxious to see you."

"Is my father in the hall?"

"Aye, my lady. He has just returned from a morning's search for you. I am sure he will be quite pleased His Eminence has brought you back to us. Praise God."

The last was said with emphatic relief.

"Have my sister or brothers arrived?"

"Nay, my lady, nor are they expected."

Her hopes for her eldest brother's help dashed, Claire sent Miles off to see to lodgings and food for the escort, then placed her hand in the crook of Bishop Walter's arm.

"Straighten your miter, Your Eminence, and remember it was your idea to bring me home." She waved a hand at the stairs. "Shall we?"

"As Daniel into the den?" he teased.

"One never knows," she answered and ushered him up the stairs and into the hall.

'Twas crowded as Dasset's hall had never been, at least not in her memory. Lords and ladies, knights and squires, milled about the hall. Pages and servants wound their way through them, pitchers in hand, filling cups and goblets. From the far end of the hall came the sounds of a harp. A troubadour? Marshall must have brought the entertainer along, she decided, and her father had been forced to submit.

Heads began to turn her way. Voices dimmed to whispers. Claire took a deep breath and looked about for her father. She needn't have. He was plowing his way through the crowd, Eustace Marshall at his heels.

For the moment she ignored her father's scowl and studied Marshall. A handsome man, of delicately carved, almost boyish features and midnight black hair. Marshall's lips were pursed and brow furrowed slightly, as if annoyed. He walked with a supple grace in sharp contrast to her father's headlong charge.

Her father came to a halt before the bishop. His bow was both slight and quick. "Your Eminence. Do enjoy the hospitality of my hall with my thanks for bringing my errant daughter home. Claire, we need to speak."

His hand shot out to grab her arm. Claire stepped back and Bishop Walter stepped sideways. Unable to reach her, her father's scowl deepened. Her stomach churned.

"Setton, do restrain yourself," Marshall ordered in his oh-so-genteel voice and stepped forward, further blocking any move of her father's. "Lady Claire, since Lord

Odo seems unable to perform the civilities, would you do me the honor of presenting me to His Eminence?''

Claire was no fool. If two men wished to act as her shields against her father, she would use them both, for now. As she made Eustace known to the bishop, she glanced about for her mother. Lady Leone wasn't known for bravery and, as Claire suspected, her mother hovered about the hearth mostly ignoring everyone in the room, including her returning daughter.

The Lord of Huntingdon and the Bishop of Durleigh exchanged a string of mannerly pleasantries and good wishes. Her father paced to wait them out. Eventually, the conversation turned to her ordeal, as Marshall termed it.

"'Tis a long, harrowing story,'' the bishop said and patted her hand, still grasping his arm. "To spare her further, I suggest we all remove to a place of privacy. Setton?''

In a huff, her father led the way to the guardroom and ordered out the few men who lingered there. He slammed the door and turned on her.

"Where the hell have you been, girl? I have spent the past few days searching under every stick and rock between Dasset and Durleigh looking for you.''

"We never left Durleigh,'' she said.

"Hah! Never made it out of the town, did he? Good. Now that we are finally rid of that knave we can get on—''

"He is not dead, Father. As much as you wish otherwise, Bernard Fitzgibbons lives.''

Setton put his hands on his hips. "Dead or not, he is no longer a concern of mine. You are home. On the day after next you will wed Marshall—''

The bishop raised a hand. "Ah, Setton, there is some

question as to whom your daughter should wed, I believe. 'Twould seem you have betrothed her to two men.''

''I did no such thing!''

''I surely hope not, for your sake, Setton,'' Marshall intoned, and for the first time Claire sensed danger. From Eustace Marshall. The man wasn't as meek as she'd thought him.

''Claire is formally and firmly betrothed to Marshall, here,'' her father told the bishop. ''Fitzgibbons can take his outrageous claims to the devil.''

The bishop tilted his head. ''Fitzgibbons feels he already has—and suffered for it since, as has Lady Claire.''

Marshall crossed his arms. ''What claims?''

''Father promised Bernard a reward—''

''Shut your mouth, Claire! You already have a lash coming for interfering in my dealings with Fitzgibbons. Say more and it will go worse with you.''

Claire steeled her resolve and focused on Marshall. ''—a reward of land and my hand in marriage for going on Crusade, to serve a penance imposed on him by Bishop Thurstan. When Bernard returned, Father denied the reward and tossed Bernard in the dungeon.'' She aimed an appeal at Marshall. ''Can you imagine, a knight and hero of the Crusade treated no better than a crofter?''

At Marshall's frown, her father cried, ''Fitzgibbons threatened my life!''

''You were in no danger,'' Claire said. ''Truly, there were several guards in the hall and Fitzgibbons was unarmed. What threat there?''

Oh, how it galled her father to hear it, to see Marshall's disapproval.

Claire continued. "I could not bear to see Fitzgibbons treated in such a manner. When I feared Father would do him further harm, I went to the dungeon and let Fitzgibbons loose. So began my adventure."

"There is *no* reward due him!" her father cried.

"I believe there is," Bishop Walter commented. "I heard the story from Bernard Fitzgibbons himself. It rings of truth, and smells of your betrayal."

Setton scoffed. "Hero of the faith indeed. The boy only went on Crusade because I gave him the wherewithal to go. And how does he thank me? He makes outrageous demands, sets the place afire and then makes off with my daughter and tries to sell her back to me. This is your hero of the faith? Bah!"

"His demands are not outrageous," Claire said. "He asks only for what was promised."

Setton turned on her. "He gets nothing that is mine, not land and not you."

Claire didn't see his hand coming, only felt the blow that sent her reeling and tumbling to the floor. Her knees and hands hit the stone hard. She tasted blood, and fought to stay conscious. Above her, she heard a man shouting, her father—asserting his right to punish her as he saw fit.

Marshall protested another strike.

Bishop Walter bent down to help her up. Knowing she couldn't stand on her feet without wobbling, Claire slid from the man's hands to sit on the floor. She'd been hit harder, but never with quite such stealth that she wasn't prepared.

"Claire?"

The bishop bent over her, both angry and concerned.

"I will be fine in a moment. Just a moment."

The bishop straightened. "Setton, I brought your

daughter home as an act of good faith on behalf of Bernard Fitzgibbons, who wishes this matter settled in an honorable manner.''

"The matter *is* settled. She marries Marshall.'' Setton turned on his heel, yanked open the door and was gone.

Marshall scrunched down next to her and gently turned her face. "A nasty bruise you will have, my lady.''

"Not the first.''

He smiled wryly. "I imagine not.'' His smile faded. "I have been here for several days, and heard the story of you being taken hostage from both your father and others.''

"I hope you believed the others,'' the bishop grumbled.

"I am inclined to.'' Marshall tilted his head toward Claire. "I gather the matter is *not* settled.''

"Bernard Fitzgibbons will be here on the morrow to restate his claim to his reward,'' she said.

"Your father does not seem in a mood to change his mind.''

"Then Bernard will challenge him for it.''

Claire didn't have to explain the consequences. Marshall got up and reached down to help her up.

"Might I suggest, Lady Claire, that until the matter is settled, you stay far out of your father's reach?''

"A suggestion I shall heed, my lord.''

And she would. She'd done what she set out to do—ensure Marshall knew of the seriousness of Bernard's claim, and that a high official of the church believed her father had duped one or the other man. From now on, the matter was in Bernard's hands.

Chapter Eighteen

Bernard hit the ground. Even while he rolled in the dirt, he decided he hadn't fared too badly. He'd sparred evenly against Hugh until the fifth pass.

He sat up and removed the borrowed helmet. Hugh stood towering over him.

"What did you learn?" Hugh asked.

"That I should unhorse my opponent by the third pass or I will be unable to keep the lance tip steady on the fifth."

"And?"

"That you are still better than I am?"

Hugh smiled. "Never a doubt there. What else?"

Bernard bowed his head and pondered the last pass of lances. He'd done everything right, until the twitch in his side had jerked his body and the lance's balance shifted. The tip had skittered off Hugh's shield and left Bernard open to a full hit. He'd fallen, landing correctly, and then…

"I should have gotten to my feet right way and drawn my scimitar, just in case. I swear to you, Hugh, I will remember if it happens in the tournament."

"You always were a pleasure to train."

"Let us hope this is the last time."

Bernard pushed himself off the ground. "Time for a bite of bread and ale. Then I intend to sleep until first light."

"You could use another go or two."

"No time. I must leave early if I am to collect my chain mail in Durleigh and still make it to Dasset tomorrow eve."

'Twas now late afternoon. Bishop Walter and Claire must be at Dasset by now. Claire was home and would eat her evening meal in the company of her family and the man she was to have married. Eustace Marshall. Bernard crushed a twinge of jealousy, keeping his feelings toward Marshall under tight rein. Emotions had no place in the lists. They led to mistakes, and Bernard couldn't afford to make a mistake.

They cared for the horses then made their way to the keep. Maudie greeted him with hugs and baby kisses. Elena had anticipated his needs and put out food and ale.

"A lovely woman, your Elena," Bernard said.

Hugh shrugged a shoulder. "In her way, I suppose."

Again came the feeling something was amiss between Hugh and Elena. They treated each with cool courtesy, but Bernard sensed a tension between them he couldn't explain.

'Twas certainly none of his business, nor did he have the time to figure it out. And Hugh was capable of dealing with his own problems, if there were any.

"Bernard, why not use my chain mail? Then you would not have to go into Durleigh first? Save you some travel time."

"Nay. I have mine own."

"I remember yours. Use mine."

"I already have your old lances and a practice shield and helmet. If I lost those—"

Hugh gave him a sharp, warning look. Talk of losing wasn't allowed. However, in any tournament the winning knight was entitled to the losing knight's armor. Bernard wasn't sure he would have the funds to buy Hugh's chain mail back should the worst happen.

"I want nothing of yours that you will miss if you do not get it back."

"All the more reason for you to use mine. 'Twill give you another reason to win, and a reason to come back and thank me for how well I trained you."

Maybe Hugh was right. Maybe the dread of having to return to Halewell without Hugh's armor would add incentive.

"Then I take it, with my thanks, my friend. Though I still need to leave early. I must stop at Faxton. I need someone to serve as my squire, and I have a friend who will be sore put out if I do not ask him to perform the honor."

Garth would leap at the chance, and Bernard couldn't think of a better way to thank his childhood companion for covering his back in Durleigh. Garth may have disobeyed an order, but Bernard couldn't fault him for it.

"Then you should have all you need," Hugh said. "You know, I have been training you all this time, yet you have never said who your opponent might be."

Bernard shrugged. "'Twill depend upon who Odo Setton chooses as his champion. My guess is he will choose Eustace Marshall, to whom he betrothed Claire. The man may even insist on it as a matter of honor."

Hugh whistled between his teeth. "Marshall, hmm?"

Bernard didn't like the sound of it. "Have you fought against him? Something I should know?"

"I have, and unhorsed him a time or two. Have him down by the third pass, Bernard. The man is very good."

"But he can be beaten."

"Oh, aye, but not easily. You might also keep in mind that he has unhorsed me a time or two."

Bernard cursed softly. "I wish you had not told me."

"You needed to hear it. Keep your wits about you. You will need them."

Bernard gave Maudie a last squeeze and kiss, and thanked Elena for her hospitality. Hugh walked him down to the guardroom and pulled shining chain mail from a chest. Bernard carefully stuffed it into his pack, then turned to Hugh for a farewell.

Hugh wrapped Bernard in a bear hug. "Take some bandaging with you. Be sure your wound is bound tightly before you enter the lists."

A last piece of advice from the man who'd taught him to fight like a warrior, to whom Bernard owed his life many times over.

"You take care. I will be back."

"Make it soon."

Hugh went back up to the hall. Bernard stretched out on a pallet but couldn't sleep.

He missed Claire. Tomorrow afternoon he would arrive at Dasset, see Claire again, give his challenge. The day after he would go up against whomever Odo chose as his champion.

After, when Claire was finally his—where then?

Truly, the destination didn't matter. So long as he had Claire with him. He'd find a way to build a life for them, to take care of her.

Bishop Walter seemed to think the reliquary of St. Babylas was worth quite a lot. Enough to purchase land—somewhere. A peaceful place where he could build a stone manor and raise wheat and hunt with his hawks. A place where he and Claire could raise a brood of children. Where love would flourish.

First, he had to win Claire. Without Claire, none of the rest of it mattered.

He laughed at his musings, remembering when he'd thought the land the vital part of the reward. Now he was willing to forgo it for love of Claire.

She'd snuck under his guard, wheedled her way into his heart, forced him to acknowledge that her love was worth any hardship or sacrifice.

Soon he would have his dream—or nothing at all.

Garth rode the mule as upright and prideful as if he rode a warhorse. He'd fair jumped with glee when asked to serve as squire. Bernard's only condition had been that this time Garth would do exactly as told. With no time to train his new squire, Bernard spent part of the ride to Dasset explaining the duties to Garth. The most important would be those during the tournament, the most crucial the care and handing up of the lances.

Garth swore to guard the lances with his life, and Bernard hoped the two of them might find a quiet time this evening to practice the handling. If not, he'd trust to Garth's observation of how the other squires handled their knights' weapons and hope for the best.

Likely, Bernard's match would be last, as those to settle disputes between knights usually were—as those were the matches the crowd most anticipated and wagered on highly.

Bernard noted the large, brightly colored tents in the fields surrounding the castle. Pennants bearing the knights' devices waved greetings in the breeze.

He wore no personal color nor chosen device, trusting

to his tabard of gray, his devices a black rose and a red cross. He needed no others.

"Stay close," he told Garth, then guided Cabal over the drawbridge and toward the gate. He looked up to see Henry waving down at him.

"Hail, Bernard. Are you sure you want to pass through?"

"Aye. One more time. How does the arm?"

Henry waved it around. "Working. If you are determined, then see Old Peter. He will show you where to put your mount."

Memories haunted the ride between the gate and the stable, both of coming in filled with hope and going out seething with anger.

Unlike last time, however, he had to pick his way through the crowded bailey. Old Peter looked harried, directing his stable lads here and there to care for a full stable of horses.

"Gonna try it again, are you?" the stable master asked.

"Aye, that I am. This time I will have a care not to burn down your stable."

Peter smiled. "'Tweren't so bad. Got more stalls out of the bargain." The old man nodded toward the castle. "You know where to find him—same place, more contrary than ever."

"I gather this time I am expected."

"Oh, my boy, they await you with breath held and coin in hand. Best give over that heathen blade o' yours. No sense getting your blood spilled until the morrow."

Bernard unstrapped his scimitar and handed it to Garth. "Guard my things well. No one is to touch anything, especially the lances, except you or me."

Garth tilted his head. "Do you expect treachery?"

"I have learned to expect most anything where Odo Setton is concerned."

Garth nodded. "Have a care in there."

Bernard turned back to Peter. "Did Julius make it home?"

Peter shook his head. "Nor did Geoffrey or Jeanne come. A shame, that."

After what Claire had told him of her siblings' dealings with their father, Bernard wasn't surprised they'd stayed away, though he'd hoped Julius would return.

Bernard strode from the stable to the castle, a knot forming in the pit of his stomach. Once more he would petition Odo Setton for a reward, but this time he'd settle for no less than Claire. And he'd win. He had to win.

He stepped through the doorway and looked about the room. Men in rich garb mingled with jewel-bedecked ladies. The strains of a harp wafted over the laughter and chatter of those assembled.

Claire's childhood dream. Her grand court.

He'd asked Claire to trade her dream for his. Would she someday have regrets? Mourn what she could have had if he hadn't roared into her life and turned it all upside down?

Bishop Walter came toward the doorway, garbed in gold-trimmed white robes, more the deceased Thurstan's style than Walter's. Bernard hadn't given much thought to why the bishop had offered to bring Claire to Dasset. Whatever the man's motives, Bernard could only be glad he'd been willing to help.

"There you are, Fitzgibbons," Bishop Walter said. "I was beginning to despair of you."

"I stopped at Faxton to fetch a squire. His mule travels slower than a horse. Tell me, how are things here?"

The bishop glanced around the hall. He shook his

head and leaned toward Bernard, as if to impart a secret. "Utterly abuzz. I had forgotten how fiercely rumors spread among idlers with no more to do than gossip and speculate."

The hall was going quiet. The bishop hadn't been the only one to notice him. Bernard ignored the stares aimed his way.

"Where is Claire?"

"Upstairs in the solar with her maids and mother and a few other attendants. I have not seen Claire since our confrontation with Setton yesterday." With a touch of ire, he added, "'Tis wise of her to stay far away from him."

Bernard agreed.

"Setton was not pleased to see his daughter?"

"Humph. Not that one could tell."

"What about Marshall?"

The bishop's brow furrowed. "Hard to say with that one. Good looks. All polish. A nice man, I think, if a bit cool."

The hall went dead silent. The sea of people parted in two directions, to the opposite sides of the far end of the hall. At the end of one path stood Odo Setton. At the end of the other path stood Claire.

He knew he should go one way but was drawn to the other.

Thankfully, Claire took the decision from him. She walked toward him with regal grace, her amber gown and veil shimmering in the torchlight that brightened the hall.

Beautiful. Precious.

She must have been watching out the solar window, waiting for him. Zounds, but knowing she'd kept watch for him, missing him, fed his sense of self-worth. He must have some merit, or Claire wouldn't wish to be his lover, his wife.

This lovely woman loved him, and he couldn't be more proud of her than now, or want her more. Despite the crowd around him and the trials before him, the urge to take her in his arms and kiss her senseless surged through him hot and hard.

'Twould have to wait, until later, until he got her alone and in some private place where he could ravish her sweet body until they were both replete. He had to believe the time would come or he'd go mad.

Here and there Claire acknowledged greetings or comments from someone along her path, but she didn't slow her pace. A few steps away from him, she put her hands out, palms down, for him to take. He minded his manners and took no more than offered.

He clasped her hands, then saw the bruise on her cheek.

She'd covered it with a chalky powder, but the dark shadow beneath hit him in the heart.

"That son of a bitch," he spat out, managing not to shout.

Claire squeezed his hands. "Truly, my cheek looks worse than it feels. Pay it no heed."

He shot a scathing glance at Bishop Walter. "You were supposed to protect her."

"'Tis not the bishop's fault," Claire said, tugging his hand to regain his attention. "I got too close. I should have known Father could not resist, even with His Eminence and Marshall standing right beside me."

Bernard shoved decorum out the door and kissed her bruised cheek. "Never again, Claire. Not while I draw a breath."

"I will hold you to that, my love." She sighed. "I do

not suppose we could simply walk out the door and ride out the gate?''

"I may block the door after you," the bishop commented.

He knew they were both teasing, trying to calm him down. He drew a deep breath. "I am tempted, believe me. Claire, you stay here—"

"I go with you. He wishes me to cower and I refuse."

She might not have cowered but she'd hidden.

"Yet you kept to the solar."

"Oh, that." Her smile widened. "My maids and I have been busy. You will see tomorrow. Shall we get this over with?"

With Claire's hand in his, Bernard turned toward Setton.

Gads, he could cheerfully kill the beast, but then he'd be in more trouble than he was already.

"Did you purchase new chain mail?" Claire asked. "You fair glitter."

"Hugh's. He insisted I use it."

"Nice. No holes, I hope. How is your back?"

He smiled wryly. "Looks worse than it feels."

She giggled. "My, but are we not a pair?"

"We are. Let us inform your father."

The first step was the hardest. Claire's diversionary chatter had worked its magic. With each step his anger faded, replaced by the cool calm he strove for in battle. Behind him he could hear the swish of Bishop Walter's robes. A good man to watch his back.

"Next to my father, in black—Eustace Marshall."

Bernard took note of the man to whom Setton had hoped to give Claire. Tall. Lordly. Good looks—as the bishop had seen fit to point out. Not a hair out of place, nor flicker of emotion on his face.

Bernard kept his attention on Setton, his immediate adversary whose emotions ran rampant. The old lord's eyes narrowed to slits. His hands clenched, then opened, then repeated the motion. Bernard came to a halt several feet away from Setton, more for Claire's sake than his own.

Though it galled him, he gave Setton the mannerly honor of a slight bow. "Lord Setton."

"Unhand my daughter, knave."

Bernard ignored the insult, and since Claire's hand didn't even twitch, he held tight.

"I think not. You see, all the while Claire was in my care, she suffered not a scratch. Her sniffles even ceased. I send her home and what do I find? An ugly bruise on her lovely cheek. I do believe I will keep her close."

"You dare disobey a direct order from your overlord?"

"Overlord? Lord Setton, when I made the oath of homage, I swore my loyalty to you and yours, upon which you swore to my protection and maintenance. Within moments afterward you denied me the maintenance to which I am entitled—the reward due me for service in the Crusade. You broke faith. I feel no obligation to obey any order of yours."

Setton glared at Claire. "Move away."

Her hand tightened on his. For strength?

In a clear voice she said, "I see no reason to move away. You are only my father. Bernard is my betrothed. Better, I say, to cleave to the man I am to marry than the father I gladly put behind me."

Marshall didn't even raise an eyebrow at Claire's declaration. Apparently he'd been told of Claire's belief in Bernard's claim.

Snickers from the crowd didn't sit well with Setton. He took a step toward Claire.

Bernard pulled Claire closer. "Try it, Setton. Be warned, *I* will hit back."

Setton heeded the warning. "The chit seems to suffer confusion over the name of her betrothed."

"'Tis you who seems confused. I had hoped your memory had improved after our last disagreement over to whom Claire belonged."

Setton sneered. "As I remember, you were willing to give her up rather quickly last time. You were most interested in the land."

"A mistake for which Claire has forgiven me."

"So we return to where we started, you making a demand for a reward never granted you."

"I make my demand for a reward you granted to me in the presence of Bishop Thurstan, may he rest in peace."

Bernard didn't like the tilt of Setton's smile. "Aye, may he rest in peace. Again, I tell you I granted you no reward, and again you will see the inside of my dungeon. Only this time, you will not escape."

Setton opened his mouth to call for the guards. Bernard battled the blood rush of a call to arms.

Eustace Marshall interrupted. "Might I have a word here?"

"To what purpose?" Setton asked, suddenly wary.

Marshall ambled toward Setton. "I find it interesting you deem it necessary to send Fitzgibbons to your dungeon—again. I see nothing he has done to warrant such treatment."

Bernard recognized the irony of having his rival for Claire become an ally, of sorts. Of course, several people had told him of Marshall's wide chivalrous streak. Truly, right now he'd take any help he could get.

Setton wasn't pleased with Marshall's meddling. "The man obviously opposes your marriage to my daughter. Is that not reason enough to keep him out of our way until the ceremony is over?"

"I should think that would depend upon whether or not Fitzgibbons's opposition is valid."

"It is not," Setton stated.

The faint spark of hope Bernard had harbored that Setton might admit to having granted the reward faded and died.

"Were the reward not valid, I would not have come back to make the claim. Indeed, I would have refused to go on Crusade all those years ago."

Marshall clasped his hands behind his back. "Which brings us to the part which confuses me. Fitzgibbons, the reward you claim is extremely rich. I find myself wondering why a lord would offer such grand enticement to a mere squire."

"I wondered, too," Bernard admitted. "Only after an enlightening talk with Bishop Walter did I begin to understand. Consider. Setton was on his deathbed, or so he thought. Whatever sins he confessed to Bishop Thurstan prodded the bishop to impose a heavy penance—send a man on Crusade. Not only was the penance stiff, but the bishop demanded restitution. I believe Setton's sin was against me." Bernard turned to stare at Setton. "After returning to Faxton, I also believe I now know the nature of the sin."

Setton blanched, but recovered quickly. "Fitzgibbons has completely lost his wits. He spouts drivel."

"Drivel? We will see. I have asked the sheriff of Durleigh to investigate my suspicions."

"He will find nothing."

Bernard feared Setton was right, but if anyone could prove Setton responsible for the death of Granville and Alice Fitzgibbons, Simon Blackstone was such a man.

"What do you suspect?" Marshall asked.

Bernard wanted to shout it out for all to hear, but knew he didn't dare. He couldn't accuse Setton of murder without a shard of proof to present.

"I will not accuse Setton of a crime for which I have no proof. 'Tis in the sheriff's hands."

Marshall seemed to accept his position, even approve. "I see only one flaw in your argument, Fitzgibbons. If marriage to Claire and land on which to settle was demanded as reparation, then why send you on Crusade?"

"Because he was certain I would not return to collect. He almost got his wish. Indeed, last fall he received word that the entire company of Knights of the Black Rose had fallen. Freed of his obligation to me, he began a search for a husband for Claire, and found you."

Setton shook his head vehemently. "I refuse to listen to these accusations further. Fitzgibbons, get out—"

Marshall turned on Setton. "If you do not wish to listen then take yourself elsewhere because I intend to hear him out!"

Bernard was dead sure that no one had ever invited Setton to leave his own hall. 'Twas a mark of Marshall's high noble rank that he would dare.

Claire's fingers tightened on his hand while they waited for Setton's answer to the stunning blow. Setton neither moved nor answered, but stood stock-still in utter disbelief.

Marshall waved a hand at Bernard. "Go on."

Bernard gathered his thoughts and picked up the thread of his tale. "Setton came to a bargain with you while he thought I was dead. However, Claire tells me he received my message to the contrary several days before you and he agreed to terms. With Bishop Thurstan dead, and thus no one to hold him to his obligation to me, he betrothed Claire to the high-ranking nobleman instead of settling for the lowly knight.''

Setton tossed his hands in the air. ''Enough! All right. Since everyone appears so insistent that Fitzgibbons should have some reward, I will give him one. *Sir* Bernard, I give you the manor at Faxton. In return you owe me one knight fee and thirty barrels of eels each year. Now get out of my sight.''

The hall went so silent Bernard could hear himself breathe what little breath he could manage.

Faxton. His home. Had Setton offered him the manor on the day he'd returned, he would have taken the offer and run.

Bernard glanced down into Claire's amber eyes. Today, Setton's offer wasn't enough, not if it didn't include Claire.

''A generous offer, but I must refuse. I claim first right to Claire. I say your promise to me holds sway over your bargain with Marshall.''

''I made you no promise!''

''Then I challenge you to a contest of arms as an honorable way to settle the dispute. You may, of course, name a champion.''

Setton studied him for a long moment. ''When you lose, you will slither away from Dasset and bother me no more?''

''I will abide by the outcome. Will you?''

Setton turned on Marshall. ''Since you were so determined to deal with this knave your way instead of mine, I think it fitting you stand as champion.''

A wry smile touched Marshall's mouth. "I have half a notion to tell you to do it yourself, but I will not. Fitzgibbons deserves a true test of his honor and honesty. For that reason only, I accept."

Chapter Nineteen

Bernard brushed Cabal, preferring the solitude of the stable to watching the other knights joust. Garth had wrapped Bernard's wound tightly, then gone off to observe the squires handling the lances.

All was ready. Last night he and Garth had taken turns standing guard over the lances and Cabal. No one had attempted to tamper with either, but Bernard felt better knowing for sure.

Early this morning he'd gone out Dasset's gate to the field designated for the tournament. He'd walked along the viewing stand with its brightly colored, flapping banners. At each end of the field stood tents where a knight could spend a few moments in quiet contemplation or receive treatment if wounded.

The ground looked even and cleared of anything over which a horse might stumble. By the time he fought, the dirt would be chewed up by horses' hooves. Still, Bernard approved of the conditions.

Soft footsteps alerted Bernard to someone entering the stable. Eustace Marshall.

Marshall dipped his head in greeting. "Fine horse."

Bernard kept at his chore, wondering what the devil

his rival for Claire's hand was doing in the stable. Marshall's steed had been led out earlier by two squires to be brushed and exercised before the tournament.

"Come to look over your competition, Marshall?"

"In part, perhaps, but I have other reasons for seeking you out," Marshall said. "After I remarked to Setton last eve that I wished your test to be fair, I wondered if I overstepped. I assumed you possessed skills similar to mine rather than Setton's. My apologies if I judged wrongly."

Bernard wondered if he'd just been insulted. If what Hugh and the bishop had told him about Marshall was correct, however, then the man was genuinely concerned.

"As much as I would like to have knocked Setton off his horse and into the netherworld, you judged correctly. Truth to tell, 'twas you I assumed all along Setton would name as his champion, though for different reasons than he gave."

"Ah, well then, I am content." Marshall clasped his hands behind his back. "Then there are but the two things I wished to tell you. 'Twould seem we have a mutual friend. Ranulf, the earl of Chester. He was most pleased to have heard that a few of the Knights of the Black Rose survived, in particular one man upon whom he had conferred knighthood, one who prefers a scimitar to a sword. That would be you?"

The earl was hardly a friend. Ranulf had been one of the high commanders in the Crusade, the man who tapped Bernard on the shoulder with a sword and conferred knighthood. The earl, and Marshall, moved within the circles of royalty and high nobility. Far too high for Bernard to call either of them friend.

"That would be me," Bernard finally answered.

"You have a staunch supporter in the earl, Fitzgibbons. If events do not run in your favor here, go to Ranulf. He would be most pleased to take you into his service."

If Marshall assumed he would win today, he'd best think again.

"We truly have two friends in common, my lord. I spent the past few days at Halewell. Hugh was kind enough to lend me a few lances and a shield, and spar against me to get the feel of them again. He speaks highly of you."

Marshall glanced at the lances standing points up in the corner of the stall before answering. "A good man, Hugh. We have met each other in the lists several times."

"So he told me."

"I gather my concern for your skills was unwarranted."

"Unwarranted, but appreciated." Bernard tossed the brush into his pack and left the stall. "Is there aught else you wish to know?"

Marshall shook his head. "Nay, but I did wish to set your mind at ease over Claire. 'Tis clear the lady has a preference for you. I want you to know I will not hold a whim of her heart against her. She will want for nothing, nor will she ever again suffer a bruise, not from her father or from me. You need not concern yourself with her safety or well-being."

Bernard's mind was anything but at ease. Couched in assuring terms, Marshall clearly issued a warning to stay away from Claire.

Whim of her heart. She will want for nothing.

Not trusting himself to speak, Bernard merely nodded.

"Till later, then," Marshall said, and left the stable.

Bernard wrestled with doubts. With his whole heart he knew Claire loved him. For Claire's love, he would do most anything. Defy her father. Match wits and lances with Marshall.

Let her go.

If he lost, he'd have no choice. He'd agreed to abide by the outcome of the contest of arms. If he lost, he would have to leave her to Marshall, never see her again. Never hold her, kiss her, love her.

"Nearly time, Bernard. Ready?"

Garth's intrusion into his musings brought him up short. He'd been mulling over the consequences of losing.

He wasn't about to let that happen.

He *was* ready, in all but his mind. He remembered another tournament, long ago when he'd let his anger interfere with his skills, and now could kick himself for allowing Marshall to get under his skin.

With a deep breath Bernard cast aside his doubts. He couldn't afford the distraction. Only one thing mattered—knocking Eustace Marshall off his horse.

Claire sat in the viewing stand next to Bishop Walter, hardly knowing which knights opposed each other or who was winning. She cared about only one knight in one match.

He'd given up Faxton.

There had been a time when Bernard would have taken the lordship of his home and been content. Last eve, when her father made Bernard the offer, she'd been torn between wanting him to take it and praying he'd refuse.

Then he'd looked down at her. A hint of wistfulness had crossed his face, then vanished. His love for her shone in his eyes, in the gentle squeeze of her hand, in his resolve to demand a contest of arms.

Her future hinged on a joust between Eustace Marshall and Bernard Fitzgibbons, and there wasn't a thing she could do to help Bernard—save believe in him.

He needed her to believe, or so he'd told her before leaving for Halewell to train with Hugh.

Despite the heat of the mid-August day, she wore her cloak. Under the cloak she wore the gown she and her maids had been feverishly sewing and embroidering— its unveiling a surprise for Bernard. Within the cloak's pocket nestled the scarlet veil he'd given her. Soon now she would give it back, if she could calm her trembling hands.

Only a few days ago Bernard had taken an arrow in the back. He'd brushed off her inquiry last eve, just as she'd dismissed the pain in her cheek. Was he still in enough pain to put him at a serious disadvantage?

A knight went down, a cheer went up.

"Oh, good show!" Bishop Walter cried.

Claire had to smile. His Eminence was having a grand time. He'd planted himself between her and her father, then settled back to enjoy the festivities. The guests, too, reveled in the excitement, with coins changing hands as the knights won or lost. Everyone, of course, had saved a coin or two for the last match of the day.

A hush came over the crowd. On one end of the field, with Bernard's lances tucked under his arm, Garth led magnificent Cabal to the front of the tent. The horse pranced and tossed his head, anticipating an upcoming battle. Bernard followed close behind. He carried a shield. A silver helmet swung at his side in casual fashion from his gauntlet-covered hand.

Claire shivered with the thrill of Bernard's imposing

presence. Erect, those broad shoulders back and squared, his long sable hair caressed by the breeze, Bernard strode onto the field with a confident, determined air.

His cherished tabard covered his chain mail. His scabbard hung on his left side. The hilt of the exotic, curved scimitar gleamed, awaiting its master's hand, if necessary.

Bernard put the helmet and shield on the ground, then reached up to rub at Cabal's neck to calm the horse down. Garth arranged the lances.

A knight ready for battle. A man determined to prove himself in the right. Her lover resolved to claim her before God and his human witnesses.

Claire gave a quick glance to the other end of the field where Marshall prepared for the joust in similar fashion.

She jumped when Bishop Walter patted her hand.

"Almost time," he said.

Claire centered on calming her nervousness before Bernard came to the viewing stand. He mustn't see her fears.

Mounted on their great horses, blunted lances pointed toward the sky, both knights made their way to the viewing stand for the short ritual before their joust. Eustace was jovial, relaxed and enjoying the cheers of the crowd. Bernard wore a hard expression, withdrawn into his own thoughts.

They pulled up to the viewing stand. As was proper, both men dipped their heads to Odo Setton, the tournament's host. Her father merely scowled at them. Bishop Walter rose and gave the knights the same blessing he'd given to all of the knights, calling on God to protect them both along with his hopes for an honorable outcome.

Two lances tilted forward to rest on the railing.

Her hands no longer trembling, Claire clutched the precious veil, unfastened her brooch and let the cloak fall away. She heard the gasps of the crowd and her father's curse, but ignored it all in favor of glorying in Bernard's reaction.

Bernard could hardly believe what Claire had done. She stood before him in a slightly frayed, gray work gown adorned with trimmings of red and black. Along the hems of the skirt and sleeves ran tiny red crosses interspersed with black roses.

His colors. His devices. His woman.

She took two steps forward and tied a token of gauzy red fabric to the end of his lance. It took him a moment to realize it was the veil he'd given her at Faxton.

"Have a care with this, Bernard," she said quietly. "I want it back to wear tonight."

The vision of his beautiful Claire covered in nothing but filmy scarlet warmed him clear through, kicking his heartbeat up a notch. Now was not the time to tell her how much he loved her or to comment on how short a time he'd have the veil off of her and himself inside her. He'd tell her later when Claire was finally, completely his to have and hold, forever.

He backed up Cabal, and with a slight motion of his knee, ordered the horse into a deep bow. He heard the cheers, but focused on the surprised and well-pleased smile that lit Claire's face.

Bernard pulled Cabal upright, gave a brief nod to Marshall, then galloped back to where Garth stood over the lances. He tipped his lance down for Garth to untie the veil, which Bernard then tucked up under his tabard and secured under his belt. 'Twas as if her love and faith rode with him. He wouldn't disappoint her.

Garth handed up the helmet. Bernard settled it square

on his head, blocking out everything but what he could see through the eye slits. With the shield in his left hand, the lance firm in the grip of his right and tucked solidly against his side, Bernard studied his opponent.

Marshall sat at the ready, his shield partially covering the device on his tabard, a griffon. Bernard noted the set of the shield and narrowed in on the griffon on Marshall's chest. He chose his target, the griffon's head. He set the angle of the lance, feeling the tug at his wound—a reminder of his disadvantage.

Three passes, no more.

On the very edge of his limited vision he saw a man step forward from the viewing stand and drop a yellow flag. Cabal's muscles bunched. Bernard kneed him to a full charge.

Lance tip up. The griffon. Closer. Ever closer. Knees tight. Shield steady. Bernard braced for the hit.

Marshall's lance skittered off Bernard's slightly tilted shield. Bernard hit Marshall's shield squarely and hard.

The lance shattered from the blow, throwing Bernard off balance. Not good, he thought as he struggled to regain control of horse and body.

Claire covered her mouth to hold back the scream that gathered in her throat. A scream from her would distract Bernard, who already teetered precariously in the saddle. He managed to right himself, but too slowly for her peace of mind.

"Marshall will have him on the next pass," her father said.

"Do not count Fitzgibbons out yet," Bishop Walter answered.

Claire hoped the bishop knew what he was talking about. Bernard could draw his scimitar, if he chose, and take the contest to a higher level of danger. He never reached for it. He'd decided to pass Marshall with only his shield, no lance. She held her breath as Marshall bore down on Bernard. She closed her eyes, heard the crash of wood lance against metal shield.

"There, did I not tell you?" Bishop Walter gloated.

"Marshall takes his chivalry too far," Setton complained. "He barely touched the knave's shield."

"Humph. So you say."

Upbraiding herself for cowardice, Claire opened her eyes and blew out a relieved breath. Bernard had reached Garth, who handed up a lance as if he'd trained for this duty all of his life. Bernard wheeled and charged at an already oncoming Marshall.

The crowd roared to life and to its feet, all knowing this might be the deciding pass. Cabal gained full speed. Bernard set his lance. Claire's nails dug into her palms.

They hit with a force that sent lances flying and horses reeling, kicking up a shower of dust. Both men fought for balance, both tilted sideways in their saddles.

One, or both, were going down.

Bernard felt himself falling. The hand that had held the lance grappled for Cabal's mane. He dropped his shield. His back burned with the strain of his awkward position. The crowd was cheering, anticipating his downfall.

He couldn't fall. Falling meant losing the match, losing Claire. He had to get himself upright and face Marshall once more. Yet he could only cling to Cabal.

On the very edge of his restricted field of vision he saw two of Marshall's squires sprint past him, which could only mean that Eustace Marshall was on the ground and not moving.

With a relief he hadn't the time nor words to express,

Bernard kicked his foot from the stirrup, and slid, albeit with little grace, off Cabal.

He'd won, and the prize he'd won was climbing over the viewing stand's railing with far more grace than he'd slid from his horse.

Grinning, he pulled off his helmet, then went ice-cold with fear. Claire held her skirts up, running toward him, smiling, crying, unaware that Setton followed her—furious, with a sword in his hand.

Dear God, would Setton kill her rather than hand her over?

Bernard took slow steps toward Claire, his arms extended, urging her to faster speed, not daring to draw his scimitar or rush forward—either of which might slow her. Thank heaven for her younger legs and eagerness to reach him.

She meant to embrace him. He sidestepped, grabbed her arm and swung her behind him, drawing his scimitar as she swept past. Setton didn't halt, as Bernard expected, but charged onward with the sword poised for attack.

Bernard understood, then, who the old man meant to kill. Not Claire, but Bernard Fitzgibbons.

Bernard raised his scimitar to fend off Setton's punishing slice. Steel met steel with a ring of finality that Bernard welcomed. Finally, he and Setton would settle old scores.

He faced Setton with the surety of winning, his scimitar flashing to meet each thrust. Odo Setton might be showing his age, but he'd not gone to seed. He could yet wield a sword with authority, but not enough.

"Ready to die, Setton?" Bernard taunted. "Persist and this could be your day."

"Not hardly," Setton spit out and brought his sword around in a well-aimed cut.

Bernard countered it, ducked under and threw his shoulder into Setton's chest. Setton back stepped, but kept his feet beneath him.

"Why, Setton? Marshall has already lost. Claire is mine. Why bother?"

"You have been a thorn in my side for far too long. Today I pluck it out."

Setton attacked with renewed fury. Bernard met hot rage with cold calm, deflecting each strike. Waiting. Knowing the moment would come when Setton would falter. When it came, he took full advantage.

Bernard knew the precise moment when Setton realized he was in trouble, that Bernard's scimitar might slice him in twain. 'Twas likely petty to enjoy Setton's discomfort, but he'd waited so long for some show of anything other than disdain from Setton that he toyed with his victim a while longer.

His wound told him to end it, so he listened. He backed Setton up to where Bishop Walter stood at the rail of the viewing stand. With two quick blows and a swift sweep, Bernard disarmed Setton. Before the man could recover, he placed the flat of his scimitar on Setton's throat.

"Have a care. I doubt anyone here would fault me if I separated you from your head."

"You will not," he proclaimed, but Bernard heard his panic.

"Believe me, Setton, I am not averse to drawing your blood."

Setton swallowed, carefully.

"Now, as to the matter of my reward. You and I both know you made me a promise, and I have just proven, beyond doubt to all gathered here, that you broke faith. That Claire belongs to me is no longer in question.''

''Take the chit and go.''

''Oh, have no fear on that score. I most certainly will. Yet, what bothers me is why you offered me a reward at all.'' Bernard pressed the blade higher, reminding Setton of his peril. ''What sin did you commit that warranted such a hefty reward? Did you order my parents murdered? The truth, Setton, or bleed—heavily.''

For a moment Bernard thought Setton wasn't going to answer, then he said, ''Your parents were not supposed to die. You were.''

Of course. He should have guessed. Not even Wat had suspected Setton of sending a band of men after a mere boy.

With his son dead, Granville Fitzgibbons would have no reason to rebel over his son's right to inherit Faxton.

His mother had known. When the mercenary had swept him from his feet, his mother had screamed his name—not in a plea for help, but to alert his father. Once rescued, his father had told him to run, then his parents had fought to cover his escape.

Dear sweet heaven, they'd given their lives to protect his.

On the verge of extracting revenge, Bernard remembered that Setton was Claire's parent. No matter how vilely the old man had treated him, or his own daughter, Claire didn't deserve the memory of watching her father die a horrible death.

''Know this, Setton. You owe your miserable life to Claire. For her sake alone I do not slit your throat,'' he said, then forced his feet to back away. He looked up at Bishop Walter, who leaned over the viewing stand's railing and assumed the cleric had heard all that Setton had confessed. "Bishop Walter, you will see this wretch serves a suitable penance for his confession?"

The bishop glared at Setton. "No penance, but a hefty penalty. Of the lands Dasset holds of the bishopric of Durleigh, several have fallen to misuse. One of them, Faxton, has been without a lord in its manor for many years." Bishop Walter shifted his attention to Bernard. "Sir Bernard Fitzgibbons, if you would do me the honor of swearing to my service, the manor is yours. Do you accept?"

Setton cursed, softly and with despair, not daring to further anger the bishop who could take away more, if he wished. Dazed, Bernard opened his mouth but closed it again, too stunned to speak.

"Bernard accepts," Claire said. Her hand slipped into his and she gave a tug. "Take me home, love."

At her side, Cabal snorted, as if to agree.

Home. Faxton. Claire. A dream become real.

Bernard decided to move, and fast, before the bubble burst.

He twirled Claire around and boosted her into the saddle.

"Fitzgibbons!"

"Your Eminence?"

"What of the wedding?"

Bernard swung up behind Claire. "Do you mind not staying for the festivities, my love?" he whispered near the delicate ear he planned to nibble on later.

She laughed lightly and snuggled back into his embrace, where she belonged. "Nay, but we had best let the bishop have his way. He is our overlord, after all."

"Best be quick, then," Bernard called out, then side-stepped Cabal over to face Bishop Walter.

"Quick, hmm? Well then, Lady Claire Setton, are you

sure you want to be tied forever to this stubborn knight?''

"Forever, you say?''

Amused, the bishop sighed. "Aye, my lady, that is the way of it, I fear.''

"Ah,'' she said, and reached back to skim her fingertips along his jaw. "Forever it is then.''

"Sir Bernard Fitzgibbons, lord of Faxton, you have gone to a lot of trouble to win this lady. Still want her?''

"For as long as she will have me. Are you done?''

Bishop Walter signed a cross in the air. "Go with my blessing, but be sure you show up at my palace day after the morrow to make all of this legal.''

"And collect on St. Babylas?''

"That, too.''

Bernard wheeled Cabal, set him to a trot and circled the field. Marshall had gotten up off the ground and appeared to be standing under his own power. Garth had gathered up Bernard's belongings and was packing the mule.

"Anything within the castle you want to take with you?'' he asked Claire, his arm pressing on her midriff.

"I do not come to you barefooted in my chemise, Bernard. I have chests full of clothing, linens, pottery…but nothing I cannot do without for several days.'' She caressed the back of his hand with her palm. "All I truly need, I have right here.''

They'd have to come back with a wagon and probably argue with Setton over every scrap of fabric or household furnishing Claire claimed as hers. Bernard didn't relish dealing with Setton again, but Claire deserved her belongings, so he'd wrestle them from the old lord.

Right now, however, he wanted to take Claire home,

rest and heal, and show Claire there was nothing wrong with her coming to him barefooted in her chemise.

"Then hold tight," he said, and reared Cabal high into the air.

He didn't hold the pose long—his back hurt too much—but it produced the desired effect. This time, as he rode away from Dasset, he did so to cheers for a winner, not curses at a loser.

Claire giggled as she settled back. "This is much better, Bernard. No gate to pass under and no arrows at your back. I could become accustomed to this."

"How dull."

She was quiet for a moment. "I can hardly believe 'tis over and we won. I was so afraid..."

At the catch in her voice, Bernard reined the horse to a halt. "Come here, wife."

Claire turned sideways and tilted her face upward for the kiss he'd meant to claim. As always, the taste of her pleased him, her passion thrilled him. She kissed him desperately, as if she feared there wouldn't be another. Desire coiled in his loins and seized him hard. 'Twould be a long, painful ride home.

He broke the kiss and gathered Claire in a tight, enveloping embrace.

"Not over, Claire, just begun. You said you would stay with me forever, and I intend to hold you to your vow."

"No escape, hmm?"

"None."

"In that case, get us home. I have plans for you and a certain scarlet veil."

Epilogue

Bernard sat with Simon Blackstone and Nicholas Hendry at a table in the Royal Oak Tavern, sipping at ale while the three wives visited Durleigh's many shops.

Bernard had given Claire a heavy purse and set her loose with an order to purchase something nice for herself. Linnet Blackstone and Beatrice Hendry had gleefully offered to ensure Claire followed orders.

Bernard wished them luck. If anyone could convince Claire to spend a coin or two on herself, Linnet and Beatrice were up to the task.

He silently thanked St. Babylas for the use of his arm bone. The bishop had bought the reliquary for more money than Bernard had hoped to see in a lifetime, giving him the means to give Claire a part of her old dream. The keep being built at Faxton would be lavishly furnished with dark oak furniture, colorful tapestries and whatever else Claire wanted.

Bernard hoped today's shopping excursion proved pleasurable for his wife. Claire deserved a carefree afternoon after all she'd been through this morning.

Simon Blackstone's zealous pursuit of finding evidence against Lord Odo Setton had produced astonishing results. Not only had he found one of the mercenaries involved in the long-ago attack on Faxton, but his digging unearthed others who'd suffered mightily due to Setton's greed. So many charges had been lodged that the king's justiciar and the bishop had held a joint court in the cathedral to settle all of the matters quickly.

In the end, both judges had despaired of assigning penalties and fines. They'd simply stripped Odo of lordship of Dasset, giving it over to his son Julius, who hadn't yet returned to England. Odo was now confined to the bishop's jail, there to await his son's return and hope for Julius's charity.

The biggest shock had been Claire's mother. Lady Leone had found the courage to quit the marriage she'd never wanted. Leone announced she would spend the rest of her days in the peace of a convent—a life she said she'd been called to but never given the chance to choose.

Tonight Claire intended to write letters to her siblings, informing them of what had transpired. 'Twould be hard on her, so he hoped she enjoyed this afternoon's respite. Being with Linnet and Beatrice would help.

Simon pushed his ale aside. "If they do not come back soon, I may be tempted to send men out to search for them."

"Worried about Linnet?" Nicky asked, shifting a sleeping little boy to a better position on his lap.

Nicholas's son, Owen, a boy of four years, had sprouted since Bernard had last seen him only two months ago. Bernard hadn't realized children grew so fast until he'd witnessed the changes in Nicky's Owen and Hugh's Maudie.

"Linnet sometimes tries to do too much. In her condition, she should slow down some. Just try to tell her that, however.''

Bernard smiled, hoping Claire would soon be in the same condition—swelling with child.

"Beatrice and Claire will watch over Linnet. If she tires, they will sit her down or bring her back,'' Nicky said. "You always did worry a thing to death, Simon. Relax.''

"Hah. Just wait. Your turn is coming. *Then* you can tell me not to worry, if you can.''

Nicky ran a gentle hand over Owen's hair. "I cannot wait,'' he said softly. "I missed so much with Owen.''

Owen was Nicky's son, but not by Beatrice. Apparently Nicky hoped to rectify that situation soon, too.

Bernard leaned forward. "Simon, how can you tell? How did you know with Linnet?''

He groaned. "'Twas awful. She wept. Happy. Sad. Did not matter. I walked into her shop one day and found her crying so hard as to break your heart. Scared me witless. When she finally calmed down she said she'd realized what was wrong with her. I was prepared for the worst, that she'd caught some fatal disease.'' Simon's expression softened, as did his voice. "She smiled up at me and told me she was carrying our child. Could have knocked me over, then.''

"Crying, hmm? Claire hasn't been overly weepy.''

"You think Claire…already?''

He'd absconded with Claire in early August. 'Twas now mid-September.

"Claire has not had her woman's time since we have been together, at least not that I know of.''

Simon raised an eyebrow. "Fast work.''

"Not fast, just often. You see, I bought her one of those harem veils and—''

"Time to change the subject," Nicholas stated, ruffling Owen's hair. "Owen is growing up fast enough as it is."

Owen yawned, not yet completely awake, but enough to talk of other things more suited to young ears. Soon now, Bernard hoped, he would have a little boy or girl to nap in his arms, too.

"Maudie is growing up fast," Bernard told his fellow knights. "She was so little when Hugh brought her out of the prison with him. Now she is walking and climbing."

"When do you leave for Halewell?" Nicholas asked.

"On the morrow or mayhap the next day." He hadn't yet returned Hugh's chain mail and other tournament equipment. Knowing Claire could use further distraction from her family's problems, they were taking an extended holiday. "I wish I had better news to give him about Guy and Gervase."

"I had expected Guy and Isabella to find Sir Edmund by now," Simon said. "But apparently not. None of them has returned from London."

"Gervase should have his sister's future settled soon," Nicholas said. "Perhaps we will hear from him again before he leaves England to join the Knights Hospitaller."

"Well, finally," Simon said softly, looking toward the door.

Bernard turned to see their wives, who'd stopped to have a word with Mistress Selwyn. Beautiful, strong, loving women all.

Claire was smiling, her arms filled with bundles, though Bernard suspected whatever was in them wasn't all meant for her. She would have bought something for him, something for Lillian and mayhap Garth.

Nicholas put Owen down, who ran over to Beatrice, asking if she'd bought anything for him.

"Bernard, when there is time, you will tell us more of that harem veil," Nicholas said.

Bernard laughed and raised his tankard. "I do not know how the three of us managed, but we all got more than we deserved. To our roses, good sirs. May they flourish."

"To our roses."

* * * * *

Looking For More Romance?

Visit Romance.net

Check in daily for these and other exciting features:

Hot off the press

View all current titles, and purchase them on-line.

What do the stars have in store for you?

Horoscope

Hot deals

Exclusive offers available only at Romance.net

Plus, don't miss our interactive quizzes, contests and bonus gifts.

PWEB

One small spark ignites the entire city
of Chicago, but amid the chaos, a chance
encounter leads to an unexpected new love....

THE HOSTAGE

As Deborah Sinclair confronts her powerful
father, determined to refuse the society
marriage he has arranged for her, a stranger
with vengeance on his mind suddenly appears
and takes the fragile, sheltered heiress hostage.

Swept off to Isle Royale, Deborah finds herself
the pawn in Tom Silver's dangerous game of
revenge. Soon she begins to understand the
injustice that fuels his anger, an injustice
wrought by her own family. And as winter
imprisons the isolated land, she finds
herself a hostage of her own heart....

SUSAN WIGGS

MIRA

"...draws readers in with delightful characters,
engaging dialogue, humor, emotion
and sizzling sensuality."
—*Costa Mesa Sunday Times* on *The Charm School*

On sale mid-April 2000 wherever paperbacks are sold!

Visit us at www.mirabooks.com

MSW592